SAILCAT

D. J. Vaughan

May 8, 2011

Standard Copyright

Chapter One

Carl Seizer, Everett Foss, and Ron Stone had just rounded the abandoned factory and slid down the red cinder embankment that led to the river. There were usually four of them on most days, but today Dicky Williams had to go with his mother to help carry groceries home on the bus. The three-mile trek from their home on Fairfax Avenue to the banks of the Ohio River was almost too much for Everett, the youngest of the three. He was pale and toe headed just like the rest of his family and proud of his Scandinavian roots. Whenever the boys played war he always wanted to be called Everett the Viking. Carl and Ron were eleven but Everett was only nine.

It wasn't considered cool to hang out with a nine year old in most cases, but Everett's case was different; he always brought the cigarettes and sen-sen, stolen from the red velvet drawer in his mother's china hutch; a vice she kept from her husband.

Carl took out the box of matches and handed them to Ron. Carl was, slightly heavy with straight brown hair, he could have disappeared into any crowd, except for the fact that he couldn't keep his mouth shut. He was too quick and loud with his opinions, sometimes pushy and arrogant, especially with those younger or smaller.

"Give me the cigs," Ron said, holding out his hand.

Everett did as he was told and watched as Ron flipped three between his lips and lit them. Ron took a deep pull off the Pall Mall and exhaled in one smooth motion. Everett and Carl however, fought off coughing as long as possible but finally succumbed, and fell into uncontrolled convulsions.

"These Pell Mells are better than the Camels huh?" Carl asked, in a raspy high-pitched voice. He had managed to regain partial composure: enough to complete a sentence and try to impress Ron, --- the leader. Ron was tall, dark and usually quiet among those he didn't know. To those he did know he was a natural leader, demanding respect without force.

After retching in the reeds at waters edge Everett too managed to stand up and take a simulated drag from his cigarette. To save face, a genuine puff was required in the beginning, but small cheek filled draws was tolerated afterward to finish the experience and maintain acceptance. Being accepted was all-important. He had proven his worth by supplying the smokes and never failing to at least try anything the older boys did.

Standing in a cloud of eye stinging smoke they watched the river as the brown afternoon slowly turned grey. The Ohio River in the fifties was smoky and smelled of diesel and coal. This place where old industry once filled the air with pollution and smells of sweaty working men, was now deserted. It was the perfect place for boys to get away and do what boys do; push their boundaries.

"Where do you think all those barges go?" Asked Everett looking to Ron and pointing to the rust colored hulk lumbering up river.

"I don't know Parkersburg, Wheeling maybe… could be all the way to Pennsylvania… who knows?" Ron answered, clearing his throat and spitting into the water. The other two boys followed suit. If Ron would have unzipped his pants and urinated instead of spitting, the other two would have also tried to work up a pee.

Carl was dizzy but no longer coughing. Everett removed his cigarette to make an adjustment to the paper which was now soggy and falling apart.

"Damn Everett you nigger lipped it again, you dumb shit. You ain't supposed to suck on it," said Carl laughing.

Both Ron and Carl laughed. Everett, however, stood stone faced with smoke tracking up his face, burning his nostrils and eyes. Trying to appear older was hard work.

All the boys were sick, even Ron, though he would never admit it. It was difficult for them to understand what adults saw in this behavior, other than looking cool, but they were determined to find out. Dicky Williams always said, "Why sneak down to the river if you don't do something cool." Just the fact that they were there meant a whipping; and if you're going to get a whipping anyway, you might as well deserve it.

Rock throwing was a frequent occurrence after the smoking and puking were done. Every pane of glass on the old factory was gone, thanks to the boys. But now they mostly skipped the flat ones or found targets in the water for the rest. There was always trash of some kind floating by to providing ample targets. During the rainy season the storm drains and sewers would overflow and dump debris of all kinds as well as raw sewage. Hitting a moving turd with a rock was considered an experts shot. The older boys made this shot more than fifty percent of the time.

A two-foot fragment of wood, which had caught on a reed, became their target of the day.

"I bet I can break it loose," said Carl, winding up like Reds pitcher Art Fowler, and then missing the wood by a foot.

No sooner had Carl made his prediction that Everett launched his own stone missile that did knock the wood free.

"Yes," he shouted, holding up both arms.

Ron shoved Carl. "You just got chopped by a runt. Way to go Everett!" He said laughing

Carl said nothing, but he didn't like being bested by a "little kid." Everett would now become the brunt of all his practical jokes and bullying; at least until he had paid the price for overstepping his station. It wasn't Everett's intention to best Carl at anything but he would gladly take the praise. Kudos from Ron were rare.

Then suddenly and without warning the three boys were under attack by a barrage of rocks coming from the hill behind them. One rock hit Carl in the back while another ricocheted off the ground and caught Ron on the calf, drawing blood. The boys turned quickly in the direction of the incoming rocks and ducked. On the hill stood four, teenage boys relentlessly throwing rocks and insults.

"This is our river, twerps, get out!"

" Fucking punks!"

"Get lost! Beat it!"

"Let's go," said Ron slapping the rock from Everett's hand before he had the chance to return fire. "It's the Gunther gang."

The younger boys fled up river away from the old factory until they came to a rotted wooden house surrounded by an equally rotted fence. The dampness of the river land and lack of attention had taken its toll on the old house. There weren't many houses along this stretch of river, but like the industry that once thrived here, they were mostly all rat-infested skeletons, decaying reminders of another time.

Rocks continued to rain down on them until they were inside the fence, where they stopped to catch their breath. Ron stuck his face between two boards to get a look behind them.

"It's Ok, they're not following." he said and slumped to a sitting position on the ground.

"Who's the Gunther gang?" Asked Everett.

"They're a bunch of tough guys mostly from high school. Nobody messes with the Gunther gang. Some of them even have cars," Ron said.

"All the times we've been coming here, we ain't never seen them before, how can they say this is their river?" Asked Carl.

"Because they're big kids and they're mean and they can take anything they want," said Ron.

"Even the river?" Everett asked.

"You want to go back and argue with them about it?" Ron asked frowning.

"No," said Everett breaking eye contact. "So does this mean we can't come down here no more then?"

"This means we got to be careful when we come down here from now on. We got to keep an eye out for them, that's all," said Ron. "It's just like looking out for grown ups."

"Yea except grown-ups don't throw rocks," said Carl.

This was a new experience for the boys. This was something new to fear; like parents and cops and anyone older who threatens. But it was also a new kind of authority to rebel against. Ron wasn't about to give up their little piece of the river so easily, and he knew that the other boys would go along as long as they didn't get hurt.

Chapter Two

The walk home took them the long way around. They weren't going to take the chance of running into the Gunther gang again. It was dusk and the boys were hungry. Carl was already late for dinner and he was not looking forward to facing his father. Ron lived with his mother, but she would still be at work at the restaurant and would have no Idea he'd been out late.

Everett would only be in trouble if his father were already drunk. He knew that if he could sneak in undetected his father wouldn't know he had ever been gone. Dinnertime wasn't a big family thing at his house. Most of the time he and his other siblings, two brothers and a sister, got their own supper. Everett's mother never really seemed drunk, although she took nips all day. Coming in late was risky and if he were caught he would surely face his father's belt, or worse.

The boys said nothing until they were sure they were far enough away from the river to be out of earshot.

Finally Carl broke the silence. "What if we get Dicky Williams, he's older than us? Maybe he could get some guys from his class to come down and help and we could kick those Gunther guys asses?"

"Dicky's only thirteen and there ain't nobody at his school who's crazy enough fight the Gunther Gang, so forget it," Ron said frowning.

He knew how dangerous the gang was. He'd seen them in action first hand after his cousin had dissed one of them at school. They caught him at Hoffman elementary waiting for Ron to finish and intramural basketball game. Ron stood terrified as he watched them beat his cousin unconscious and then repeatedly kick him afterword. One of the boys grabbed Ron by the shirt and threatened to kill him if he squealed. Since then he'd heard stories about them and how the police suspected them of killing a man. The word on the street was they killed him and dumped him in the river. He wondered what the man had done.

Suddenly Everett's eye's lit up like Christmas morning and he yelled like a lost sailor who has just spotted land, "Sailcat."

The other two boys reacted by following Everett's gaze to the opposite side of the road. Everett bolted across the quiet street, followed by the other two. Whoever called it first got the first throw. Everett was on it first and quickly looked around for a stick to pry it up. He spotted a dead branch in the gutter and retrieved it.

The three boys stood grinning over a flattened dried carcass of a cat.

"I saw it first. I dibsed it," said Everett as he worked the stick under the cat, prying it loose from the concrete.

After several attempts, working the stick from three different angles he finally freed it. The cat was stiff and flat. It had obviously lain in the road for several days being continuously hit by passing cars and then dried by the sun. What once was a fluffy living thing had been reduced to a fur outline stuck to the road. It was perfect.

Everett took the cat between his fingers and, with a side arm throw, sailed the cat upward into the air. Spinning like a pie pan, it gained altitude and then spun gently to the ground.

"Did you see that," said Everett as he ran to retrieve it.

"That was shitty, give it to me, I'll show you how to do it," demanded Carl.

Everett picked up the cat, but instead of handing it to Carl, he stuck out his tongue and then handed it to Ron. Carl was infuriated and popped the younger boy on the forehead with his palm. Everett came back at him with a barrage of flailing arms causing him to take a step backwards. Before Carl had the chance to slap him again, Ron dropped the cat and stepped in between them, grabbing them both by the shoulder.

"Enough of this shit, you want to fight go back to the river," he said.

The intervention by Ron always defused minor flare-ups between the other boys in the neighborhood. Even Dicky, who was older, gave in to Ron's authority.

Ron picked up the cat but did not immediately throw it. Secretly he admired Everett's resolve to stand up to Carl. In an attempt to defuse the situation he turned and spoke to Carl.

"My birthday is next week, Everett just gave me an early birthday present," he said holding the cat above his head. Then turning his attention to the road ahead he started walking in the direction of Fairfax Avenue, swinging the cat at his side, and paying no further attention to the boys. When they reached the top of the hill looking down Fairfax, they could see their houses at the bottom where the street leveled off. When they came to the first house on the right, just past Owls Nest Park, and one block from home, they noticed clothes still hanging on the line in the back yard.

Ron stopped for a moment fixed on the white bed sheets billowing in the wind and then down at the cat in his hand. The sweat from his fingers had moistened the cat skin just enough to bring out a stronger odor of decay than before. This was the perfect time for a launch. Then without a word he began swinging the cat over his head, around and around at least ten times before releasing it. The cat sailed through the air like it was meant to fly, riding a thermal breeze like an eagle. It gained altitude with every rotation until it was twenty feet off the ground. It then banked slowly to the left and descended over the back fence like an alien spacecraft on a mission, straight into the side of one of the clean white sheets. The boys smiled broadly and let out a cheer of delight when the cat made contact. This was the best sailing of a dead cat any of the boys had ever seen. If a record book existed for such things it would have listed it as legendary. It was also another way to poke back at the system, which held their contributions as minimal. In other words, they were tired of being on the low end of the ladder.

The boys walked on past the house by the park and then home to whatever fate awaited them. No matter what else came down on them that night they had delivered a Sailcat to a most righteous target.

Chapter Three

Carl's father was sitting on the front porch steps with belt in hand waiting for him to come home. Carl knew what this meant but he didn't know was how severe the whipping would be. It was not uncommon for children to receive this kind of corporal punishment in this neighborhood, even on the front porch for all to see.

The boy's stomach fluttered as he got closer and saw the look on his father's face. He tried hard not to start crying but closer he got the worse he felt until finally a long mournful wail left his lips and his face contorted into sobs that sounded like a wounded beast.

"Shut up! Crying won't do any good," his father spat as he grabbed Carl's left arm and held it above his head, almost lifting him off the ground. His humiliation would be complete, everyone within earshot would either be listening or watching.

With Carl dangling like an eel in a fish market, his father began to lay stripes on his body with the belt. He jumped and flinched with every lash. Sometimes his father would go into a kind of frenzy and wouldn't stop until his arms grew tired or his son reduced to silent screams with mouth agape.

"I'm sorry," Carl screamed with every strike. His father only flailed harder using his threats as cadence to the lashes.

"I'll be- damned- if I'm -going to -have -a son -living under – my roof –who doesn't -respect -my rules. Do- you- understand?" Asked his father.

"Yes," he managed to answer, his voice unrecognizable.

"Do you, huh! Do you?" His father shouted.

"Yes Dad I swear, I swear," Carl squeaked, his voice broken.

Finally the crazed look diminished and he let go of Carl's arm. The boy slumped to the ground as if he were boneless. This wasn't the worst he'd been whipped nor was it the worst he'd witnessed in the neighborhood.

"Get inside wash up and get to bed. You don't deserve no supper tonight. Carl picked himself up off the ground and slowly walked past his father, afraid to make eye contact.

"I bet you won't be late for supper again, will you?" His father snapped as he past.

Carl walked by his mother sitting on the couch sewing, but she never looked up. He went upstairs, washed his face and hands and slipped into bed. His last thoughts, before falling asleep, were of the cat sailing over that backyard fence.

Ron waited up for his mother as long as he could, but it wasn't unusual for her to sometimes be gone all night, especially if she had a date or met someone nice. She used to bring them home until the one time his father showed up drunk demanding sex and got into a fight with the man. Ron remembered that night like it was seared into his brain. All of the shouting and broken furniture, the blood, and his mother begging them to stop and all of it ending with the police arresting both men. That night and the night his father left them for good, he would never forget.

Ron fixed himself a peanut butter on toast and went to bed. The creaking of the house at night used to scare him but he was used to being alone now even though he still slept with the hall light on and with his bedroom door open.

Everett managed to enter his house through the outside cellar door and then up the stairs to the hallway between the kitchen and the living room. He rounded the doorway at the top of the stairs, looked both ways and ran silently up another flight of stairs to the bedroom he shared with his two brothers. He could hear his brothers in the hallway bathroom splashing in the tub. He changed into his pajamas and went downstairs to see if he could find something to eat. Halfway down the stairs he heard his father snoring from in the living room. Before heading into the kitchen he looked in to see his father passed out in his favorite chair, surrounded with empty beer bottles. He didn't see his mother or his sister but assumed they went upstairs when his father became drunk and belligerent.

Sometimes he would stop off at a bar with his friends and be drunk when he got home. Everyone held their breath then, to see what kind of drunk came home. Sometimes he was funny and made everyone laugh, but sometimes he became dark, angry and loud scaring them all. Sometimes he also became violent and slapped his mother. Lately she managed to stay away from him when he was like that. Everett was glad he came home when he did. If he hadn't found the Sailcat he would have walked right into the worst of it.

Everett found dinner cold but still on the table. The spaghetti tasted like rubber straight from the bowl but he ate it anyway and went upstairs. His mother was coming out of the bathroom where his brothers had just finished bathing. Her eyes were moist; he knew she'd been crying. Everett had been through all of this before. She had started drinking socially at first and then with her husband at his request. He didn't like drinking alone. Now she nipped all day just to get through it, but unlike her husband, rarely appeared drunk.

"Where have you been?" asked his mother.

"Just out playing with Carl and Ron. You know it's Ron's birthday next week? I already gave him a present though, I found a Sailcat," he said.

"Oh Everett, you didn't pick it up did you?" She asked.

"Well, just a little, then I gave it to Ron. Sorry I'm late Mom," he said.

"I was worried about you, but you're home now," she said leaning to kiss his cheek.

Everett could smell the sweet smells of wine, licorice, and lilac.

"Was it bad tonight Mom?" He asked.

"It was.... everything is fine now, you'd better get to bed before your father wakes up," she said, picking him up to give him a hug. She started to make excuses for his father's behavior but stopped. What could she say that would make things better? Her sweet Everett was only nine.

Everett kissed his mother and went to his room where his two younger brothers were in bed, but still whispering. His brothers were six and seven and, as usual, not sleepy at bedtime. They knew that their father was passed out drunk, but they also knew to be quiet if they heard his heavy footsteps on the stairs. For now they were safe. Everett however, was tired and had learned to tune out the world around him years ago. Once under the covers he drifted off.

Chapter Four

Dicky Williams had accompanied his mother downtown to do some needed shopping, both grocery and to the five and dime. It was a three-block walk to the bus stop, then a transfer to the streetcar just to get to Peoples Corner. The trip home was especially strenuous carrying two full bags of groceries and notions. Dicky didn't mind it though. He enjoyed accompanying his mother on her shopping trips. They always stopped for lunch at a downtown diner across from Fountain Square where he would order his favorite hot dog and orange soda.

Shopping was easier before his father lost his job. In those days they had a car. He was able to get work at G.E. for a while until they went out on strike. His dad got quiet after that, withdrawing from the outside world. The curtains were seldom open anymore, his father preferring a darkened house. Three months ago he had a stroke and now spent most of the time in a wheelchair staring into the darkness. He never seemed to be able to focus on anything. He would respond with his eyes when spoken too or when his mother hand fed him but otherwise everything that he used to be was gone.

By the time Dicky and his mother reached the front porch of their two-story row house, the grocery bags were beginning to tear from the constant jostling to readjust the load with their knees. Dicky followed her into the kitchen and sat the bags on the table. The kitchen was the only room where the curtains were ever open but the sun had already gone down. The only light came from the bare bulb on the ceiling. Dicky was putting the canned goods in the pantry next to the cellar door when he heard a loud noise coming from outside. Stopping to listen he heard it again. It sounded like someone wailing in pain.

Following the sound he walked to the front window and pulled open the curtain. He saw that the noise came from Carl's house across the street and in front was his friend, dangling from his fathers arm, being lashed with a belt. It wasn't the first time he had seen this happen. It made him angry to watch the ordeal. Carl's father was quick to deal out harsh punishment, even for minor infractions. "Spare the rod and spoil the child," was a popular mantra In their neighborhood.

Neither he nor his older brother Danny had been a recipient of such corporal punishment for quite a while, not since his father got sick. For Carl however, it was practically a weekly occurrence. As much as Carl was afraid of his father it was hard to imagine that he would continuously, and knowingly break his father's rules, but Dicky knew that he did. ---- They all did. The only difference was that his mother seldom questioned where he went or what he did. He and his brother were keeping the family afloat. They had assumed all of his father's responsibilities. This earned them more trust than the average thirteen and sixteen year old. Danny had to quit school and take a job as a mechanic's apprentice at Fisher's bakery. Dicky had a morning paper route and took care of everything around the house.

Finally and mercifully the whipping was over. Carl lay in a quivering heap on the front walk while his father still assailed him with curses and insults. Tomorrow was Saturday, after mowing the lawns and repairing the back fence he would be free to get out of the neighborhood with his friends.

Chapter Five

Saturday morning was beautiful. The sky was a clear deep blue, filled with white billowy clouds rolling lazily past in the direction of the river. The air was filled with the thick sweet smells of summer. By the time Carl got up and looked outside, Dicky Williams had already mowed the front and back yard and fixed the fence. He was sitting on his front porch looking down the street toward Owls Nest park at the cluster of cars parked near the gate to the baseball field.

Carl got dressed and went downstairs to the kitchen. His mother had fried bacon for his fathers breakfast and left two slices for him draining between a folded dishtowel. Carl wrapped them in a slice of bread and went out the front door and on across the street to Dicky's house, while he ate.

"You just getting up, you lazy shit?" Asked Dicky.

"What time is it?"

"Ten o'clock or so, I think."

"I had a bad night last night, man!" Carl said.

"Yea, I know I heard it," said Dicky. "What did you do, man, he burned your ass?"

"Went to the river and missed dinner."

"You go with Ron?"

"Yea, and Everett."

"Oh! You guys went down there to puff," said Dicky smiling. Was it worth it?"

"Up until I got whipped," he said stuffing the last of his bacon sandwich in his mouth. "Man I wish I was you, you don't have to worry about whippings no more huh?"

Dicky thought about it for a moment, recalling the times before his father got sick. He would have given anything to have his father back the way he was, even if it meant the occasional whipping. But his answer to Carl's question was just, "Yea."

Next door, Ron Stone appeared on the porch shirtless, stretching and yawning. He glanced to his right and saw Dicky and Carl sitting on the steps. All of the houses on this stretch of Fairfax looked alike; two story, narrow row houses built sometime around the turn of the century.

"What are we doing today?" Ron shouted.

Dicky and Carl turned and yelled, "We're going up a pig's ass for a ham sandwich."

"Dicky!" his mother admonished from inside the house, causing him to cringe.

"Sorry Mom I didn't know you were there," he said in a low voice.

Ron laughed and went back in his house to get a shirt. By the time he emerged from the house wearing a striped t-shirt, he spotted Everett coming down the sidewalk wearing a helmet and pulling a wagon. Everett's father returned from the war with souvenirs he'd taken off dead Germans; the oversized helmet Everett wore was one of them. His eyes were barely visible at times peering out from under it.

"Hey you guys want to play Army?" he asked coming to a stop in front of Dicky's house.

"Got any smokes?" Carl whispered.

"No but I can get some, but we have to play war first," Everett answered.

Ron stepped over the two-foot high hedge separating his yard from Dicky's and joined them on the porch steps.

"Why don't we go down to the river and play war then have a smoke?" he suggested.

Everett thought for a long moment before answering. He was dreading the walk to the river. He knew that if he didn't go along though, he might be called a baby, or even worse, a chicken, and nobody wanted to hang out with a chicken.

"All right I'll go get the cigs but you guys have to go get your army stuff," he said turning his wagon around, putting his right knee inside and pushing off down the sidewalk. The other boys watched as he rode, one leg pumping, down the street to his house before they dispersed to retrieve their own gear.

The boys had an odd assortment of items that qualified as Army gear. Dicky returned wearing his father's old Kaki uniform, and with the exception of the rolled cuffs in the pants and sleeves, almost fit. Carl had a canteen belt and a marine fatigue hat. Ron wore an army class A soft cap, which his father used to call a "Cunt Cap," and a bayonet stuck, in his belt. When Everett finally returned, besides the helmet dangling on his head, he wore a strap across his chest attached to an olive drab pouch. The strap had been adjusted to the shortest notch but it still bounced heavy below Everett's buttocks.

"What's in the pouch, the smokes?" Asked Carl.

"Yea and a surprise," He answered smiling.

"Better let me carry it then," said Carl reaching for the strap.

"No you don't," said Everett ducking away from his grasp.

"Well if we see them Gunther guys again you won't be able to outrun them, but I can," said Carl.

"Yes I will, I can out run you," Returned Everett frowning. He was getting tired of Carl's constant harassment. He would show him at the river. He would show them all at the river.

"What Gunther guys?" Asked Dicky.

"Oh yea, we forgot to tell you, we got chased away from the river yesterday by the Gunther Gang," Ron said.

"Shit, what did you do?" He asked.

"They through rocks at us so we ran like hell, that's about it," Ron answered.

"Did you guys do something to piss them off?"

"Nothing, we were there, that's all," Ron replied.

"I wanted to throw rocks back but Ron wouldn't let me," said Everett.

Ron and Dicky looked at each other and laughed.

"So you're a tough guy too?" Asked Dicky.

"Yea he's our secret weapon," said Carl joining the laughter.

"Maybe I am, maybe I'll show you I am," said Everett indignantly. "C'mon let's go."

The other boys laughed but followed. Everett did have the cigarettes.

The trek to the river started with one of several shortcuts, first walking toward the back of Dicky's house and then through the hollow that bypassed the crowd at the park.

The good weather did not carry to the river, which was still hazy in the midmorning sun. The boys found several empty metal drums in back of the old factory and rolled three of them to the cinder embankment and pushed them off. Once down by the shoreline they were strategically placed to provide cover for the mock firefights that ensued. Ron and Everett were one army and Carl and Dicky were the other. Once they had each tasted victory and been shot down at least a dozen times each, they grew tired of playing war and finally Ron called a truce at the riverbank.

"C'mon Everett lets see the phags," called Carl. The three older boys stood together at water's edge but Everett stayed behind the drum he had used as cover.

"No I haven't showed you my secret weapon yet," said Everett from behind the drum.

"We're tired of that, we want to have a smoke, now get your ass over here," said Carl.

"No," come and get me," demanded Everett.

"Everett come on," said Dicky.

"No"

"All right Everett what'cha got? Asked Ron. "Go see Carl."

"Damn it Everett you little twerp this better be good," cursed Carl as he walked closer to the drum.

Carl stopped just in front of Everett's cover and waited a moment before kicking the drum and almost knocking it on top of the younger boy. Everett shifted to his left away from the teetering drum and pointed a gun at Carl and pulled the trigger.

The shot was deafening, it echoed off the water and the empty building behind them. Carl dove to the ground screaming.

"Fuck"

The bullet had only missed him by a breath. He was visibly shaken but not hurt. Dicky and Ron were by the river and had also hit the ground. The bullet made a zip sound as it passed Dicky's ear.

Everett had dropped the gun as it discharged and now sat wide-eyed and stunned.

"Everett, what the hell are you doing man?" Carl shouted, afraid to move.

"Everett, don't shoot anymore, Ron shouted while he and Dicky crawled behind an overturned barrel.

Everett only heard part of what Ron said because the blast had rendered him partially deaf. Finally he stood up. He was shaking and confused.

"I'm sorry," he said looking down at Carl. He then looked up at Dicky and Ron peering around the barrel and said, "I'm sorry, I'm sorry, I didn't know there were bullets in it. When the realization that he could have killed somoone finally set in he began to cry. "I'm sorry, I'm sorry.

Ron was the first to get up. He walked slowly over to Everett and looked down at the gun. Dicky followed but Carl lay where he had fallen still shaking.

"Where did you get this?" Asked Ron bending down to pick it up.

"It's my Dad's, he says he took off a dead German.

Carl managed to get up now and joined the boys by the drum.

"It's a Luger, I've seen pictures of them," said Dicky.

Everyone's interest was now on the weapon, momentarily forgetting the danger they were in only minutes before.

"Wow that's really cool, can I hold it?" asked Carl, now standing.

"You ever handled a gun before?" asked Ron.

"Just my BB gun," he replied.

"Then no not till I figure out how to get the bullets out," Ron answered.

"Do you know how to take the bullets out?" Ron asked.

"No I never thought my dad had any," said Everett. "Sometimes he takes it out when he's drunk and says he's going to shoot my Mom but we all know he won't, we thought it was empty. I think my dad thinks it's empty cause once he said it was all jammed up inside."

"Yea well it ain't jammed now," said Ron.

It occurred to Carl again that he'd just been shot at.

"Hey you little shit you almost killed me," he said shoving Everett.

The younger boy lowered his head and again apologized, "I said I was sorry."

"Yea, you know Carl's pop would beat his ass if he ever came home dead." Dicky laughed.

Ron smiled and said, "If your Dad thinks it's empty then let's empty it."

"Yea, let's empty it," repeated Carl.

"Ok Everett? Asked Ron.

"Yea, sure," Everett said.

Ron turned the drum upside down and began to survey the ground. At last he spotted and old root beer bottle and set it on the drum

"Look for bottles," he shouted.

The boys dispersed to hunt for targets and soon came back with armloads. Ron set up four bottles on the drum and moved back about fifteen feet with the other boys behind him.

"You don't know how many bullets are in here, do you?" Ron asked looking at Everett.

"No," he replied.

"Ok we each get a shot and we keep on shooting till we run out of bullets, Ron said. Everyone nodded.

You get bypassed on the first round Everett since you already took a shot," said Dicky.

"Yea," said Carl, scowling.

Since Ron already had the gun he raised his arm and squared his shoulders. He carefully tilted his head slightly and squinted down the sight. Remembering how loud it was, Everett immediately covered his ears.

Ron squeezed the trigger. The gun bucked in his hand and another deafening blast echoed across the river as the green soda bottle exploded in a cloud of sparkling shards.

"Whoa, that was cool cat, good shot," Dicky said reaching for the gun.

Dicky repeated the stance and took aim. Again another blast from the muzzle but this time no exploding bottle. Dicky looked puzzled for a moment, then turned to Ron.

"I wasn't ready let me have another shot," he pleaded.

"No," Ron said, "one shot whether it's a hit or a miss. Next!"

It was Carl's turn now. Everett's first shot had rattled him causing his hands to shake a little when he tried to sight down the barrel to take his shot. He dropped his hands to his sides and took a deep breath, standing motionless for a few moments.

"Come on Carl, Granny was slow but she was old," Dicky said.

"Wait a minute, damn it," Carl growled.

Carl again raised the gun to shoot but this time he held his breath. The gun barrel wavered back and forth between the second and third bottle. Finally he fired and shattered the third bottle. The explosion sent the glass in a sideways trajectory knocking over the second and forth bottles. Carl was elated that he hit something.

"I did it! Did you see that? I got three with one shot." Carl turned excitedly to get Ron's approval, but as he did, the gun barrel followed and in his excitement the gun bucked again in his hand.

In that instant of unbridled joy, the boy who was Ron ceased to exist. The bullet had ripped a hole through the side of his head at the temple spraying Dicky and Everett with blood and grey matter. Everett gasped and covered his mouth. Carl stood frozen for a long moment and then began to scream.

"Aahh! Aahh! Aahh!" He looked quickly at Dicky through squinted, tear-laden eyes and continued screaming.

Dicky Williams had stopped breathing the split second the luger bucked as his face became instantly covered in the warm wetness from his friend's brain. Ron slumped to the ground as though he were made of rubber.

Carl turned to the boys and held out the gun, butt first, begging with his eyes for someone to take it. Dicky took a deep breath and jerked the gun out of Carl's hand. They stood and watched as the blood gushed from Ron's head and pooled on the dirt in a dark ruby halo.

"You fucking idiot," Dicky screamed, his face contorted with the pain of reality. Dicky eyes darted back and forth between Carl and the gun, his expression growing angrier.

"I'm sorry, I'm sorry," wailed Carl. He sounded like a man in flames.

Dicky's anger grew with the moment until he finally burst the silence in a scream of rage and pointed the gun towards the river and squeezed the trigger three more times, but the Luger was quiet except for the clicking sound of a hammer striking empty chambers. The last bullet had killed Ron. Dicky dropped to one knee, exhausted, beside Ron's body.

Everett had taken several backward steps as if maybe distancing himself from the scene might make a difference. He was crying and taking heavy breaths.

"What do we do?" He said finally, looking to Dicky for direction.

"I don't know yet, let me think," he said wincing.

"I can't go home and tell my Dad I did this, you guys, I just can't," Carl cried. He looked at Dicky and said, "I'm really sorry, I really am, but I'm scared of what my Pop might to do."

"He'll have you put in jail maybe," said Everett.

No one spoke for a few moments as they assessed the gravity of their situation and the desperation of a no way out scenario sunk in. Dicky forced himself to calm down and Everett had stopped crying.

"Hell, man, we're all going to be in big trouble. None of us should be here," said Dicky finally. "They're going to say it's your fault for swiping your dad's gun and they're going to say it's my fault because I should have stopped everything cause I'm the oldest," he said looking at Everett. "And you..." he said shaking his head at Carl.

"But if I tell them that it was an accident and I didn't mean to, they can't put me in jail, can they?" Carl asked.

"The hell they can't. My Dad's cousin got into a fight with some guy at a bar and hit him too hard so it killed him. He didn't mean to kill the guy either and he got sent to jail for seven years. Seven years man!" Dicky answered.

"What am I going to do then?" Carl asked, now crying again.

Dicky looked upwards towards the old factory and then down to the riverside. He wiped off the empty gun with his shirttail and handed it back to Everett.

"Nobody meant for this to happen, but it did. What we need to do is make it like it never happened," said Dicky. "No matter what we do we can't bring Ron back."

"So what do we do then? Asked Everett.

"You're going to put this thing back where your Dad keeps it and none of us are going to say nothing to nobody. Do you understand?" he said looking at Everett and then at Carl.

Both boys both nodded. Carl was guilt stricken but also eager to make it all go away. Everett was sickened at the thought of what they must do and only wanted to crawl into his mother's arms and confess. But he also knew he would go along with the older boys, he always did. Everett put the luger back in the ammo pouch and buttoned it tight.

"What about Ron? Asked Everett, starting again to whimper.

"I'm sorry Ron's dead, he was my friend too but he wouldn't want any of us to get in trouble would he? Would he?" Dicky asked.

"No," said the boys.

"Then we're going to give him a sea funeral, I mean a river funeral and then we're not going to tell anyone ever," Dicky said.

"What do we have to do," Carl asked almost afraid of the answer.

"Let's take him over by the river," he told Carl. "And you," he said pointing at Everett, "kick some dirt up here and cover up the blood."

Dicky hesitated a moment and then slipped his hands under Ron's limp arms and lifted. Carl grabbed his feet and they carried the body to the water's edge. Everett watched them for a moment but did as he was told and kicked dirt over the blood stained ground until there was no sign that a killing had taken place. When he joined the other two at the river, Dicky had already removed Ron's bloody hat and bayonet and laid them on his stomach.

"We got to drag him a little ways into the water," Dicky said looking Carl in the eye.

"Don't we say something first, you know like at a funeral?" asked Carl. "We can't just put him in the water without saying some words or something."

"Ok, yea, we need to say something. Ok---We each say something and then we all say goodbye and then--- we put him in the river," Dicky said.

The boys stood at attention as though it was a military funeral. Carl straightened his marine hat and Everett steadied his helmet.

Dicky Williams started things, his voice quivering "Ron was my best friend. He was always there if I needed help or anything and I'm going to miss him a lot."

He looked at Everett who was crying again.

"Ron was my friend too. He always knew what to do when I got confused, and he made me feel safe all the time." Everett said. "I'm sorry Ron, I'm sorry I brought this stupid gun."

Carl was trembling. He tried to say something several times but choked on his tears each time. Finally he dropped his head and said, "I didn't mean it, I'm so sorry. And, just know I don't want to put you in the river either, but we have to. If you're in heaven I hope you like it there."

Before they pushed the body in the water Dicky noticed a few drops of blood on Carl's shirt. He then took inventory of his own clothes and found that he too was blood spattered.

"Take off your shirts and cover Ron with them," he ordered. Being the first out of his shirt Dicky laid his it gently over Ron's face. No one admitted it but they were glad not to have to look at Ron's face anymore.

When they had covered his body from head to foot Dicky and Carl waded into the river and gave Ron's body a gentle shove. Once having released it to the river they snapped to attention and saluted. The body floated for a few moments and then disappeared beneath the murky waters of the Ohio.

Chapter Six

Behind the William's house, on the far side of the wooded hollow, stood the ruins of an old stone cabin. Overgrown and hidden it became the boy's private meeting place where they could talk and share secrets away from adults. They called it the Fort. All that remained were the stonewalls and fireplace. Except for the fruit crates the boys hauled in to serve as a table and chairs, anything else made of wood had long since rotted away.

Shirtless and quiet on the long walk home they headed in silent agreement straight for the Fort. Once inside, Carl had pulled the boxes together and they sat, grief stricken staring at the dirt floor. He was also the first to break the silence.

"What are we going to say when people ask if we seen Ron?"

"We say we ain't seen him since we quit playing army. We played army then Ron went home and we ain't seen him since," Dicky said.

"What do you think will happen when he don't come home? And what's his mom going to do?" Asked Everett.

"I don't know, she'll probably think he ran away or got kidnapped or something. Nobody's going to think he's..." Dicky paused unable to finish the sentence.

"Ron told me that sometimes his Mom don't even come home everyday anyway. She might not even know he's gone yet," said Carl.

"My Dad says she's a floozy," said Everett.

"Shut up! You don't say nothing bad about Ron's Mom. You ain't suppose to say nothing bad about somebody when they're... dead." Again Dicky had trouble saying the word.

Everett's eyes welled up. "I just said my Dad says it."

"Probably next week everybody will figure he's just gone. They'll probably think he just decided to take off, and then things will get back to normal again," said Dicky.

"How can things be normal, Ron's dead?" Everett asked, blurting out the word Dicky had trouble saying, the word that no one wanted to say.

"They just will that's all," Dicky shouted. "It's like when my Dad had his stroke. At first we didn't know what we were going to do, but then we just got used to it. I wished things could be like they were, but they never will, and you just get used to it."

Carl watched Everett closely as the younger boy tried to regain his composure. He began to worry about Everett's resolve to keep quiet.

"And you better keep your mouth shut, you hear Everett?" Warned Carl.

"Yea, you better not squeal," said Dicky. "A squealer gets in just as much trouble as everybody."

"I ain't no squealer," Everett shouted.

"Well if you do, we'll just tell'em it was you that done it. You brought the damn gun anyway," spat Carl.

Everett jumped off his box and shoved Carl to the ground. Before Carl could recover Everett was on top of him with fists flying. Carl tried to get up but Everett was in a rage and stronger. He tried to grab his arms but Everett managed several hard punches to the face causing him to pull his arms back to block the blows.

"You killed Ron! You killed him! You killed him," he screamed like a child possessed. "You don't ever say it was me"

The whole flair up only took seconds but it seemed much longer to Carl before Dicky was able to grab Everett's arms and pull him off.

"Stop it Everett! Stop it!" Dicky yelled shaking him.

Dicky wrapped his arms around him and held him until his breathing returned to normal and his muscles relaxed.

"Take it easy, nobody's going to say nothing, right? Right?" shouted Dicky, shaking Everett once. "Right Carl, nobody's saying nothing, right?"

Everett was the first to speak, "Ok."

"Right Carl?" Dicky repeated louder.

"Yea, right, I was only saying if," said Carl.

"Shut up Carl, ain't nobody saying nothing," Dicky ordered.

Carl finally stood up and dabbed his bleeding lip. He was taken by surprise by the younger boy but what surprised him the most was his inability to overpower him once he'd begun. Completely loosing face however was not an option.

"All I can say is, it's a good thing Dicky pulled you off cause I was getting ready to kick your ass," he said unconvincingly.

"We all calm now?" Asked Dicky.

"Yea," said Everett.

"Ok, that's good. Then Everett, you better get home and put that gun back. And Carl you better get home before your Dad beats your ass again," said Dicky. We'll all meet up tomorrow. Everything's going to be all right, you'll see." No one really believed everything would be all right, including Dicky. In times of tragedy people feel compelled to say it and the grief stricken want hear it. But though they might get use to it, nothing would ever be all right.

Chapter Seven

As he passed, Danny kicked his brother, still in bed. He was in his work uniform on his way to the kitchen for breakfast. Dicky, startled awake, raised his head to see Danny's smiling face.

"Asshole," Dicky said under his breath.

"I heard that! Get up you lazy bum," Danny shouted from the stairs.

Danny was blonde, tan and nice looking. He also looked older than seventeen. Becoming the family's sole breadwinner at sixteen had taken his teenage rebelliousness and replaced it with a grown man's calm. Whatever dreams he might have had before, were now just dreams. He was resigned to his fate and doing fine.

Dicky Williams hadn't slept well, he would have preferred to lay in bed all day and tell his mother he was sick, but he felt the need to see his friends. Yesterday, needed to be talked about. He needed reassurance that they also had made it through the night and were still in agreement.

Once showered and dressed he went to downstairs for breakfast.

"Dicky, do me a favor and go next door and ask Ronny if they can spare some butter till tomorrow," his mother said when she saw him in the kitchen doorway.

"What?" he asked. He had heard the words but froze as she spoke them.

"You heard me go next door and borrow a cube of butter?"

Dicky stayed frozen in the doorway trying to think of a good enough reason not to obey.

"Now," she insisted.

He couldn't speak, but when saw the look on his mother's face he bolted for the front door. Once outside he went down the front steps and across the yard to the small hedge that separated the two properties. He stopped just the other side of the hedge and looked back at his own house and then at the steps leading up to Ron's front door. He didn't want to go to the door but then he thought; What if his mother is home?

What would he say if by chance Ron's mother was home? He walked to the front door and stood in front of it for a long moment and then gently rang the doorbell.

After a few seconds he felt sure that she wasn't home. He felt relieved. The small corner market was just two blocks away. Instead of going back empty handed and having to answer questions about Ron, he bolted and ran to the store.

With one pound of butter in hand he returned home and gave it to his mother.

"I said a cube, not a whole pound Dicky," his mother scolded.

"I know mom but they had plenty, he said just to take it."

"Well, ok I guess. I was only going to buy a cube but I suppose we can afford a whole pound. Did Danny tell you he got a raise?

"No," he replied.

"He's been there a year now and his boss says he's doing real fine. He told Danny he's better than some journeymen he has on he job," she said, proud of her son.

It felt strange engaging in small talk with his mother. Ron is dead and his brother got a raise. Ron is dead and he's talking about the price of butter. Ron is dead and it's going to be another scorcher. Dicky didn't feel very talkative. He wished it was all a bad dream but what he felt was worse than any dream. He needed to talk to the boys.

Carl's Father gently shook his son to wake him; The Weekly Sun newspaper awaited delivery downstairs.

"Hey Sport, I made us some pancakes this morning, hurry up and get dressed," said his father. Carl's Dad was in a good mood most of the time. He showed his love in many ways; he took Carl to see the Reds play now and then and he never forgot a birthday, but the biggest reason, above all else, was that he stayed. No matter how much his Dad may have been unhappy with his marriage, and his life, he stayed. Carl saw how much Ron's life was torn apart when his father left, how insecure, vulnerable, and alone he had been. He never wanted that. Carl would endure whatever he had to endure as long as his father just stayed. Yes, he had rules, and those rules were chiseled in granite, not to be broken. His punishments at times were extremely harsh, but nonetheless he believed that his father did love him, and Carl also loved his father, even though he feared him.

After breakfast, his father left for work and Carl loaded his bike and delivered his papers. When he got home he spotted Dicky on the front porch.

"Hey," he called as the Schwinn skidded to a stop in front of Dicky's house.

"Hey Carl, you Ok?"

"I guess so, my dad fixed me pancakes this morning. It was really cool. I forgot for awhile, you know?"

"Not really, my mom sent me over to borrow butter from Ron this morning,"

"Oh shit man!"

"Yea! I didn't know whether to shit or go blind." I ran to the corner and bought some with my movie money. I didn't know what else to do."

"Nobody's ask about Ron yet?" Carl asked. A flood of emotion coursed through his body when he spoke Ron's name. Even though he fought it, he looked away in case he started crying again.

"No, I guess maybe his Mom didn't come home last night. I don't know. Least ways nobody said nothing," Dicky answered.

"She get's up late too, so she could have thought Ron just got up early and was gone someplace," said Carl.

"Yea maybe."

"You seen Everett yet?" Carl asked.

"No, why don't you go down and knock on his door and see what he's doing? Dicky suggested.

"No, why don't you go down there?"

"Cause I'm thirteen, It's going to look funny if a thirteen year old wants to play with a nine year old. You,--- your still young enough so it don't look weird."

Carl hated it but Dicky was right, a thirteen year old couldn't do that. He set the kickstand and walked down to Everett's house and knocked.

Everett's mother was a plain looking woman; thin with hair so blond it was almost white. When she opened the door she smiled at Carl.

"Hi Carl, Everett isn't up yet," she said, looking at her watch. "If you want to wait a few minutes I'll wake him."

"Oh, it's ok, I was just wondering what he was doing, that's all."

"Well, how about I wake him and I'll have him come look you up."

"Ok thanks, tell him I'll be at Dicky's house," Carl said. He thought, it was just like Dicky said; everybody is doing everything they always do, just like normal. He started feeling a little better at the thought of things getting back to normal. They could get through this. It was possible to hold it together, and everyone would just think he ran away; after all, his dad did.

Everett had been up for hours before his mother came in to wake him. He had lain in bed thinking about Ron; Remembering the times he had defended him against Carl; remembering all the times playing kick the can or catching lightning bugs. And the perfect throw Ron made sending the Sailcat into the middle of clean bed sheets. It was the best throw he'd ever seen.

Thinking of the good times helped ease the ache in his stomach. If he let his thoughts render images of Ron from yesterday, the ache was so bad he couldn't breathe. Maybe getting up and talking to his Mom would help. He knew he didn't want to talk to Carl.

Down in the kitchen his mother had left a plate of scrambled eggs on the table before returning to her room. Everett popped a slice of bread in the toaster and stood at the counter waiting. He would have liked the comfort of his mother's company this morning but he wouldn't again go knocking at her door and disturb her unless he knew for certain that she was not having one of her spells. She would sometimes stay in her room all day, coming out occasionally only to disappear in the basement to smoke a cigarette. On those days he and his siblings had to fend for themselves.

The toast was hot and the eggs were cold, but shoveled together with ketchup, it was all good. Everett went to the front windows and pulled back the drapes. Scissors of light from the morning sun assaulted the dark room prompting him to quickly close them. He didn't want to see Carl but he did want to talk to Dicky. Yesterday Dicky was reassuring and Everett needed more.

His every instinct told him to tell an adult, to confess the whole horrible tragedy to someone. But he couldn't. He had made a promise to his friends that he would not tell. Squealers got into as much trouble as everybody.

Chapter Eight

Dicky and Carl sat side by side on the front steps watching Everett walking towards them squinting into the sun.

"Hey Everett you Ok man?" Asked Dicky sounding concerned.

"I guess so," he answered toeing a pebble with his sneaker

"You ain't ratted me out yet have you twerp?" Carl asked sarcastically.

"Shut up Carl!" Dicky scolded. "Why are you being such an asshole?"

Carl withdrew, laying back on the porch. Everett had always gotten on his nerves, but his grief over Ron's death had him blaming Everett for bringing the gun. Shifting the blame eased his conscience a little. But still, he felt that the nine year old held his life in his hands ad he feared that. He thought about how when he woke up yesterday, he just wanted to have a little fun with his friends, but now because of Everett, his whole life had been turned upside down.

"Nobody knows he's even missing yet. It might be a week before somebody asks where he is," said Dicky, snapping Carl back to the present.

"You remember what you're supposed to say don't you?" Carl asked Everett.

"I ain't seen him since we got back from playing Army yesterday," Everett answered.

"That's right," Dicky said. "You just stick to that story and everything will be ok."

"So what are we supposed to do now, you know until we get asked by somebody?" Asked Carl.

"We just go on like we always do. We play kick the can, we shoot marbles, we play Army, only we want to do it here where people can see us. We play cowboy, we hunt Sailcats--- Yea that's what we should do, and if we find one we'll make sure everyone sees us with it. We're just three kids doing what we always do," said Dicky.

"How long do we keep doing what we always do, forever?" Everett asked.

"What do you mean?" Dicky asked.

"You said we have to do what we always do, so when can we stop doing what we have to and start doing what we want to?" Questioned Everett.

"What?" Asked Dicky with a tone of disbelief. "We do what we have to do until we don't have to do it anymore. We act normal until we're sure everything's cool, until nobody's looking for Ron no more. Do you want Carl to go to prison? Do you want to go to reform school and only see your Mom and Dad on weekends?"

"No, I didn't say I can't do it, I just want to know, how long does it take before it's going to be all over?" explained Everett.

"I don't know, not very long," said Dicky exhaling deeply. His patience with Everett was running thin. "Can't you just shut the fuck up about it and just do it. If you want to hang around with us you can't be a baby, you have to do what I say."

Carl felt now that he had good reason to worry. Everett was too much the Mama's boy he thought. The truth was, it had been a long time since Everett's mother had been capable of giving him enough of her time. When she wasn't cloistered in her room, or waiting on his father hand and foot, she was tending to the younger children.

Carl decided to keep quiet and let Dicky do the talking, even though he felt that a good thumping should be the tactic used to insure Everett's compliance. This however might turn Dicky against him and he desperately needed his support just to keep his own resolve from crumbling.

The boys walked single file up and down the surrounding neighborhoods looking for feline remains. With eyes downcast scanning the streets in silence, an invisible fog of emotions fell over them; guilt, remorse, and the inescapable images of Ron during the last seconds of his life; the images that replayed like a never ending loop inside their heads.

Almost without realizing it on a conscious level, they had made their way to Madison, the edge of their neighborhood. What lay beyond, for the most part, was unfamiliar except for the few streets they had been on many times, the streets that led to the river.

Still silent they stood on the curb and looked across the street like they were on the edge of the world looking into no man's land; a boundary not to be crossed.

"I want to go back to the river," said Everett breaking the silence. His suggestions were usually met with scorn and ridicule, especially from Carl, but not this time. Both boys looked to Dicky for an answer but he said nothing.

After a few moments he just stepped off the curb, looked both ways and ran across. Everett immediately followed but Carl stood frozen on the curb until they reached the other side.

Dicky turned back and looked toward Carl. "You coming?" He yelled.

Carl shook his head and said nothing. He then turned back toward home and ran. He ran hard and fast making a moaning sound that kept time with his footfalls. Everett and Dicky watched as he slowly disappeared down Madison.

"Is he scared, do you think?" Asked Everett.

"Aren't you?" Dicky asked.

"No I ain't scared," Replied Everett trying to stand taller.

Dicky looked Everett directly in the eyes for a long moment. Everett felt as though Dicky could see inside his mind, and he was afraid of that.

"Ok, I guess I'm scared maybe a little but I ain't going to run like Carl, he said.

"Yea well you didn't shoot him either, did you? It wasn't your finger on that trigger was it?" Asked Dicky, penetrating Everett's false bravado.

"No," the boy replied meekly.

"Then don't go bad mouthing Carl, He's got more to carry than you do."

"Sorry," said Everett, looking towards the direction of the river.

"Let's go then, I got to do this now before I chicken out," said Dicky.

He turned towards the river and started walking. Everett was surprised to hear him talk about being chicken. No one would ever admit to being chicken, even if they were, and especially an older boy. But he also understood that this was different. Other than his Father talking about killing Germans, no one that he knew had ever killed anybody. Only bad guys were supposed to be killed, and Ron was a good guy. Everett gasped when he thought about that. He wanted to cry again but fought it off. If Ron was a good guy, he wondered, does this mean we're the bad guys?

Chapter Nine

The river seemed lower than usual when the boys arrived. They stood at water's edge and gazed at the same spot where they last saw their friend. The clouds were dark and slow moving, ready to fill the thick sticky air with rain.

"Do you think the river took him all the way to the ocean?" Asked Everett.

"Naw, not yet, it's only been a few days, he ain't had time," Dicky said. There was along pause, and then he said, "Maybe by next week, he'll be there."

"I ain't ever seen the ocean, have you?" Everett asked.

"No, just in pictures, but some of them people out there in California ain't never seen the Ohio neither, except in pictures," answered Dicky. "It all depends on where you hail from, unless of course you're rich, then you got the money to go everywhere and see everything."

"How about Ron do you think he's ever...? Asked Everett.

"Nope, this'll be his first time if he makes it."

"Then I'm glad we gave him a river funeral."

Neither boy took his eyes off the water. Wind started to blow in off the river brushing their hair back off their faces while sheets of tiny raindrops appeared on the rippling surface. The wind blowing on the surface of the water made the river appear to be running backwards.

For the first time since the tragedy the boys felt a little better. It was like they were in Ron's presence and he was listening. Dicky told the story of how Ron had helped carry his sick father in and out from the taxi before they got his wheelchair. Everett told of how he was the first person to talk to him when his family moved on the block, and how he always defended him against bullies. He was mainly referring to Carl though he didn't say so.

"You know man, this is the first time in a couple of days I've been able to breathe," said Dicky.

"Me too," Everett replied. "Too bad Carl ain't here hunh. I wonder where he went?"

"We'll make him come next time, " Dicky said smiling.

Everett couldn't remember the last time he saw anyone smile or laugh. He smiled too and turned his face back to the river. It felt good.

Chapter Ten

On the way up the cinder embankment to the old factory, they heard voices coming from down river---- young voices. They walked to the other side of the old building and looked down at another small stretch of shoreline. There on the beach were four teenage boys throwing rocks into the water. They were yelling and laughing like the crowd at a baseball game. Dicky and Everett positioned themselves behind a horizontal metal drum about thirty feet away and watched the older boys as they tried to hit an object in the water. From atop the hill it looked like it was perhaps a ball stuck in the branches of an overhanging bush about twenty-five feet out. They would all cheer when one of them hit it. The object looked to be possibly a beach ball or maybe a basketball.

One of the boys wore a leather jacket like Brando in the "Wild One." The other two wore just white tee shirts and jeans. The boy in the leather jacket found a large rock that filled his entire hand and threw it. The ball made a hissing sound and bubbles could be seen coming from under the water.

"Suddenly the boys demeanor changed from laughter to scowling and cursing.

"Ah shit man you did it now. Whooh!" Said one of the boys covering his nose.

"Oh God, that smells like dog shit," said the other.

The boy in the leather jacket just laughed, pointing at the other two, as he retreated further from the river.

"I guess you were right," said one of the other boys.

"I told you it was man, I told you, didn't I?" Taunted the boy in the jacket.

"I wonder who it is?" Asked one of them.

"I don't know man, but it sure ain't the first one I've seen floating in this river, that's for sure," said the leather jacket.

"Let's go it's starting to smell really bad here. I got a date later man, and I don't want to have to go home smelling like a god damn corpse," one said.

The tree boys turned and headed further downriver and then turned landward and disappeared.

Dicky and Everett stayed hidden and silent until after the other boys had gone. Neither wanting to say what they were both thinking.

Everett was the first to move to a standing position. Frowning at the ball in the weeds, mouth open, he asked, "Is that

Ron, do you think? I mean it doesn't look like Ron from here Ron wasn't fat. It just looks like a big black ball with some rags on it."

Dicky came from behind the drum, sat down, and began sliding down the embankment to the river. He walked closer to the object straining his eyes to see and at the same time holding his nose to block the stench.

At first Everett was opposed to joining him at the water's edge but finally relented to his curiosity, knowing that all the good feelings he had felt earlier were about to disappear.

When he finally stood next to Dicky he noticed his friends eyes were wet.

"I don't know for sure, I can't remember what he was wearing that day, do you?"

"Cut offs and a white shirt," replied Everett. "But he didn't wear no black and I see black, don't you?"

"Yea, but I can see a white tee shirt maybe. It's just really dirty that's all," said Dicky. "But I don't see no Levi's though."

"But what about the black and he didn't have no big belly?"

"I don't know," Dicky whispered. "Maybe it's just some dead nigger, that fell in the water drunk or something."

"Yea that's it, it's just some dead nigger and Ron's on the way to the ocean like we said," said Everett convinced.

Dicky was starting to have second thoughts however about Ron's trip to the ocean.

"Hell Everett if this guy can get hung up in these bushes here, then Ron might be hung up in the bushes someplace else and if he is, then maybe somebody will recognize him. If they find him like he is, shot and everything, Carl is going to come apart man, and tell everything. You saw him, he's just barely holding it together."

"What do we do then?" Everett asked.

"We need to walk as far as we can down river and look to see that he ain't hung up someplace."

"Ok," said Everett reluctantly looking downriver.

The rain worsened as they climbed over bushes and old iron railings leftover from some long ago barge ramp. Sometimes they had to wade into the river to get around fenced property, but after three hours of walking Dicky held up his hand like a cavalry commander and stopped. Everett had long ago past his endurance level but followed anyway without complaint, now he faced at least a six-mile trek home. He slumped on the sandy bank and lay back exhausted with his mouth open, trying to quench his thirst under the summer cloudburst.

Dicky was a runner at school, he could have gone on another three miles but he saw the younger boy struggling and decided call an end to the search. The river made a sudden turn to the left and widened reveling at least another mile of shoreline free of brush. The riverbank was clear as far as he could see.

"If he made it this far, it's a straight shot to Louisville. See that channel of fast water in the middle," said Dicky pointing down river.

"Yea," Everett replied without moving from his prone position.

Dicky noticed his lack of attention and smiled. The rain was coming down harder prompting him to copy Everett and tilted his head to catch rainwater in his mouth.

Both boys lay soaked to the skin gulping their fill of the sweet tasting rain and recharging a second wind for the walk home.

The walk back upriver seemed easier than the trip down. The boys were tired and had lost the sense of urgency that consumed the hunt for Ron's body. But despite the belief that Ron, had at least made it past Louisville, they were plagued by the existence of the other unidentified body. Though neither would admit it then, they had to make sure.

They could smell the object long before they reached it but it hadn't moved from the spider's web of branches that held it in the shallows. The object floated on the current like a river buoy, constantly in motion but anchored in place.

"Hey Dicky, are we sure that's even a body, it still looks like something with a bunch of rags over it?" Everett asked hoping they had been mistaken.

The object had changed shape slightly looking more like a body floating face down. Dicky recognized the head bobbing separately from the torso. He knew then it was definitely a corpse.

"I'm sure it's a body but there's only one-way to find out," Dicky replied.

"I want to go home, I don't want to go in the river."

"Don't be a baby. --- You and me, we'll go in together Ok? It ain't like we're going to get any wetter."

The older boy twisted a branch off a nearby bush held it out in front of him like a sword.

"We'll use this and just poke it a little till we see," said Dicky.

"What if it's him?" Everett asked.

"Then we get him loose and send him on down the river like he's supposed to. Don't you want to him to make it to the ocean?" Argued Dicky.

"Yea, I guess, but Carl ought to be doing this. Not me!"

"Well, Carl ain't here and besides you saw how he was, we got to do it and that's just the way it is," he said frowning.

The boys waded out in the water walking slowly towards the body. The smell worsened the closer they got, even though they tried to cover their noses. Everett turned his head away and wretched into the water, letting Dicky have the lead.

Stopping several feet from it Dicky snagged the cloth covering the ball and pulled it towards him. As it got closer Everett turned and headed for shore.

"Get your ass back here," shouted Dicky.

The younger boy turned again and faced his friend. Dicky struggled with the object trying to free it seemed to be hung up on something below the water line.

"What's wrong?" asked Everett.

"It's caught on something, we have to reach under and untangle it," he said.

The younger boy began to whine, "I can't Dicky I can't touch it."

"Look you little shit, this could be our friend caught in here and you're going to get over here and help me pull him loose."

A large ripple washed ashore without warning causing the corpse to pitch to the left and roll over. For a split second the head of the corpse to broke the surface. The skin on the face was a bluish white, otherwise void of color. The eyes were open but also held no hint of what they once were.

Dicky dropped the stick and jumped backward, knocking Everett off balance. He fought for a moment to regain his footing but managed to stay on his feet.

"Did you see, was it Ron, was it?" cried Everett.

"I'm not sure," shouted Dicky.

Suddenly the water next to corpse exploded like a depth charge. This was followed by voices yelling at them from shore. The boys turned quickly to see four teenage boys hurling rocks; the same boys they saw earlier. They had to be part of the Gunther gang, Dicky thought.

Without a word he grabbed Everett's arm and pulled him. As fast as he could he dragged Everett through the water and behind the same bush that held the corpse. The bushes were especially thick here and Dicky knew that the teenagers would have to go around the old factory before sliding down to the river.

"Are those guys the Gunther gang?" Everett whispered.

"I think so, so be quiet," Replied Dicky.

When they came to the thickest part of the brush, where it made contact with the river they lowered their bodies so that only their heads were above water. They could barely see through the brush when the other boys made it down. With rocks in hand they scoured the bank in both directions.

The two boys remained still and quiet.

"Where the hell are they," one boy yelled.

The voice was familiar and Dicky recognized it as the one with the leather jacket from earlier.

"We got to find them, they've been messing with our dead body," he said.

"What do you think they were doing out there next to it, I mean man, that would make me puke?" one of them asked.

"I don't know, but we got to find them before they tell somebody," said leather jacket. "Let's split up, you two go down river and Jake and me will go up river. If you find them before we do, you hold them till I get back."

Dicky and Everett sank deeper until only their noses were above water. They heard the footsteps of the other boys disappear in both directions.

After a few minutes Dicky lifted his head and made his way to the edge of the brush to where he could see a clear path up to the old factory and beyond.

With a tug on Everett's arm he pointed to the shore and then brought his finger to his lips to signal quiet. Slowly they made their way past the corpse, taking another look as they past, and then to the shore.

Dicky looked first to the left and saw no one. He then looked right and, in the distance, saw two figures running in their direction.

"C'mon let's go," he said and began scrambling up the bank still dragging Everett.

They heard the other boys yelling, "stop if you know what's good for you", but they did not stop.

They made it to the top of the twenty-foot embankment and on around the old factory by the time the other boys made it to the bottom of the hill. They ran across Riverside Dr. and down Collins to Taft before they dared to look back. No one was behind them anymore.

Everett slumped to the ground completely exhausted. Dicky leaned against a mailbox to catch his breath before continuing on.

"Do you think they gave up?" asked Everett, breathing heavily.

"Yea, there's no way they could see which way we went even if they did follow us up to Riverside," said Dicky. "You ready to go now just in case I'm wrong?"

Everett groaned but slowly stood up. Dicky put his arm on Everett's shoulder and walked beside him all the way to Madison and Owls Nest Park.

Sitting at the entrance leaning against the park sign was Carl. When he saw them crossing the street, he stood, holding up one arm with something in it. He smiled as they got closer and waived a dried carcass like a railroad flagman.

"I found one!" He said excitedly. The object was flat enough but just a little too big to be a cat Dicky noticed. After closer inspection, he smiled at Carl and said, "You do know that's a dog right."

"No it ain't it's just a big cat," insisted Carl.

"It's just a small dog; a poodle maybe," said Dicky.

"We could still sail it," said Carl looking disappointed.

"I ain't sailing it," said Dicky.

Carl then looked to Everett who had just, again, slumped to the ground.

"What's the matter with him?" Carl asked.

"It's a long story," replied Dicky.

"Well shit," Carl said, twirling the carcass over his head with hopes of watching it sail high over Madison and land softly on the other side. It might have actually done that if the leg he was holding hadn't detached, causing the mummified remains to slam into the side of a passing car.

Chapter Eleven

It had been three days since the shooting and the boys had not heard a word about Ron's disappearance. Every morning Dicky would walk out on his front porch with coffee expecting to see Ron's mother frantically canvassing the neighborhood, but as yet, this hadn't happened. Keeping quiet about Ron was maddening. It would have been easier to just say he didn't know what happened to him and get on with his life, instead of worrying about what he would say or how he would say it. He wished he could go on record now and forget about it. (Don't ask Dicky he already said he doesn't know anything.)

He rolled out of bed and sat rubbing the sleep from his eyes when his brother Danny opened the door wrapped in a towel.

"Shower's all yours shithead," he said, as he stripped off the towel and snapped his brother with it.

"Ouch!" cried Dicky, rubbing the red mark on his chest.

Dicky was still deep in thought and didn't respond with his usual caustic remarks.

"What's the matter are you sick or something?" His brother asked.

Dicky did not acknowledge his brother except to brandish a middle finger as he lay back on the bed, his legs still on the floor.

"Ok, what is it little brother, did somebody run over your pet frog or something?" Danny asked sarcastically.

"Don't you have to be at work or something?" Dicky snarled.

There were disadvantages sharing a bedroom with his older brother; for one thing Danny always knew when something was wrong. Most of the time he didn't care one way or the other what Dicky was worrying about, but sometimes he did, and then he was actually helpful.

Dicky thought about getting his brother's advice without actually telling him anything. Maybe with a hypothetical question, he thought. He gave up on that idea after thinking about it for a few moments, for fear his brother might connect the dots later when Ron's disappearance was common knowledge. He did, however decide to ask him about another problem.

"You know about the Gunther gang right?" Asked Dicky.

"I know enough to stay the hell away from them, you remember what they did to Cecil?" he answered referring to the beating they had given Ron's cousin.

"Yea I know, but is it true that they kill people and drop the bodies in the river?" He asked.

"Why do you want to know that for?" Danny asked.

"I want to know if it's true, that's all."

"I don't know, maybe I guess--- Yea I heard that, but I don't know if it's true. I wouldn't put it passed them though. Everybody says they did, why?"

"Cause Ron and Carl and Everett ran into a bunch of them the other day down by the river and they got chased," replied Dicky.

"Everett still stealing his mom's cigarettes?" Asked Danny smiling.

Dicky nodded but did not make eye contact, nor did he smile.

"Yea it's something to worry about, but they aint going to kill you and throw you in the river. They might kick your ass though. Did those guys do anything?"

"No they just said they were on their spot. They threw rocks and everything," Dicky replied.

"Tell those guys not to worry about it too much. Just stay away from them, that's all. I did hear a couple of those guys carry guns, but as long as you guy don't fuck with them, you'll be all right. They ain't likely to be after no kids"

After listening to his brother's advice Dicky went downstairs. He sat sipping a cup of coffee on the front porch while his mother was in the kitchen busy frying eggs. He sat for a few minutes enjoying the morning before he noticed the grey Buick parked in front of Ron's house. Since she didn't own a car he figured it belonged to one of her boyfriends. A tree blocked his view slightly but he thought he saw movement inside.

Dicky moved to the other side of the porch for a better look and could clearly see two people very close together in the front seat. At first he couldn't make out what they were doing and then he did; they were kissing. It wasn't the first time for that. Ron's mother didn't seem to care who watched. She always seemed oblivious to anything going on around her.

After several minutes she emerged from the car disheveled, pulling and tugging at her clothes. She was barefooted, carrying her panties and bra in one hand and her purse in the other. This is why Ron hadn't been missed yet; she was just getting home from one of her trysts. As she turned to walk to her door she noticed Dicky on the porch. He smiled and held up his cup as a gesture of hello but she didn't respond. She hurried to the front door and went inside, without a word or a smile.

Elaine Stone was a tall thin woman in her mid thirties. With dark hair and brown eyes she was fairly attractive, but not what Dicky would call a looker.

Dicky gulped the last of his coffee and turned to go inside when he came face to face with his mother standing on the other side of the screen door. May Williams was a stout woman in her mid forties with dark hair that hung out from her head in a triangle like the sphinx.

"Elaine just getting home?" She asked.

"Yea,"

"It's a damn shame how she leaves that boy alone all the time. I feel sorry for him, does he ever say anything about it?"

"Naw, he don't never say nothing," he replied.

"Well the next time she does that, you tell Ronny he needs to come over and spend the night here," she said.

"Ok, I'll tell him," he said in a low voice avoiding eye contact.

Even when Ron was alive he wouldn't have taken her up on the offer. He had been a very private person and not in the habit of doing sleepovers.

The sudden sound of the phone ringing interrupted their conversation and while May left to go answer it, Dicky went to the kitchen to eat his breakfast. After a few minutes she returned with a puzzled look on her face.

"That was Elaine. She says Ron's not home and she wanted to know if he was here. I told her that he wasn't, then she asked if I would ask you if you knew where he was. Do you?"

"No, how would I know where he's at I've been here all night," he answered slightly defensive. Maybe he just got tired of being left alone all the time and just decided to split."

"Has he ever told you he felt like that?" She asked.

"Well not just that like that but I just figured, you know?" Dicky said sounding a bit irritated.

"Hmm!" she grunted, puzzled with the tone of her son's answer. "Well when you go outside make sure you ask Carl and Everett if they know where he went, now I'm worried."

"Why are you worried, his mother darn sure ain't, she's been gone for three days, Ron could have died for all she cares," Dicky said realizing immediately that he'd said too much.

"How do you know she's been gone for three days--- Ronny tell you that?" She asked.

"No, he don't have too I got eyes I can see when she ain't home," he said, sounding more defensive.

"I didn't realize you kept such close tabs on the comings and goings of Elaine Stone," she said frowning.

"I don't Mom, jeez! I'm just saying I noticed this time, I don't notice all the time, but this time I did. I mean they live right next door for craps sake!" he said, his voice getting louder.

"Don't you get ticked off with me, Richard Williams, You finish your breakfast and go out there with the rest of the boys and see if you can find Ronny, so Elaine can have piece of mind before she goes to work."

Dicky put the last of his breakfast in his mouth and left the room feeling a little irritated but for the first time since the shooting he was feeling the full weight of the secret. Confession would cure everything but he felt it was too late for that now.

Once outside he sat on the steps to ponder his next move. After a few moments he got up and walked across the street. He could see that the front door to Carl's house was open. He stood at the bottom step and shouted.

"Hey Carl, can you come out?"

He heard movement inside and then Carl's father, Bert was at the door.

"Carl went with his mother down to Peoples Corner, they should be back in about an hour," Bert said. "By the way how's your dad doing?"

"He's about the same, I guess," Answered Dicky.

"Well that fact that he hasn't gotten any worse is a good sign, don't you think? What's it been now, almost a year?

"Yea, I guess," Dicky said but he didn't feel optimistic. His father hadn't gotten any worse because he can't get much worse unless he's dead, he thought. "Well I'll just come back later then, he said leaving"

He walked to the middle of the street and looked towards Everett's house. He thought about going down to get him but then he thought; he's nine. He then walked back to his house and sat on the porch to wait, and let them come to him.

Chapter Twelve

When Everett woke up and went downstairs for breakfast he noticed the cellar door was open. This usually meant it was washday unless it was the weekend and then it was his father working in his shop. He walked to the edge of the steps and looked down into the pale light coming from a single bulb with a pull chain. It was a weekday and he could usually smell the strong odor of bleach wafting up from the cool basement, but this time he smelled nothing. He could hear movement downstairs so he decided to take a step down.

"Mom are you down there?" he called out.

At first there was no answer and then his father's husky voice said, "Don't bother us Everett… leave us be we're talking."

He thought he could hear the muffled sound of his mother crying. This thought terrified him. Many times he had seen his father's drunken rages turn loud and violent, usually at his mother's expense.

"Mom, Is that you? Are you ok?" He called again.

"God damn it Everett, what did I tell you? Huh! What did I tell you," his father bellowed.

Everett could hear his footsteps getting closer to the stairs. Suddenly he appeared, red eyed and angry, looking up from the basement. Everett took a step back up into the kitchen as his father took a step up.

"Don't you touch him, don't you dare," he heard his mother scream from somewhere in the basement.

His father turned to look at her and stepped back down. And then with the look of surprise he took another step back away from the stairs and then held up his hands. Everett's mother, armed with a large pry bar, came into view and stepped backwards onto the stairway. Everett couldn't see her face but by the sound of her voice he knew she was angry: angry enough to defy her husband, which she only did when protecting her children. The woman never took her eyes off her him as she made her way up the stairs one slow step at a time.

"You are going to stay down here you son of a bitch until you sober up," she said making her way all the way up the steps and then quickly closing the doors. She slid the pry bar through the handles of the two cabinet style cellar doors.

His father tried to rush up the stairs before she had secured the door but he was too late. He hit the cellar doors with such a jolt it shook the kitchen.

"When I get out of here you're going to be damn sorry, you stupid bitch," he yelled while continuing to batter the doors.

His mother turned towards the sink and grabbed a butcher knife from the dish drainer. Everett could clearly see the cuts and bruises on her face. This was the worse beating he'd ever seen.

His father continued to batter the doors until he grew tired and his voice grew raspy. All the while his mother maintained her armed vigil in front of the basement doors.

When all was quiet she put the knife on the kitchen table and turned to Everett. Everett stared at the knife saying nothing at first.

"What happened Mom? It's morning, why is he drunk already, why ain't he at work?" Questioned Everett.

His mother pulled Everett to her and held him close. He buried his face in her terry cloth robe and cried. He tried to understand why his father was changing, but he was only nine. The pressures that motivate adults were still foreign to him but he did understand what it was doing to the family and especially his mother. What also scared him was that he knew sooner or later he would get out and when he did his mother would again pay for her defiance.

"Shh, don't cry, everything's going to be all right," she whispered running her hand through his hair.

"But what happened Mom?" He asked again, looking up at her.

"Your father lost his job this morning. He didn't come home right away. When he did he went to the basement to be alone. It was my fault this time I should have let him alone but I didn't. I went down there and I shouldn't have. She started crying now and opened a cut on her lip. As she wept she could taste the salty mixture of tears and blood, both staining the yoke of Everett's shirt.

"Don't worry," she kept repeating, "we're all going to get through this."

Everett felt secure in his mother's arms. Many times he had thought of going to her and telling her about the shooting. He saw himself confessing it all and being held in the softness of her robe filled with her smells and being told everything will be all right. That was impossible now and he knew it. He couldn't burden his mother with anything that horrible, especially while she was going through a hell of her own.

After a few moments she took him by the shoulders and said,

"I want you to go out and play now and don't come home till this afternoon, by then your Dad will be sober and everything will be all right."

She wrapped four pieces of bacon in a thick slice of white bread and gave him a full bottle of orange pop.

"Go on now, come back this afternoon," she said.

Everett took the sandwich and soda and walked out to the front porch to eat. He sat down on the steps but found that he wasn't hungry. After staring at the sandwich for a moment he laid it down on the step beside him. He did take a couple of gulps from the soda and wiped his lips with his forearm before setting out to find his friends.

On the way to Dicky's house he saw the checker cab stop in front of Carl's house and watched as Carl and his mother got out carrying packages. They had been shopping, he concluded, and by the looks of the packages they had spent a lot of money. Carl's Dad hadn't been laid off.

Carl glanced over and looked at Everett and then saw Dicky sitting on his front steps. Without acknowledging his friends, he turned and followed his mother inside. Carl's mood had grown darker with every passing day. He found that all the things that used to give him pleasure now seemed like useless wastes of time. A mixture of anger, guilt and frustration, festered inside him. He needed some kind of release before it completely consumed him.

Chapter Thirteen

By the time Carl had finished helping his mother Everett was already sitting on the steps beside Dicky, his soda half gone and his upper lip a bright orange.

"What are we doing?" Carl asked.

"We're going to go to the fort for awhile, we're suppose to be looking for Ron. His mom came home this morning.

"Oh shit, what do we do now?" Asked Carl looking worried.

"Like I said, we're going to the fort," replied Dicky.

He noticed that Carl was worse than when he saw him the day before. Even Everett could tell that something wasn't right with Carl.

"I need to talk to you guys," Carl said. "I think we ought to---.

"Not here, not now!" Dicky interrupted. "Not until we get to the fort."

No one spoke as they walked across the hollow to the old stone ruins. This was usually a happy place where they would come to play out any number of scenarios from war to cowboys to Tarzan. But the boys hadn't laughed or played together since the shooting.

Once they were settled on their wooden crates Carl couldn't wait any longer.

"I think we should tell what happened," he said. His eyes were swollen like puffy little bags.

"You know you look like shit Carl. You look like some little old man who pees his pants," sneered Dicky poking his finger in Carl's chest.

"I don't care man. You were right Everett, we should have told, we should have told right from the beginning," he said.

"No! We can't tell now," said Everett, surprising both Dicky and Carl. "We can't tell now. If we tell now it's going to mess up everything."

Carl was speechless for a few moments. He had counted on Everett to back him up to out vote Dicky.

"What happened to you, you wanted to tell as soon as it happened?" Asked Carl.

"No man, what happened to you? We agreed to keep our mouths shut mainly because of you. We did it to keep you out of jail mostly but now you want to go to jail now, is that it?" Dicky asked exasperated.

"I don't care anymore. I don't care if they send me to jail, I can't take it anymore man I just can't," Carl whined, his voice quivering. "I can't sleep anymore. My mom keeps asking me what's wrong and I keep lying. I've told so many lies I can't remember what I told anybody. I killed Ron, I did it," Carl said with a tear in his voice.

Dicky went over to Carl and put his arm around him. Everett followed and stood on his other side.

"It wasn't your fault though Carl. It was a accident and all we did was to give Ron a funeral so he could go to the ocean. Come on man we all have to stick together. This is all going to be over soon, you'll see. And if you tell now it won't bring Ron back. It won't change anything. And it would probably be harder on Ron's Mom to know he's dead right now. If she thinks he ran away then at least she thinks he alive and she can still hope that she'll see him one day. Don't you see?"

"Hey if it were Ron instead of you, he wouldn't tell. If he's in heaven he knows it was a accident," said Everett.

Carl stretched the sleeve of his tee shirt and dried his eyes. The boys had made him feel better. He lifted his arms and hugged them both squeezing until his arms hurt. For the first time Carl knew the difference between playmates and friends. The boys had set him free and he wanted to thank them. He wanted to apologize to Everett for every hurtful thing he had ever done or said, but he didn't. He didn't do any of it; he just held them close and cried.

Chapter Fourteen

By four o'clock Elaine Stone had gotten only five hours sleep and was up ready to go to work. Before going downstairs she checked her son's room again, but again he wasn't there. Since Ron wasn't much for cleaning his room, it was hard to tell the last time he'd slept in his bed.

She glanced at her watch; her ride would be there in five minutes. Once dressed in her frilly waitress uniform she went to the front porch and looked both ways, hoping to see Ron playing with his friends. She was beginning to worry. He was resourceful and independent so she felt confident that wherever he was, she could rest assured that he would have a good explanation. Still she was worried and she felt a little guilty for staying gone so long. This wasn't the first time by any means but he had always been home before.

Elaine returned to the living room and called the Williams again, but this time got no answer. Before hanging up she heard three loud toots of a car horn from out front, her ride was there.

She would have to deal with him later. She would call him on her break and he would be home, very apologetic for making her worry and everything would all right again, she told herself.

Before going out the door she quickly wrote a note for Ron to stay put when he got home and wait for her call. The horn from the impatient driver sounded again prompting her to stuff the note in the refrigerator door and leave the house running.

Half way to work she popped three aspirins and washed them down with a swallow if gin from the half pint in her purse. Her head was pounding from last night's party and lack of sleep. Worrying about her son didn't help much either.

The co-worker she carpooled with shook her head when she saw the bottle.

"Sorry honey, hair of the dog! You know," she said through a fake laugh.

The first four hours of her shift went by slowly, but at the end of the first two she had gotten her second wind and was at least feeling better. Sitting in the manager's office she dialed home.

The phone rang four times then five and six and seven. By the tenth ring she was beginning to feel the cold flush of alarm. She looked at her watch; it was 8:30 and dark out, he should be home. Sometimes during the summer he and his friends would go out at night and catch fireflies but he had to have come home for dinner. That's why she left the note in the refrigerator door. She then called the William's again, and this time Dicky picked up.

"Oh Dicky I'm so glad your home. I'm looking for Ronny is he by any chance there?" She asked.

Dicky flashed with panic. He wasn't expecting to have to talk to her, especially at night.

"Ah! No Ma'am, ain't he home?" he answered.

"No Dicky that's why I called you. Do you think he might be at Carl's house?"

"Oh, I don't know, I wouldn't think so though, he and Carl ain't that tight, you know what I mean?"

"Well did you see him last?" She asked.

"Uh, well it was yesterday sometime, I think, I'm not sure." he replied.

"You don't remember the last time you saw him?" She questioned. "How can you not remember the last time you saw him?" She asked, now irritated.

"Because I have to go with my mom when she goes shopping and sometimes we're gone a long time," He answered defensive and surly.

"I just think it's strange that you can't or won't remember when you saw him last, I'm worried Dicky. If you're not telling me everything..."

"Look Mrs. stone I told you what I can remember. Do you remember the last time you saw him?" He lashed out.

The question hung in the air and stung as she stumbled to answer.

"I— I --- It was--- never mind," she hissed and hung up. Dicky's sarcasm hit her hard. Now she was worried and feeling nauseous with guilt. She took another deep pull on the gin bottle from her purse and sat alone in the room trying to decide what to do.

Finally she came to the conclusion that Ron was off doing something he shouldn't and that's why the Williams boy had been so rude. Anger flooded her thinking, momentarily pushing worry aside; she would have deal with him when she got home. After being gone for two days, she couldn't afford to loose another shift. One more drink and Elaine Stone returned to the floor

Chapter Fifteen

Sergeant's John Mapes and Herb Porter turned off of U.S Highway 52 and then drove left past St. Rose Church before parking facing the river. Officers of the Cincinnati police had already secured the scene, their white-topped service hats clearly visible from the road.

John Mapes was a heavy set man with almost thirty years on the job and Herb Porter had just past the sergeants exam last year and was new to homicide. Neither man spoke as they exited the vehicle and walked the hundred plus yards along the river to where the body was found.

"What do we have here?" Mapes asked the ranking officer standing next to a distorted white corpse lying on the sand.

"It looks like a male Caucasian, maybe in his teens to early twenties. It's hard to tell, he's been in the water at least a week," he answered.

Mapes squatted down for a closer look. Pieces of flesh were missing from the face and hands, which he attributed to a weeks worth of jostling by river currents and scavengers.

"Who found the body?" He asked.

"That gentleman over there," said the officer pointing to a shabbily dressed man carrying a gunnysack. Mapes pegged him as a river bum; a person who scavenges the riverbank for anything he could pawn, sell or cash in.

The man sat on a log next to two more officers about ten yards past the body. Walking towards him he glanced back at Porter who had covered his mouth with a handkerchief.

"You get use to it," he shouted.

Porter nodded and followed the older detective towards the witness. Another older officer standing next to him looked up and recognized Mapes.

"You still on the job Johnny?" He asked.

"Me! What about you? You were around when they arrested Jesus, and you're still here," said Mapes smiling.

The older man grunted a laugh and looked down at the man on the log.

"This is Julius Speck he says he's a beachcomber. I told him he's a long way from the ocean but he says he's just up from Miami via the interstate rail system and he came across the body this morning being attacked by a dog."

"Yes that right," the man said. "I chased away the dog with rocks and I called the police from the church."

"Because he's an upstanding citizen," said the older officer sarcastically.

"Well not exactly, I was actually heading for the church when I came across that unfortunate man," he said.

"You were on your way to the church, why?" Asked Mapes.

"Because the padres there are kind enough to give unfortunates like me a little food and odd jobs."

"Tell me what you saw exactly, this morning. You were walking upriver towards St. Rose church and then---?"

"And then I see this dog pulling at something in the water and when I get close I see it's a body, so I chased the dog away with rocks like I said,"

"Did you see anyone else on the river besides the dog?"

"Well not today, no, but last night I stayed in that old building up there," he said pointing to the old factory, "and I saw some boys throwing rocks at something in the water."

"Throwing rocks at the body, do you think?"

"Yes, I suppose they could have been," he answered.

"Can you give us a description of these boys?" Asked Mapes.

"One was wearing a leather jacket, you know--- like a motorcycle jacket. And the other boys wore tee shirts and jeans, I think. They were too far away for me to get a good look at their faces."

"One more question, and you better not lie to me, did you touch the body at all?"

The man looked down at the dirt between his shoes for a moment before answering. He then reached into his jacket pocket and pulled out a gold wristwatch and handed it to Mapes.

"I found it in his front pocket," he said.

Mapes took the watch and inspected I closely. I was a Bulova with a gold case and band.

"It doesn't work I already tried to wind it. It seems to be wound too tight. It doesn't tick," said the man.

Mapes instinctively held the watch to his ear but the man was right, it didn't tick. Mapes thanked him for being honest and then told the older officer to let him go.

On the way back to the car Sgt. Porter asked, "Do you think those boys might know something about the body?"

"Maybe, there is a rumor that the Gunther gang killed somebody and dumped him in the river. We don't know if it's true or just something the gang made up to impress people."

"There aren't any missing persons to match up with the story?" Asked Porter.

"Of course there is! In a town this size, there's always somebody missing; Take your pick. Even if you could I.D. somebody, there ain't any evidence to link it to the gang, it's just one of those conundrums."

"Conundrums?" Porter laughed.

"Yea, you'll find a lot of those in homicide. Where did you say you came from?" Asked Mapes.

"Vice, why?"

"Didn't you have any conundrums in vice?"

"I don't know, we had a lot of condoms," he replied with a smile.

"I mean didn't you have any cases that just kept you running in circles because you couldn't find the what you were looking for? Well! That's a conundrum,"

" I guess I did--- a few cases, yea. Mostly all I did was pop hookers and junkies who kept showing back up on the street twenty-four hours later."

"Hooker's and junkies! That's what they had you doing? Anybody over there trying to collar any bad guys?" Asked Mapes.

"I got to hope so, but I never saw much of it. That's why I wanted in homicide. I figure here I could do something, you know."

"I heard you passed the sergeants test with flying colors on the fist try, that's probably what got you in homicide."

"Like I told you, I wanted in bad. I studied my ass off."

" I got to pull over up here, I got to grab a pack of smokes," said Mapes.

"Yea sure, I didn't know you smoked."

"Only when I drink," he said smiling.

Mapes pulled to the curb and went in the liquor store.

"John, you're early today, how's the cop biz?" Asked Chuck, the middle-aged ex-cop turned liquor storeowner.

"You know, same ole same ole, said Mapes

"The usual?" Chuck asked.

"If you please sir," replied Mapes.

The man threw a pack of Chesterfields on the counter and bagged a six-pack of Weidemans long necks with a pint of hundred proof peppermint schnapps. Mapes scooped up the cigarettes and stuck them in his jacket pocket.

"See you Chuck," he said, twisting the top of the bag into a handle and walking back to the car carrying it at his side.

Walking quickly behind the car so that Porter couldn't see he popped the trunk and placed the bag inside.

"Sorry it took so long I decided to pick up a few incidentals while I was there," he said as he slid in behind the wheel.

The older detective went through his usual ritual of pounding the unopened pack against his palm several times in a hatchet motion before opening, and after a flip of his Zippo he took a deep draw.

"You a drinking man Herb?" he asked after driving down a deserted alley behind a gutted Victorian building.

"Not much, I can take it or leave it," said Porter.

"You a judgmental man?"

"It depends, I got my pet peeves like the next guy."

"I need to stop a minute here and have a quick snort, does that bother you Herb?"

"I don't live in your skin and you don't live in mine."

"Good answer," said Mapes as he stopped the vehicle.

Mapes got out of the car, opened the trunk and opened a beer. Porter remained in the car and said nothing. Mapes took several pulls off the schnapps, downed the beer and finished the smoke. He tossed the empty bottle down the alley and after crushing the cigarette out with his foot, got back in the car.

"I ain't a drunk," said Mapes, but his partner said nothing. "I just drink enough to numb the beast, that's all. I figured if we're going to work together you needed to see the whole picture,"

"What if I'd been a prick and decided blow the whistle?"

"Nobody would believe you. Everybody knows you can't trust those reefer addicts in vice, besides I got twenty eight years on the job. I'm gold plated," said Mapes laughing.

After a long moment Porter said, "Understand though, if you can't hold it together out here I won't jeopardize my career."

"Understood," replied Mapes. "You like baseball?"

"Yea I'm a Reds fan," Porter answered.

"Good, why don't you tune in the ballgame they're playing the Dodgers this afternoon," said Mapes rubbing his eyes.

The tires squealed slightly as they made a left on Taft and headed for Walnut Hills. Porter cranked the window down and took a deep breath.

"Let's go find this gang then," he said.

Chapter Sixteen

Elaine Stone made one more call before leaving for home but again there was no answer. The anger had changed again to worry but she still held out hope that he was just asleep and didn't hear the phone.

Her ride was Stan the cook, co-worker and sometimes boyfriend. This week he was just a ride home. He pulled the car out of the parking lot and headed toward Victory Parkway.

"Want to stop off for drink someplace?" He asked putting his hand on her thigh.

"Not tonight I have to get home there's something going on with Ronny," she answered removing his hand and placing it back in his own lap.

"Yea, what is it, has he been having broads over while you've been gone." Stan laughed.

"Stan I appreciate the ride home, but do me a favor and shut the fuck up. I'm not in the mood."

"Ok, ok, I was just trying to lighten up the mood a little, you know. I was thinking we might listen to the radio and mess around a little at your place."

"I told you Stan I'm not in the mood," she said just as they pulled up to her house.

The house was dark, with not even the porch light on. She sat in the car for a few moments staring at the blackened windows before opening the door.

"I changed my mind Stan could you please just go in with me until I check out what's going on. This isn't like Ron, he always leaves a light on somewhere, --- I'm scared."

"Yea sure," Stan said exiting the car and falling in behind Elaine on her way to the front porch. She unlocked and they both walked in. The old house had a small foyer with a stairway to the upstairs bedrooms to the right and pocket doors opening to the living room, dining room and kitchen to the left. Elaine and Stan stood at the foot of the stairs and looked up.

"Ronny," she called but there was no answer.

"Ronny," she repeated turning on the hall light and running upstairs.

Frantically she ran to his bedroom and flung open the door. Finding it empty she checked her own room, turning on lights as she went. As a last resort she followed the small stairway to the attic where Ron sometimes played on rainy days but she found this room also empty.

"Ronny!" she screamed, "God Damn it where are you."

Elaine was becoming hysterical now as she brushed passed Stan on the stairway to check the first floor. Putting her hand in the brass cup on the Pocket door she flung it open revealing another darkened room. She also could see that there were no lights on in the dinning room or the kitchen either. Just as she did upstairs she went from room to room turning on lights. Stan followed closely now. He could see that Elaine was on the verge of an emotional display, as he called them, and decided to cool his jets and just try to be her friend tonight.

When she reached the kitchen she opened the door to the cellar and flicked on the light. She was crying now and afraid to go down for fear of what she might find, or wouldn't find.

"Stan could you?" she whimpered.

Without an answer he pushed her aside and went downstairs and disappeared into the dark basement. After a few minutes he appeared at the foot of the stairs and shook his head. Elaine was crying harder now.

"What about his friends?" Stan asked. "Maybe he's spending the night with a friend."

"I already checked they said they don't know where he is." She sobbed, and slumped down in a kitchen chair.

"So what do you want to do babe?" He asked.

"I don't know yet let me think a minute, ok!" She snapped. Stan had seen her like this once before when she became jealous of his attentions to another waitress and knew to keep a low profile until she got passed the hysterical stage. He stood quietly by her chair listening to her cry.

Chapter Seventeen

The boys plan to stay visible in the neighborhood only lasted for a few days. Everett was usually the first on the street in the morning, taking his mother's advice of being out of sight out of mind when his father was on a binder. This happened a lot more frequently since he got laid off. Walking the picket line in the morning and getting drunk in the afternoon became his daily schedule. The beatings his mother had to endure were getting more frequent as well. Since locking him in the basement he made sure she paid the price for her insubordination.

One or two days a week he was more sober than drunk and on those days he was attentive and apologetic to Alice for his violent behavior. This conversation was also followed by a string of promises to become a better husband and never again hit her. Everett quickly learned that those were hollow promises.

His other siblings spent most of their time sequestered in their room as part of another out of sight out of mind solution.

Carl had taken a vow of total obedience to his father. He was slowly coming to terms with the incident, but he still feared that if he provoked his father into another whipping, he might, under the stress, be brought back to his original state of mind and spill his guts about the killing. Everything in Carl's life now was held precariously together by his pact with Dicky and Everett. Occasionally he still had bad dreams and something as slight as a word or phrase could remind him of Ron and stagger him momentarily. But he was getting better. The phrase, "Time Heals All Wounds" became his mantra, especially when he was alone in the dark. The daily meetings at the fort were more like a support group gathering; each telling their individual experiences about how they are able to stay sane and appear normal. Everything was going along as planned until Elaine Stone filed a missing persons report.

Two days after Elaine finally came home and discovered him gone, the police were knocking on doors and talking to neighbors. Dicky had just finished cleaning the basement when his mother called for him to come upstairs. When he got to the front door he saw two uniformed police officers standing on the porch.

"This is my son Richard," she told the police. "Richard these officers would like to talk to you about Ronny."

Dicky felt the muscles in his stomach tighten, but he tried hard to appear like nothing was wrong.

"Richard do you happen to remember the last time you saw your friend Ronald?" The heavier officer asked.

"I guess it was a few days ago, why?"

"You do know your friend is missing, right,"

"Oh I didn't know he still was, so he hasn't come back?"

"Come back from where?" The officer asked.

"From wherever he was," said Dicky now feeling the pressure of the questioning.

"Do you know if he was planning to go somewhere that his mother might not approve of?"

"I don't know sometimes we used to go to…" Dicky stopped himself and glanced back at his mother.

The officer noticed the look and said, "Excuse me Mrs. Williams but could we speak to your son in private?"

"No you may not," she said indignantly.

"It's ok mom," said Dicky stepping out on the front porch and closing the door.

Dicky felt if he appeared to be cooperative they would have no reason to suspect anything.

"We used to go to the river and smoke sometimes," he said.

The thinner officer smiled and said, "Yea me and my friends use to do the same thing. That riverbank must have a million butts by now. The senior officer frowned at the remark and continued.

"Do you know if Ron was happy at home?"

"Well I know his Mom, she's gone a lot," he said deciding to throw them another fact to show his cooperation.

"You mean gone to work?" the thinner officer asked.

"Yea that too, she does have to work a lot since his Mom and Dad split up. But I know she has boyfriends and sometimes she's gone, you know overnight, or even a couple of days sometimes."

The two men looked at each other. The heavyset officer folded his notebook and shoved it in his back pocket.

"Thanks for your cooperation, if we need anything else we'll contact you," he said.

"Uh do you mind not telling my Mom about the smoking part?" Dicky asked smiling.

"I don't think we need to do that," he said. "But it's not a good idea to go down to the river without supervision, it's dangerous."

The officers left the Williams, and walked to the house next door to continue canvassing the neighborhood. Dicky felt that the interview went well. The officers appeared pleased with the information he gave them; just enough to say he cooperated, but not enough to incriminate himself. Besides, he thought, even if worse came to worse it wasn't him who'd killed Ron, it was Carl. Still, being interviewed by the police was like cold water to the face; it made him think that no matter how much he wanted to protect his friends it was stupid not to have a way out.

Chapter Eighteen

Porter and Mapes contacted fellow officer Phil James from narcotics to ask him what he knew about the Gunther gang.

James told them they started out as a high school car club that now has blossomed into a full-fledged crime organization. There were twelve Charter members who have since dropped out of school and an array of members ranging from fourteen through early twenties. They are linked to several high volume drug dealers who specialize in marijuana and bennies. Most of the original twelve are now in jail except for three.

"Some of these kids are mean as rattlesnakes. The younger ones are the worst, constantly trying to prove their balls are big enough," said James.

"So you think they're capable of murder?" Asked Porter.

"Oh yea, and I know they have committed murder, I just can't prove it," said James. The word on the street is they just offed another small time speed dealer who got in over his head and couldn't pay up."

"You heard about the floater we found this morning?" Asked Mapes.

"Yea, I've asked the Coroner to keep me informed," he said. "So if you want to get a good fix on these bums, word is they're holding a street race tonight on the east side, Just outside of Batavia on 132. We plan on letting them get started before we break it up, to see what shakes loose. All we need to do is find a couple of bags of pills and we can haul them all in for mug shots."

"We got a witness who says he saw some boys throwing rocks at something the day before he found the body. We think they were throwing rocks at the body," said Mapes.

"You think they offed him then?" Asked James.

"Well we won't have an idea about that until we get an approximate time of death and when they I.D. the corpse. But my feeling is they know something," Mapes answered.

"So we going to the races tonight?" Asked Porter.

"I like watching a good race especially when the winner is going to end up being the looser," said Mapes, "What time?"

"Nine o'clock, James said.

James told them that the rendezvous spot would be about a mile down Highway 132 from where the incident is set to take place. They planned a surprise raid after they're sure everyone who's coming is there. It seemed like a well-planned raid complete with six patrol cars, a bus and tow trucks.

Mapes called Saint Rose church to see if their star witness was on the premises and was informed that the man was gardening at that moment and would be there for several more hours. Porter and Mapes then drove back to the Church to make sure that Julius Speck knew not to leave town until after he viewed the upcoming mug shots of the Gunther gang. Though he insisted he had been too far away to recognize any faces the detectives convinced him he had to look at them anyway in the chance they might jog his memory about something he may have forgotten.

Chapter Nineteen

Mapes and Porter arrived late for the initial bust but not before anyone was hauled off to lock up. The raid was successful in arresting thirty-six suspected gang members including two with felony warrants.

When they walked up to the bus, James was still collecting wallets to identify those being taken.

"I was beginning to think you weren't going to show," said James.

"We got hung up in town. I see everything went down as expected," said Mapes looking at the string of young toughs lined up facing the bus.

"Yea except a couple of them managed to escape cross country though that field," James said pointing toward the open field behind the bus.

"And I don't suppose any of these punks know who they are either," said Porter.

"No they all got amnesia, nobody knows nothing," James said. "But wait till we get them alone one by one downtown and we'll see how many stick to that story. We got over half of them on possession charges alone," said James.

Mapes noticed how many leather jackets were being worn and gave up on the idea of using that to narrow down the field. Tow trucks were busy along the highway towing away the gang's transportation.

"How many vehicles?" Asked Porter.

"Twenty four cars and three motorcycles," James answered with a grin. This will slow'em down for at least a few days."

"So is this the whole gang here?" Porter asked.

"Not even! There are at least twenty some that didn't show. The gang pres ain't here either. I guess he must have figured this was all too risky," replied James.

"Anything we can do?" Asked Mapes just as another patrol car came to a stop next to them.

An officer got out of the car, opened the back door and dragged out a boy that looked to be about fourteen. He was handcuffed and yelling," Police brutality."

He had long brown hair combed high in front and wore a leather jacket and jeans.

"You ain't got no reason to arrest me I wasn't doing nothing," the boy yelled as he was being forcefully taken to the bus.

The boy dug in his heel on the first step causing James to have assist the officer in getting him aboard. Once he was safely handcuffed to a seat, James and the officer came out and rejoined Porter and Mapes.

"A real tough guy huh?" Porter commented.

"Yea he thinks he's Brando," said the officer.

"Did he have any I D on him?" asked James.

"Yea he had a student I D card from Withrow," said the officer handing the card to James.

"Neal Slater," said James reading from the card. "I'm surprised the little shit is still in school with that attitude. Where did you find him?"

"Trying to hitchhike back to Walnut Hills," the officer replied.

"How long till we can get copies of the mug shots?" Asked Mapes.

"I'll see that you get copies sent to you by tomorrow, first thing," said James. "I'm jerking off inside I'm so happy. I hope these hanyaks keep on planning these little chicky runs. They're just making my job easier. I'll keep my fingers crossed that you get a hit on the mug shots."

"Tomorrow then," said Mapes.

Chapter Twenty

The Foss children looked almost albino in the glaring lights of the Hospital emergency room. All of their toe headedness and light skin color came from their mother. She now sat in a cloth draped cubicle getting treated for head trauma and assorted cuts and abrasions suffered from another bout with her drunken husband.

Two uniformed police stood in the hallway quietly waiting to have a word with her after treatment while Everett's sister and brothers were crying, still traumatized from their earlier ordeal.

Life at the Foss house had been getting progressively worse since Everett's father got laid off. He had just missed a beating himself a few days earlier by hiding out in a closet until his father finally passed out. His mother though had not been so lucky, and tonight's beating was the worse so far. Tonight had pushed Everett over the line. He was starting to hate his father, and no matter how much his mother tried to convince him that things would eventually get better, he didn't believe it anymore. Dicky Williams had also said that things would get better but they hadn't for Everett. He had been plagued by nightmares recently with Ron beckoning him to join him in the ocean, where everything was wonderful and far away from his menacing father.

The two officers straightened up when they saw Alice Foss in a wheelchair being pushed into the hallway by the attending nurse.

"Excuse me Mrs. Foss," said one of the officers, "I just wanted to let you know that your husband has been arrested and he won't be released until he sleeps it off. He should be fine in the morning and apologize for his behavior. I'm sure he regrets the injury he caused you. You two need to work this out on your own."

"You should lock the bastard up and throw away the key for what he's put this woman through," said the nurse pushing the wheelchair.

"We aren't marriage councilors," said the officer. "The department has a policy of not getting involved in domestic disputes between a husband and wife unless charges are filed or a felony has been committed, in which case the district attorney will decide if it warrants further action."

"You mean when he finally kills her. Do you know how many times I've treated this woman in the past year?" The nurse asked.

"I'm sorry for that Mrs. Foss I truly mean that but at this point we've done all we can," he said.

"It's all right I understand," said Alice. "I just want to get my children home now, they've had enough for one night."

"Do you have a car?" Asked the nurse.

"No, could you call me a cab?" She asked.

"Wait a minute," said the officer. "We'll take you home, we can at least do that."

The Foss children joined in behind the wheelchair as the nurse pushed their mother to the squad car parked in front of the emergency entrance.

The officer held open the car door letting the children pile in behind their mother. Everett was the last to get in and as he did he made eye contact with the officer.

"Where'd you get that shiner, at school? Asked the officer smiling and gently dragging his finger under the child's eye.

Everett immediately touched his face. He hadn't been aware that he had a bruised eye.

"No, it's summer, no school," said Everett.

The solemn looks on the faces of Everett and his mother answered his question.

"Oh Jesus!" said the officer, and reached into his pocket retrieving a courtesy card and handed it to Everett. "Here," he said, "if things get worse you call me anytime and I'll come over."

Everett looked at the card for a moment and then slid it in his back pocket.

Once home, Alice put the children went to bed, and lay down on the couch. She began to feel the enormity of her problem and how alone she was.

Everett could hear her crying from his room upstairs. He listened for a few minutes and then got out of bed and went to his parents room and retrieved the luger from his father's hiding place at the bottom of his underwear drawer. He lifted the contents out and fished around with his hands hoping to find more bullets; but there were none. He would use the gun if he had to, he thought.

Suddenly his mind was filled with random memories about his father; his seventh birthday when he got his wagon and he watched his him put it together on the living room floor; the trip to Coney Island when his father carried him on his shoulders in the big swimming pool. There were good times before the drinking took over. Killing his father wasn't what he wanted, he only wanted to protect his mother the way she always protected him. But being his protector had cost her dearly. Perhaps he wouldn't have to shoot at all. Maybe just having the gun pointed at him would make him back down, or if he did have to shoot he could just wound him in the shoulder the way his cowboy heroes did on Saturday mornings. The more he thought about it the idea scared him, he'd seen what damage a gun could do and it wasn't anything like he'd seen on Saturday morning.

Everett carefully replaced the gun where he found it and closed the drawer. Returning to his room he took off his clothes and got into his Roy Rogers pajamas. Before lying down he examined the courtesy card the policeman had given him and then stuffed it under his mattress.

Chapter Twenty-one

Mapes got to the office early the morning after the big bust and went straight to his mailbox. He found the fresh batch of gang mug shots and sat down to put them in order before presenting them to Julius Speck. The office was quiet with only the sound of his papers shuffling. When the phone rang it gave him a start. It was sergeant James.

"Homicide, Mapes speaking," he answered.

"Yea, listen Mapes, we got lucky last night. You remember that last punk who was brought in before you left?" James asked.

"The one doing all the screaming about police brutality?"

"Yea that's the one. Any way after we got him back to the precinct and started interrogating the little shit he caved and gave us some information about a recent murder he heard about where the gang dumped the body in the river."

"That's great, did he give you a name?"

"No, he said he didn't know who the guy was only that the guy owed the gang money. But he did give us a line on the shooter though. He says it's a guy they call Shark. He kind of a sergeant at arms, he doles out the gangs punishment. He wasn't there last night but we have his mug shot on file. He ain't exactly been no choirboy, he's been arrested for burglary, assault and assorted drug charges. The best thing about this guy is, he's over twenty-one. If you can pin it on him it's going to be an early Christmas."

"That would be nice," said Mapes.

At eight on the dot Porter walked in carrying two coffees and a bag of doughnuts. Mapes filled him in on his conversation with James while they had coffee.

"So what do you want to do, arrest this muke and shake his tree?" Asked Porter.

"Not yet, I want to see what the medical examiner has to say about the body first," said Mapes.

They drove to the Hamilton County Medical Examiner where they were led into the autopsy room to speak to the examiner on duty. The man didn't look like he spent his days working with dead people. He was tall good looking and tan. His clothes under the white smock were brightly colored giving him the appearance of someone who had just walked in off the golf course.

"What do you have for us on that body that washed up on the east end a few days ago?" Asked Mapes.

"Which one?" The examiner asked.

"What do you mean which one, how many do you have?" Mapes asked.

"Two," answered the examiner. "One, a male Caucasian gunshot victim with a wound to his left temple, approximately ten to twelve years of age. Estimated time of death is five to eight days ago. Sorry I can't be more specific but they were pretty much waterlogged. The second was a male gunshot victim, also Caucasian with a small caliber wound to the back of the head, looks like an execution. Estimated time of death, five to eight days ago."

"When did the second one come in?" Asked Porter.

"The younger victim came in the morning of the fifteenth and the older the night of the fifteenth," He answered.

"Night shift," said Porter

"Have you I D'd the body's?" Mapes asked.

"The older male still had his wallet in his pocket. His name was Rudolph Shultz. The younger boy we haven't managed to identify yet, but we're working on it. It takes a while to run down dental records. Anyway while you're waiting you might want to give missing persons a try," said the examiner.

"Yea, thanks for the hot tip Ben Hogan but this ain't exactly our first Rodeo," said Mapes sarcastically.

It was ten o'clock before they got back to the precinct. Porter went to talk to the detective in charge of missing persons while Mapes got an arrest warrant for Shark, who's real name turned out to be Jack Short.

Detective Bliss of missing persons reviewed the notes from the uniformed officers sent to take the initial report. He told Porter that they came to the conclusion that he was a runaway based on talking to some of the neighborhood kids who knew him.

"So what now, what does his mother say?" Asked Porter.

"She's like all mother's of runaways, she's in denial about her son having reason to leave. Christ, the woman was constantly gone, leaving the kid alone while she's out balling every Tom's Harry Dick. He's used to living on his own.

"What about the father, where's he?" Porter asked.

"He's living in Covington, I'm planning to talk to him this week just in case he shows up there to live with his dad. We talked to him on the phone and he says he doesn't know anything but I'm going to drop in on him anyway just to make sure. The mother is a basket case."

"Could I borrow this file in case we I D this kid as your runaway?" asked Porter

"Knock yourself out, if you can close this one, I'm all for it. I'm swamped this time of year."

When Porter got back to homicide Mapes had the warrant.

"Grab your jacket we're going Shark hunting," he said. "He works at a rental yard in Batavia, he's there till five."

Porter and Mapes sat in the car holding a mug shot of the suspect and watched the employees of the rental yard come and go from the yard to the office assisting customers.

"There he is," said Porter pointing at a tall young man in his twenties with dark greased hair.

Porter was the first one out and reached the man before Mapes had even closed the door to their vehicle. He grabbed the suspect from behind with one arm and shoved his badge in the man's face with the other. The suspect immediately grabbed at Porters arm and struggled to get free when the sudden appearance of Mapes's gun pushing at his nose caused him to stop struggling.

"You need to relax grease ball," said Mapes, out of breath from running to keep up with his younger partner. "It's hard to get chicks without a nose, know what I mean?"

"What's this all about, I ain't done nothing?"

"Aren't you the famous Shark man? I know you are. Hey! A shark's a fish, are you a fish, Shark man?" Taunted Mapes.

Porter cuffed one hand and then the other behind him and then grabbed his collar, almost jerking him off his feet as he led him to their unmarked car. The man said nothing until he was inside the car.

"Are you two lumps going to tell me what this is about or do I need to call my attorney?" He asked.

Mapes turned around in the driver's seat and looked him in the eye.

"Yes Mister Short we got a witness who saw you pop Rudolph Shultz last week and you're going down for murder," said Mapes.

"That's impossible you can't pin that on me, you're lying. Ain't nobody seen me do nothing cause if they said they did they'd be dead, " said Short sneering.

"Then how did we know to come to see you tough guy?" Asked Porter. "You think that bunch of pimple faced kids you call a gang are going to keep their mouths shut to save you're miserable ass? I've arrested jaywalkers tougher than you."

"And if I can connect you to the other body we found on the river I'll give you to the DA all wrapped up and tied with a bow for two murders," said Mapes.

"What other body I don't know about no other body," the man insisted.

"We can prove that you knew Rudy Shultz and that he owed you money. We already got one witness and I bet if we shake the tree a little harder we could come up with a few more who heard you brag about it," said Mapes.

"Any jury will convict you right now for the murder of Rudy Shultz and all we have to do is prove that you knew this other kid and they'll convict you of both murders without even deliberating, especially with your rap sheet," said Porter.

Short suddenly got quiet as he pondered his fate. The detectives had planted the seed of doubt, stopping momentarily to let the weight of their words sink in.

"I tell you I don't know nothing about no second body, I swear, can you cut me a deal?" he pleaded.

His tough guy persona was gone as he pleaded with the detectives for a break. The car pulled up at police headquarters and Porter slid out pulling Short out behind him. They took him inside to an interrogation room to close the door.

"You realize that even if you can prove that Shultz was rat shit a jury won't be likely to give you a break on two murders. I can see the electric chair in your future, my man," said Mapes. "But I might be able to keep the electric chair off the table if you come clean right now."

The man laid his head on his arms. The room was hot and humid. There was a small fan on a table near the door but it was turned off.

"Can I get some air?" He asked pointing to the fan.

"Sure," said Mapes.

Porter positioned the fan so that it blew on Short. They waited a few minutes waiting for him to speak.

"Ok, but no chair right?" He begged for assurance.

"If you tell us everything and don't leave out nothing, you understand?" Mapes warned.

"Ok I did Shultz, he owed me a lot of scratch from the bennies I gave him. I gave him plenty of chances you know but he just kept putting me off. I couldn't just let him go, then I got everybody thinking I'm some kind of marshmallow and pretty soon nobody pays me," he said looking up from the table.

"How'd you do it?" Asked Mapes.

"I clipped him behind the ear with a twenty two and dumped him in the river. I don't understand how you guys found him cause I weighted him down with a car wheel," he said.

"How'd you tie him to the wheel?" Asked Mapes.

"Tied his hands together through the hole," he answered.

"That's your problem you dumbass, when a body is in the water a while sometimes the hands come off," said Porter.

"Where's the gun?" Mapes asked.

"It's under the armrest in the back seat of my car," He answered.

Mapes and Porter locked eyes. Porter immediately left the room to secure a warrant for both the house and car. The older detective took out a pack of cigarettes and offered one to Short. "Thanks," he said as Mapes lit it and one for himself.

"What about the other boy, Jack, if you even passed this kid on the street and you don't tell me, I swear you'll fry?"

"I swear on my mother I don't know anything about no dead kid," he insisted.

"Ok I want you to write it all down exactly the way it happened and then sign it, you understand?" Barked Mapes sliding a note pad and pencil across the table.

"Yea I got it," he said and began to write.

Mapes left him locked in the interrogation room and returned to his desk to wait for Porter. He spotted the missing persons file on Porter's desk and reached over to get it. He flipped through the pages till he came to the original officer's notes from his neighborhood canvass. The missing boy was Ron Stone. His neighborhood friends were Carl Seizer, Richard Williams, and Everett Foss. As he read the boy's statements he noticed the similarities; they almost seemed rehearsed. Every one of them said exactly the same thing; they felt he had run away. But then, he thought, if the boy had run away he might have told them what to say. The only thing difference he discovered in their statements was, the Foss boy said that his friend Ron wanted to go to the ocean.

Chapter Twenty-two

The wooden front doors of St Francis De Sales Catholic Church looked massive to a nine-year-old. Everett Foss had managed to open one of them and now stood looking down the center isle of the main Chapel. He had never seen anything as opulent in his short life. It made him dizzy trying to make out every scroll and filigreed design on the ceiling. Tall columns that reached all the way up to arched ceiling ran down both sides of the church ending at the half rotunda behind the pulpit. Brightly colored stained glass windows surrounded the entire chapel. After a few minutes of sightseeing he focused his attention to the square structure against the wall next to the right side isle.

He had never been inside a confessional but he knew what it was, because he'd seen them in the movies. He knew it was a place where people could go and confess their secrets to someone without fear of reprisal. His aunt had told him that confession was good for the soul. Everett took that to mean that if you confess something it made you feel better. The weight of what Everett carried was just one crushing secret too many, especially with his problems at home. That life would ever go back to the way it was before the shooting was a wasted dream now. The shooting had taken the color out of his life, and his abusive father had taken the warmth. No one figures that their childhood will be over at nine, but for Everett, this was his reality.

He opened the door to the confessional and stepped inside. It was dark at first but he didn't mind. The darkness was his friend now. Darkness was silent and calming; it would hide him when he wanted to be hidden. He felt a part of it and he embraced it.

Everett sat alone in the dark for a few moments when the small window suddenly slid open, startling him.

"Yes my child," came the disjointed voice of the priest on the other side of the window.

Everett was nervous and stuttered a bit at first, but after a moment he cleared his throat and began.

"Hello father is this where I say, 'bless me father for I have sinned?'" He said.

"Yes, how long has it been since you've been to confession?" Asked the priest.

"Uh, nine years I guess. I've never been really."

"Do you go to mass then?"

"Uh no, I don't think I'm catholic but I'm not really sure. Nobody ever took me before."

"I see," said the priest. "What can I do to help you?"

"I need to tell you some sins if it's ok. Do you let people do that if they're not catholic?"

"Anyone is allowed in God's house."

"Ok, well I guess I should start with the smoking. Me and my friends went to the river and smoked cigarettes, and uh... I stole them from my Moms hutch and her Sin Sin too. It's pretty bad so far I know, but I ain't even come to the worst part yet," said Everett, with a tear in his voice.

"Take you're time," said the priest.

"Well we were all playing war one day and I brought my dads..." He was trying hard not to cry. He wanted to say the word gun, but at first it wouldn't come out. It stuck to the back of his throat like vomit; burning as it tried to exit. For he knew that once he'd said gun there was no turning back. Everything he'd kept bottled up inside would come gushing out like hot black bile.

He held his face in his hands and tried to regain his composure. The priest remained silent waiting till Everett worked it out. The man would wait as long as it took. He was experienced listening to people. Most were minor infractions that required only a few simple acts of penance to absolve them, but his ear was also attuned to recognize tragedy and desperation when he heard it, so he remained silent and listened.

"I brought my father's gun and we were only shooting pop bottles, but then it was Carl's turn and then it just went off and..." He stopped for a moment and then finished in a whisper. "It just went off... and something bad happened, something really bad."

"Can you tell me what happened my son?" Asked the priest slowly and in a low comforting voice.

Everett stared at the window and held back his words again, wondering if he should continue or open the side door of the confessional and run.

Finally he said in a whisper, "The gun went off and now Ron's dead. The gun went off and now Ron's dead," he said, this time a little louder. "The gun went off and now Ron's dead," he shouted, startling the priest.

Nothing he had ever heard in the confessional had prepared him for what he was hearing now. He struggled trying to put the right words together to absolve as well as heal the young tortured voice.

"I think that's why God is punishing me, but he's punishing my Mom too, and my brothers and my sister and they didn't do anything," he said fighting back tears.

"God doesn't punish without reason. If it was an accident then it was no one's fault. God is not punishing you," said the priest.

"Yes he is, it is my fault. The other guy's wouldn't smoke if I don't bring the smokes. I bring the matches. I brought the gun. I bring everything." He began crying. "I don't know what I should do. Can't you tell me something that makes it all better?"

"Did you tell the truth about the accident?"

Everett was slow to answer.

"No, I lied," he said swallowing hard. "I lied... we all lied."

"Then you know what you must do, don't you?"

"I can't! I promised Carl. I can't!"

"To absolve yourself in the eyes of God you must tell the truth to everyone," the priest said. "Do you know how to say, Hail Mary's?"

"No," he answered.

"Repeat after me and we will say it together."

"Ok"

The priest began slowly while Everett followed along as he did what the priest suggested.

"Hail Mary full of grace the lord is with thee. Blessed art thou among women and blessed is the fruit of thy womb, Jesus. Holy Mary mother of God pray for us sinners at the hour of our death. Amen."

This was a familiar exercise to Everett. It was like saying the pledge of allegiance, except he couldn't mouth it like he did at school. Because of a religious Aunt, he had heard a lot of those words before; like God and Jesus and sinners and of course Amen. He hadn't heard the word womb, nor was he sure what it was. Sinners went to hell and the righteous went to heaven, he remembered. His parents never spoke of such things so he wasn't sure where the line was drawn between the two. He wondered if there was a middle ground or did it have to be one or the other. His mind raced trying to understand.

"You know what you must do?" The priest said breaking the silence.

"Yes Father," replied Everett.

"You do understand that death isn't necessarily the end of the road, don't you? Asked the priest.

"Yea, It's like a sailcat," replied Everett.

"I don't understand, how so?"

"A cat has to be dead before he can fly. Ron used to say a poem. 'Sailcat Sailcat up in the sky, you have to die before you can fly'."

The priest thought about Everett's answer for a moment. He wasn't completely sure if he understood the comparison. He had never flown a Sailcat, but the thought of flying to heaven after death he could accept.

"Ron has flown to heaven and now sits in the arms of our heavenly father," said the priest.

"That's good, he must have already seen the ocean then."

"I'll pray for you", said the priest.

"Thanks," Everett replied.

Everett left the church feeling lighter. He could breathe again. The Sun light washed the streets in orange and yellows. It was like he had never noticed late afternoon before. How beautiful it is, he thought. It was also a reminder that he needed to be home soon. Coming home after sunset was risky if his father had been drinking. When he reached the corner of Woodburn and Fairfax he decided to run the last four blocks.

He thought about the priest's last words. He felt good but feeling good was a temporary condition. Even at nine, Everett knew that. A lie to prevail or the truth to destroy, those were his choices. He may not have been able to verbalize it, but he knew it nonetheless. The answer was easy, as easy as saying nothing.

Chapter Twenty-three

Fountain Square was one of Mapes favorite places in downtown Cincinnati, and like today he often bought a hot dog at the corner vendor and sat on a bench to eat it, watching the water splash off the old bronze centerpiece.

"What are we doing about our floater? Are you buying Sharks story or what?" Asked Porter between bites of his hot dog.

"We got to make double sure the kid wasn't involved with the Gang somehow. We ain't ruling out nobody yet," said Mapes.

"Double sure! What the hell does that mean?" Asked Porter.

"That means we look at it, then we look at it again. This ain't vice. We aren't popping hookers to catch some John with his dick in his hand. If we make a mistake and somebody gets fried, then we did a piss poor job investigating. What are we going to say oops! I'm sorry? Fat lot of good it's going to do that poor schmuck strapped to Old Sparky," Mapes lectured.

"Ok Mapes I get it, relax will you. You got to cut down on the caffeine in the morning." Porter replied slightly irritated. "Mind if I ask you a personal question John?"

"Shoot!"

"Why peppermint schnapps and beer, you German or something?"

Mapes stopped eating and stared at Porter for a moment trying to decide how much of himself to reveal to his new partner.

Finally he said, "Well this town is full of Germans, but no, that ain't the reason. My old Daddy once told me, peppermint cures a world of sin."

"What the hell does that mean?"

"It means all the women downtown love me because I always smell like peppermint. I never smell like beer. --- And besides I only take a nip after four."

Porter thought about it for a few seconds and then smiled.

"And it's always Four O'clock somewhere right?"

"Right," said Mapes smiling through the last of the hotdog.

He stood up, threw his napkin in the trash and took a last look at the fountain. "Let's go show the mug shots to that bum at Saint Rose before we get involved with the missing kid. My gut keeps telling me that those kids he saw throwing rocks, know something."

Jules Speck was sitting on a stonewall behind the parish school, eating lunch consisting of a bologna sandwich and Kool-Aid.

"Mister Speck, sorry to interrupt your lunch but we need you to take a look at some pictures," said Mapes in an attempt to sound cheerful but failing.

The man had made quite a transformation since the first time they saw him. Besides clean clothes and new shoes he had a fresh haircut and a close shave.

"Look at you," said Porter. "You going to stick around for a while now?"

Speck flashed a thin lipped smile and said, "Maybe."

"Well take a good long look at these mug shots and if anyone looks familiar or you get a feeling no matter how small.... You know, it might be important," said Mapes.

Speck took the mug book and began to slowly leaf though it. The two officers sat on the wall also, flanking him on both sides. When he got to the last page he looked up at Mapes.

"Like I told you man I wasn't that close enough to see faces," he said.

"Is there anything about any of these shit's that looks familiar?" Asked Porter. "Give them one more look, ok?

Speck did as he was told, not expecting a different outcome but he wanted to appear cooperative. It wouldn't hurt to have an in with the local police. Being a traveling man he was sometimes on the outside of the law. But when he got to the second to the last page he saw something that did look familiar.

"This kid here with the big hair and leather jacket, I remember one of the boys had big hair, you know like James Brown.

Mapes took the book from Speck and looked at it closely. He then handed the book to Porter, pointing to the photo.

"Remember this kid?" Mapes asked.

"Yea, it's the one who raised hell about police brutality," said Porter.

"And the one who gave up the Shark," said Porter smiling. "I had a hunch we didn't have it all yet. Let's go shake his tree a little."

The boy's home was in an affluent section of Walnut hills, not the environment one would expect for a member of a violent street gang. From talking to James, the boy was allowed to join because his cousin was a charter member and a proven solder.

Tim Pressey was fourteen, not the youngest in the Gunther's but only a year older. It hadn't been clear before if he wanted in the gang for the status or if he was as mean as his cousin. The bust, however, yielded information, as well as a picture of a kid who was willing to give information to stay out of jail. Mapes felt that if he and Porter gave him the Mutt and Jeff treatment he would probably tell them everything they wanted. Mapes would be the scary Mutt while Porter, the more understanding Jeff; Good cop bad cop.

Mapes and Porter parked across the street from the boy's house and waited. It was after two thirty and they figured to take him after he got home from school.

About forty minutes lapsed when a black forty-nine Ford pulled up and a leather jacketed teen got out. The car was filled with boys, some wearing leather and some not. After a few minutes of banter and ball busting the car pulled away, leaving the Pressey boy standing on the curb flashing the universal sign of ill will and laughing as they left. As soon as the car was a half a block down the street the two detectives jumped out and held up their shields.

"Just a minute Timmy we need to have a word with you," yelled Mapes. The boy turned to face them and upon seeing their badges bolted for the house.

"Son of a bitch, don't do that," Mapes shouted, but the boy kept running up the lawn. He yelled, "stop" and then pulled his thirty-eight and fired into the air.

The shot startled the boy as well as Porter. Pressey dropped to a prone position and froze.

"Are you crazy I'm only fourteen, my Mom will be home any minute," he whimpered.

Porter made eye contact with Mapes and mouthed, "What the fuck." He had been on the job for ten years and never fired his weapon.

Mapes gave him a shrug and continued up the lawn to the boy. He reached down, grabbed the boy's shirt and jerked him to his feet.

"Get up you little fuck weasel before I give you the back of my hand," he ordered.

"Easy John he's only fourteen we don't need to use that kind of language, besides I think he wants' to cooperate, don't you son?" Asked Porter.

"Yea I guess so, what's this all about?" Asked Pressey.

"You told Sergeant James that the Shark killed that kid and dumped him in the river," said Mapes, pulling his jacket collar.

"Yea so!" Replied the boy.

This answer prompted Mapes give him a slap to the back of his head.

"Ok how about I take you down town and throw your ass in jail until you feel like talking?" Mapes asked.

"I already told James all I know, I don't know nothing else," said the boy.

"You forgot to tell sergeant James that you were down at the river when the body was there. We got a witness who put's you there the same day as the murder. That makes you an accessory," said Mapes.

"That's a lie nobody seen me there you're just fucking with me. That's what you cops do, you love to rattle people for no reason," he said with a small show of defiance.

Mapes spun the boy around and pulled one hand back and cuffed it. When he reached to cuff the other hand Porter raised a hand to block him.

"Don't do this John let me talk to him," Porter said.

Mapes cuffed the other hand anyway and marched the boy over to the car and put him in the back seat, under the protests of both the boy and Porter.

Once everyone was inside, Mapes turned towards the back seat.

"I'm going to put you away for a long time Timmy, if you don't talk to me. We got a big black guy in lockup that just lost his punk and he's looking for a new one. I think you'll be answer to his prayers. You know he makes all his punks wear pink panties; he's crazy like that. You'll look real cute in pink panties. Don't you think Bill?" Mapes now looked at Porter.

"Come on John take it easy, cool off and let me talk to him," Asked a sincere looking Porter.

The boy looked worried by Mapes rant. He looked to Porter for help, his eyes saying it all.

"Look son please, tell him what he wants' to know and I won't let him arrest you, I promise," Porter said.

"Ok, ok, I was there, at the river, but not when he got killed. We wanted to see the body. We never seen a dead body before," The boy said.

"How did you know where it was, did Shark tell you?" Mapes asked.

"No, not even man, I don't talk to those guys, you know the older guys. We heard about it and we looked for two days before we found it. We walked about four miles down the river all together before we found it," he said.

"You and who else? Asked Mapes.

"Me and a couple of my friends from school, that's all we just wanted to see it."

"We're going to need the names of those boys," said Porter.

"Yea sure, we didn't do anything but throw rocks at it. My cousin told me when it swells up and floats you can throw rocks at it and bust it like a balloon. That's all we did."

Porter wrote down the boy's names and addresses in a small notebook and stuck it in his lapel pocket.

"These are the only boys who saw the body?" Asked Mapes.

"Yea! No!" Said Pressey.

"Which is it?" Asked Mapes.

"I mean I only took these guys, but there were these other kids we saw there."

"What other kids?"

"I don't know I never seen them before but they were younger kids. They were in the water right next to the body when we got there. We chased them away,"

"What were they doing?"

"I don't know, I think they were trying to see the face maybe. One kid he had at stick and he was poking at it or something."

"What did these kids look like?" Asked Mapes.

"There was one older kid and one younger one. The younger one was real pale looking. You know really light hair, almost white and the other one was older and taller, maybe twelve or so and he was just normal looking; brown hair I think."

"Ok Timmy, you've been real helpful. If everything you told me checks out you're off the hook; if not I'll be back, you got that?"

"Yea, no man I swear I told you the truth, I swear," replied Pressey.

Mapes got out and opened the back door. He uncuffed the boy and pointed him towards his house. But before he reached the other side of the street Mapes called him.

"Hey Tim," the boy turned around, "take my advice and get out of that damn gang before you get into real trouble. Take it from me, you ain't cut out for it. Oh and another thing, that corpse you nitwits were throwing rocks at wasn't the one you were looking for. He was just a kid who got in over his head---kind of like you."

Twenty-four

Elaine Stone stood on the front porch of the Foss house leaning on the doorbell. She had already given the bell the obligatory three quick rings with no response. Now she was serious about rousting someone. It was common knowledge in the neighborhood that Del Foss was out of work, and his wife Gloria was only seen on washday hanging clothes in the back yard. No one in the neighborhood stuck their noses in each other's business no matter what they may suspect. A man's home was his castle and domestic disputes, no matter how loud, was considered a private matter.

Elaine wasn't there to confront Del about his wife beating practices, or save Gloria from a new shiner; she was there to talk to Everett about her son's disappearance. It was four weeks since he vanished without a trace. The first few weeks she held out hope that he was just off on some lark, or maybe he wanted to punish her for being away so much, but now she was worried and plagued by guilt. The detectives told her that they were convinced he ran away, in which case he would either get tired of being on the street and come home, or possibly become a victim of the many street crimes that befall young runaways; drugs, prostitution, or violence.

Ron was not a runaway, she told herself, and she was convinced that the boys he spent so much time with knew more than they were telling. Dicky Williams had been rude and surly when she pressed him about Ron. This wasn't like the boy she knew. Something was wrong she could feel it.

The click of the door latch startled her and caused her to remove her thumb from the button and step back. The reality that she might soon be facing an angry and violent Mel Foss gave her a sudden chill. She looked around for something she could use as a weapon if it came to that, but she couldn't find anything. Suddenly the door opened and Alice stuck her nose through the crack.

"Yes, oh Elaine it's you. What time is it?" She asked.

"It's eight thirty, I'm sorry if I woke you but I haven't been to bed yet from work and I need to talk to Everett if you don't mind."

"About what, Ronny's disappearance? He already told the police everything he knows. Everett is sick over Ronny being gone, believe me. If he knew anything he would have already told someone."

"I know Alice, it just that I thought maybe he might be able to remember some small thing he might have forgotten, you know. I'm going crazy. You know you'd feel the same if was Everett gone," said Elaine with the frantic look of a person begging for her life.

Alice thought for a moment and said, "Let me wake him up, just a minute."

The door closed and Elaine waited. A few moments passed until she heard bare feet shuffling across the wood floors inside. When the door opened it revealed a weary eyed Everett Foss in cowboy pajamas.

"Hello Everett, I'm sorry I came so early but I just wanted to asked you if you have, maybe, remembered something since you talked to the police, anything, no matter how small? Anything that might help me figure things out. I—I'm confused please can you tell me anything?"

Everett could see that she was hurting. He could feel her pain. He hadn't stopped hurting since that cloudy day at the river. The truth he carried overwhelmed him. The woman was desperately looking for hope; hope or closure; to the parents of a missing child it's always hard to know when let go. He understood that knowing the truth was better than not knowing, but he was bound by an oath he could not voluntarily break.

"I'm sorry, he didn't say where he was going," he said.

"But he did say that he wanted to leave me? Did he say he wasn't happy? Did you hear him say that?" She asked.

Everett was uncomfortable. Any answer from here on he would have to embellish. He didn't like lying. To many lies were hard to remember later. Getting caught in a lie would be disastrous, yet here he was, living the biggest lie of his life.

"One time I heard him say he wanted to go to the ocean, maybe he went there," he answered.

Elaine looked puzzled, as though she didn't understand what he had just said. Her hands were trembling now. July was only days away and a heat wave had stalled over Cincinnati yet she was cold.

"Maybe he did," she said as though she were preoccupied. "Maybe he did."

Carl Seizer sat on his front porch watching Ron's mother talking to Everett. What they were talking about, he could only guess. His imagination suggested they were talking about him. It was Everett that urged him to keep quiet, when he himself weakened and wanted to tell. But Everett was only nine, he had changed his stance twice already. Perhaps he had weakened under the pressure from Ron's mother and was now telling her everything, he thought.

At last he jumped from the steps, and bolted across the street. He felt like a cornered rat, fearful and angry, lost in the fog of paranoia. Carl's mental state had degraded to an all time low. He was a time bomb ready to explode.

No one saw him approach. It was only when he leaped up from the lawn onto the front steps that anyone saw him. Both Everett and Elaine were startled.

"God damn it Carl, what the hell's the matter with you?" "You scared the shit out of me," she gasped.

"Me too," said Everett.

"What are we talking about Everett, Huh?" Asked Carl, like his words were being forced out through his teeth.

"Nothing she was just---,"Everett was interrupted.

"I was asking him if he remembered anything about Ronny since he talked to the police," said Elaine.

"You guys were sure talking a long time what did you tell her Everett?" Carl demanded loudly.

He looked almost as pale as Everett and he was beginning to sweat. His face was contorted like he was staring into the sun, yet the porch was in shade.

Everett opened his mouth to answer but Elaine cut him off.

"He told me he thinks Ronny went to the ocean, is that what you think Carl?" asked Elaine frowning.

She was suspicious of the way Carl was reacting so she decided to press him harder. The pit of her stomach told her he knew more.

"I don't know, he could have. Yea I think he did. I think he went to the ocean."

"Where Carl, what ocean?" She snapped.

The Carl who was only minutes ago in control was now on the defensive.

"I don't know, the ocean. He went to the ocean."

"Did he tell you that? Did he confide in you?" She pressed

"Yes"

"When Carl, when did he tell you he was going to the ocean?" She pressed harder, taking a step toward the now backpedaling eleven year old.

"The day he left he told me he was going to the ocean," stuttered Carl.

"That's not what you told the police, is it Carl? Why didn't you tell them you saw him the day he left? That's not what the other children said, they all say It was the day before" she pushed.

"Maybe it was the day before, you got me all confused now."

"How did he get to the ocean Carl, the ocean is a long ways away? You should know that, you sound like you were his best friend"

"Maybe I was," he said turning to look at Everett. "I was his best friend."

Everett said nothing although he wanted to. He thought of the many times Ron had saved him by standing up to Carl's bullying. He stood silent as he listened to Carl embellish.

"I think he said he was going to go down the river to the ocean, you know on a barge of something," He said, his upper lip covered by beads of sweat.

"I think you're lying Carl. I think you're all lying," she said glancing over to Everett.

Everett took a step backward into the doorway.

"You don't get to call me a liar just because you're a grownup," shouted Carl, frustrated and angry.

"You're a lying little shit Carl and I'll do anything I damn well please. It's my son who's missing and I'm going to tell the police to take you all downtown and make you tell the truth," she spat.

"Are you going to tell them how you're never home because you sleep with a different guy every night? Everybody in the neighborhood knows what a whore you are," Carl shouted.

"Carl," came the bellowing voice of his father across the street.

The shout caused him to instinctively flinch. He turned his head in the direction of the voice, but not before Elaine smacked his cheek hard with her bare hand.

The woman's eyes were glazed with tears and anger as she stood glaring at the boy. Carl's father Bert ran across the street and grabbed his son by the back of his shirt.

"What the hell's going on here?" He demanded.

"She called me a liar Papa, she doesn't get to call me a liar," said Carl twisting to get loose from his father's grasp.

The man shook his son with one violent move of his arm and Carl stopped struggling.

"What is this about Elaine?" He asked.

Everett's mother had heard the commotion from inside and was now standing beside her son in the doorway.

"I suggest you have a talk with your son Bert. He keeps changing his story about when he saw Ronny. And now he says Ronny went down river to try to get to the ocean. If that's true, why didn't he tell that to the police?"

The man frowned at his son and asked, "What about it Carl?"

"She was asking if anybody remembered anything and I just remembered some stuff that's all, Carl answered defensively.

"Your son is lying Bert I'm telling you, you better get to the bottom of this before the police get a hold of him," Elaine insisted.

"I'm not a liar, you whore. She hit me too papa," he shouted. Bert responded with a backhand across the mouth.

Carl began to cry. The blow had brought blood to his lips. His father jerked him again and turned him toward their house. But before he left he turned again and spoke to Elaine.

"I'm trying to understand you Elaine. I realize you're grieving, but you don't ever talk to my boy again without going through me first. I'll get to the bottom of what he knows or don't know, and if something comes out of it, I'll call you."

Elaine nodded and took a deep breath. She dabbed her eyes with a tissue and watched as Bert Seizer and his son walked home. She turned back to the doorway and looked at Everett, and then his mother.

"I'm sorry for the row on your front steps Alice. I didn't come over here to do that," she said.

"Elaine, nobody is judging you, we all have our own paths to follow and we all got our own devils. I pray that you find your boy."

Chapter Twenty-five

His father didn't let go of his shirt until they had walked through the house and down the cellar steps. When they reached his the workbench to the right of the stairs he was shoved into it. The back of his shirt was now twisted into a wrinkled handle. Carl watched his father slide his belt through his pant loops until it finally hit the floor like the long tongue of some horrible monster. This was a ritual that his father did very slowly for effect. As far as Carl was concerned it was the tongue of a monster, a monster that inflicted unbearable pain.

Coming next was going to be a test of wills. On any other day he might have had more confidence in his ability hold up under it. But today his nerves were already frazzled by the confrontation with Elaine.

"What was she talking about, you changing your stories?" Said his father, looking down at his son through deeply furrowed brows.

Carl had started to sniffle during the long walk to the cellar, but now he was past crying, he felt like he was coming undone, like a wild animal was ripping him apart from the inside. Because once the belt was out there was nothing he could do or say to stop what was about to happen.

"I---I just remembered he told me he wanted to go to the ocean, that's all. That's all he told me and that's all I said," Carl replied, his face contorted.

Bert stood silent for a few moments allowing time for Carl to finished speaking. Call interpreted his father's silence as an accusation of guilt and started to move slowly backwards away from the workbench. Bert's face was red and angry. He grasped the other end of the belt and held it in a loop. Carl braced himself. When his father was this angry he knew that there was no right answer to his questions. He always assumed there was more and usually Carl eventually gave in and told him what he wanted to hear no matter what the truth might be.

"Why didn't you tell the police that Ronny went to the ocean?" Bert asked.

"I don't know I guess I just forgot."

"Did Ronny tell you not to tell where he went?"

"No, he didn't tell us anything except he wanted to see the ocean.

"If I go ask Dicky Williams the same question, will he give me the same answer?"

"I don't know…. Yea he will, I'm pretty sure."

"Were you all together when Ronny discussed running away?"

"Yea I'm pretty sure we were."

"Then why did you lie to me when the police came? You told me you didn't know where he was and you didn't say a thing about going to the ocean."

"I forgot."

"You forgot! You forgot! Your famous excuse for everything! After all the whippings you got you still believe that's going to get you off the hook?"

With that Bert lashed out with the belt across his son's shoulders. The belt wrapped completely around his making a welt on his bare neck. Carl yelped in pain and took another step back.

"Answer me damn it!" Bert shouted, his voice getting higher and louder.

"No, I'm not trying to get out of anything I'm just trying to give you what you want," screamed his son wild eyed and drooling.

Smack came another lash from the belt, this time just below the hem of his cut-off jeans and around his bare legs.

Carl jumped backward and began pacing back and forth in front of the coal shoot in a frenzy. Bert had never seen Carl react this way to a whipping before. His actions infuriated his father even more.

Bert took two steps towards his son and lashed out again. Carl tried to duck under the belt but failed to clear it. This time the lash caught him across his face with such force it was left bleeding.

Carl screamed in agony. Bert stopped momentarily when he saw his son bleeding from the face and dropped the belt to his side. Carl looked like a cornered animal. The fear on his face had slowly turned to rage, a rage to match his father's. A grimace stayed on his face as he took quick breaths through his mouth like a rabid dog.

"You Asshole!" he screamed. "You're an Asshole!"

Bert was jolted by his son's behavior but only for a moment. The sneer returned to his face and he was determined to show his son no mercy. He felt compelled to crush his son's defiance for his own good. He began a mad borage of rapid-fire strikes with the belt.

"You don't ever, ever speak to me like that. You don't ever speak to any adult that way either I don't care what they say to you".

"Elaine is a whore I heard you say it," he screamed.

Snack! Smack! Smack! The belt found its mark. Carl was bleeding from the legs as well as his arms, face and neck. He continued running back and forth trying to avoid being hit, but for every strike he managed to dodge, the belt connected two more times.

Finally Bert began to show signs of fatigue. His swings were slower and with less force. Carl's fight or flight instincts had taken over on the first crack of the belt. Adrenaline coursed through his veins. He tried to run away but couldn't. His world was collapsing around him. He knew his father would not stop until he was completely drained of energy. He decided then that he could take no more. It was time to fight back.

Bert stepped to one side and blocked his son's path again. With every arch of the belt he drew closer. The final strike came totally trapping Carl in the corner of the basement by coal shoot. He was cornered with nowhere to go. When Bert recoiled the belt for another strike Carl grabbed the coal shovel, leaning against the side of the furnace and swung it wildly blocking the lash. Infuriated, his father lunged at him. Without thought Carl drew it back and swung again. Screaming at the top of his lungs like a man on fire, he broadsided his father in the face with a loud metallic bonk. Bert dropped the belt and fell back onto the dusty floor dazed and astonished. He said nothing while Carl stood over him panting, threatening to unleash another blow. Carl walked around him and took one step up the stairs.

"You want to know why I didn't tell you, and why I've been so moody? Well! It's because I'm a murderer. Ron's dead and I killed him. I did it! I... did it! And you ain't never going to hit me again. Ever!"

Carl threw the shovel across his father's prone body and left him speechless and stunned. As he ran up the stairs he stopped again at the top to look back, expecting to see his outraged father in pursuit, but the stairway was empty. Suddenly he felt sick and wretched on the top step. His body trembled uncontrollably. The child in him wanted to go back. He wished things could go back to the way they were. He loved his father and he worried now whether the last blow had injured him. He could hear his father scuffling in the coal dust and then his face appeared at the foot of the stairs. Carl realized now that he had crossed a line. He would never be the same again; His relationship with his father would never be the same again. Like a terminal infection, the killing of Ron Stone had spread into every aspect of his life.

He and his father locked eyes for a moment without speaking and then Carl bolted for the front door and out of the house. He would never go back, he told himself. He was afraid to go back.

Chapter Twenty-six

Mapes stumbled through the living room of his one bedroom apartment looking for cigarettes. He tripped over his shoes and crashed into the coffee table sending empty beer bottles flying in all directions.

"Fuck," he shouted, as he lay sprawled on the floor in front of his floor model, seven-inch Philco television. Slowly he picked himself up and then noticed an open pack of Chesterfields lying on the floor beside the couch. Mapes lit it and sat down. He spotted a lone half empty bottle of beer still sitting on the coffee table and picked it up. It was warm and stale but he downed it anyway, grimacing at the flat taste.

Sleep had been an infrequent visitor lately. He tried to drown his insomnia with alcohol with mixed results. Relief only came when he had drunk himself into a stupor and passed out. The mornings had to be treated with another shot of schnapps to take the edge off and then the roller coaster started all over again. His job was that which lay between.

Mapes glanced at his watch and noticed it was almost time to get ready for work. He started for the bathroom when the phone rang.

"Mapes here," he said after picking up.

"John this is Porter, I called Bliss last night about that missing kid on Fairfax and guess what?"

"I can't imagine"

"We got another runaway, the kid from across the street has been gone since yesterday morning. I tried to call you last night but I got no answer."

"That's because I was off duty. Do you know what that means?" That means I don't have to answer the fucking phone."

"Ok, ok, I get it but don't you think this is too much of a coincidence that two kids go missing from the same neighborhood a month apart?"

"What does that have to do with our dead kid?"

"Well maybe nothing but maybe he's the first one. What do you think?"

"Stop by the morgue on your way in and pick up a picture of the dead kid and we'll go see the mother this morning," Mapes instructed.

"Should I call Bliss and tell him what were doing?" Asked Porter

"Suit yourself."

"I think Bliss figures it's a homicide case now."

"If you call him tell him if we're going to keep working missing persons we're going to need a bump."

"What do you mean?"

"I mean that every case of his is O.T."

"Right!" Porter said sarcastically. "See you when you get here."

With the picture in hand, the detectives drove to the woman's home address first, only to find her not at home. They then drove to the diner where she worked and went inside.

The diner was full. It was the breakfast rush and two waitresses were running feverishly trying to keep up. One of the waitresses looked up from refilling coffee and yelled, "Sit anywhere you can find a spot honey."

She was a round woman with hair so perfect Mapes thought it could be carved wood.

"Were here to talk to Elaine Stone," Porter answered flashing his badge.

The woman pointed to the other woman towards the back of the diner and said, "You might have to wait just a tick honey she's running her ass off right now. Why don't you sit here at the counter and have some coffee till she gets caught up?"

The thought of a cup of coffee sounded wonderful to Mapes. He was still feeling the effects of sleep deprivation and alcohol. The two officers slid into the stools on the end of the counter and watched the smiling waitress fill two cups.

Nearly ten minutes elapsed before Elaine Stone came over to talk.

"Miss Stone, my name is Mapes, this is my partner Sergeant Porter."

"Have you found my boy?" She interrupted.

"That's why we're here, could we go somewhere private to talk?" Mapes asked.

"Yea follow me," she said walking around the counter and through the door to the kitchen.

At the end of the kitchen was a small manager's office. Mapes and Porter followed her in and closed the door.

"What's wrong, why did you want to talk to me in private? Did you find my boy or didn't you?" She questioned.

Porter and Mapes made eye contact before Porter pulled the photograph from his lapel pocket and handed it to Elaine.

"Oh my god!" She gasped, holding it away from her as if it were burning.

She looked at it for a long time, with one hand over her mouth. Tears came to her eyes and she began shaking her head.

"No! This can't be him. This isn't him. It's not him. No!" She said turning the picture away and laying it on the manager's desk face down.

"Look Miss Stone, understand that this boy was in the river for almost a week. Please look again. Do his facial features resemble your son's?" He asked.

"What happened to this boy… his head?" She asked wiping away tears.

"He was shot in the temple," said Porter.

"Did your son have any problems with a gang that you know of?" Asked Mapes.

"No, he was a good boy. He just played with the boys in the neighborhood. But you need to question Carl Seizer I'm sure he knows something. He changed his story twice yesterday when I kept asking him about Ronny going to the ocean."

"Yea I saw that in his file. Everett said he thought Ron went to the ocean," said Porter.

Elaine looked at the photograph again and again shook her head.

"I don't think this is him I really don't," she said.

"Understand Ma'am we have to make sure. Did Ron ever see a dentist?" Asked Porter.

"At school, yes," she answered.

"Does he have any distinguishing marks, like a birthmark or a mole, maybe a scar from some old or fresh cut?" Asked Mapes.

"I don't know. He never told me about any cuts and I don't remember a birthmark or anything," she answered.

"We're going to have to obtain his dental records and let the coroner make the final call," said Mapes.

"Do you happen to have a photograph of your son with you so that the pathologist can compare it the body to?" Asked Porter.

"UH yes let me get my purse."

She went to the back of the manager's office and opened a small locker. When she returned she sat a black leather purse on the desk and fished a picture out of her wallet inside.

She handed it to Mapes with a trembling hand.

"I really don't think it's him," she said, smiling sadly.

It was apparent to the detectives that Elaine Stone was in denial. Accepting that her son was dead wasn't going to come easy--- not without conclusive proof.

The two detectives hovered over the photograph and exchanged looks.

"Thank you for you time Miss Stone we'll get back to you when we know something for sure," Mapes said, squeezing her hand.

When they got back to the car they sat a minute before leaving.

"What do you think?" Asked Mapes.

"About the boy in the morgue, I'd say she's refusing to come to grips with the fact that her son is dead. This picture she gave us was obviously taken several years ago but it's the same face. I'm convinced of it," said Porter.

"Me too," said Mapes.

They got the name of the school dentist from the summer school office at the Hoffman school, and went to his home address in Norwood. They accompanied the man to a storage unit where they retrieved the dental records for Ronald Stone and then dropped them off at the coroner's office. Afterwards they decided it was time to pay a visit to the Seizer residence since Carl was supposedly missing and partly because of Elaine Stone's hunch that he knew something about her son's disappearance.

When they arrived at the Fairfax address, a woman was watering flowers in the planter adjacent to the front steps. The summer sun was straight up and the humidity was in the nineties. Driving with the windows open didn't help. Mapes got out of the car, removed his jacket and threw it in the back seat. The watering woman noticed him and turned towards the curb.

"Mrs. Seizer?" Said Mapes.

"Yes," she answered.

"Sergeant Mapes, this is my partner sergeant Porter," he said flashing his badge.

"Are you here about Carl? Have you found him?" She asked now looking frantic.

"No Ma'am, but we are on the case. We need to ask you a few questions," he said. "Has Sergeant Bliss talked to you yet?"

"Only on the phone. He's supposed to come out here though," she said.

"When did you first realize he was missing," Asked Porter.

The woman looked down at her water can and turned away to resume watering.

"Yesterday, it was yesterday, she said.

The woman's demeanor was inconsistent with someone whose child had just disappeared and both detectives noticed.

"You want to explain to us what happened?" Asked Mapes.

"You should wait and talk to my husband, he'll be home at two thirty," she said.

"We plan to talk to your husband, but right now we need to hear from you about what happened," said Mapes.

The woman put down the can and sat down on the steps her face in her hands.

"I take it we can rule out a kidnapping?" said Mapes.

"He and my husband had an argument and Carl ran off. We haven't seen him since," she said.

"Mrs. Seizer," said Mapes.

"Call me Peggy," she said.

"Ok Peggy has Carl ever done this before?"

"No he's always been a good boy. We've never had any trouble with him really," she said.

"Well pardon my bluntness, but a happy well adjusted kid doesn't just up and leave over a disagreement. What aren't you telling us?" Asked Mapes.

She took a deep breath and continued, "My husband was... ahh... administering... he was getting punished."

"What kind of punishment?"

"He was getting a spanking and he bolted out of the house and ran."

"He was getting a spanking?" Questioned Mapes.

"Yes," she said.

"With a hand, a switch, a belt, what?"

"A belt," she said.

"A Belt, he was getting a whipping then not a spanking. A spanking is what you give a three year old for running out in the street. A belt is a whipping."

"Yes," she said.

"What did he do to warrant a whipping, did he steal something, did he use drugs, what?" Asked Mapes.

"He yelled at Elaine Stone and caused a big scene in the street."

"Did she accuse him of lying about what happened to her son?"

"Yes, and my husband had to go get him, and bring him home."

"So your son was obviously agitated and upset?"

"Yes"

"Why do you think that is, Why do you think he got so agitated with a woman who is obviously distraught over the disappearance of her son?" Mapes asked, pressing her harder.

"I don't know I don't have the answer. He's never like this," she said wiping away a tear.

"Look I'm sorry Peggy, I know you're upset and nobody is coming down on you about how you raise your kid as long as he's not a victim of cruelty. I mean every kid gets a whipping now and then. That's the way it is here, right?"

"Yea," she said without looking up.

"Excuse me but earlier you said you had no trouble with him really. So you have had some trouble with him, what kind of trouble?" Porter asked.

"Fighting, he's been sent home from school a few times for fighting, but what boy doesn't?"

"How many times exactly?" Asked Mapes.

"Six times I think," she said turning her head away from Mapes. She knew what they were thinking. "But that doesn't have anything to do with him leaving."

The detectives had the same thought as they made eye contact; that children who are victims of violence at home pass it on. Without meaning to say it she had just confirmed to Mapes a what he were already thinking, that her son was prone to violence.

"How severe was the whipping?" Asked Mapes.

"You'll have to ask my husband when he gets home. I've said all I can say right now I have things to do. Besides you should be out looking for my son anyway," she said.

In the car they decided that while they waited for the coroner to compare dental records they would go back to the school and see if they could access Carl's school records.

"You know what I'm thinking? I think the kids old man gave him a lollapalooza of a whipping and that's why the kid ran," said Porter as they drove.

"Yea that's my take on it too. I can't wait to ask the old man what he found out. If he beat his ass that bad the kid must have spilled something," Replied Mapes.

"Something strange is going on in that neighborhood, that's for sure," said Porter.

Again they found themselves at the Hoffman admissions desk talking to the summer school office manager.

"Oh my! Didn't I give you the right directions?" She asked when she saw the detectives.

"Yes you did, thank you. We're here on a different matter this time," said Mapes. "Can you show us the file on another one of your students?"

"What's this about, if you don't mind me asking?"

"Well, there is another student missing, a boy who lives across the street from the Stone boy. We just need to cover all the bases, it's just routine. The name is Carl Seizer."

"I don't know these files are supposed to be private."

"Yes, I realize that but don't you see how time sensitive this is? The longer it takes to find him might make the difference between life and death. We can get a warrant, of course but that will just eat up more precious time," Mapes explained.

"Yes I suppose it's all right then. Just wait a few minutes and I'll get it," she replied.

The woman left the room for several minutes and then returned carrying two files.

"Do you want his Cume folder also?" She asked.

The two men looked at each other for a moment and then Mapes relied, "Of course let us see that too."

"What the hell is a Cume folder?" asked Porter under his breath.

They opened the folder titled Cumulative. This folder turned out to be a treasure trove of knowledge pertaining to Carl Seizer, everything from test scores, grades and any behavioral problems to pictures of him at every grade level.

Under behavioral problems they weren't surprised to find out that Carl was a bully. Most of his fighting weren't fights at all, but beatings of other younger, smaller or non-physical children administered by Carl. This problem seemed to manifest itself from day one. They learned that his mother's estimate of school trouble was much more than six times. This year he was threatened with expulsion if his behavior didn't change.

"Jesus, this kid thinks he's Joe Palooka," said Porter.

"Yea, this kid ain't just a little violent, he's a God Damn menace. If he ain't stopped he's going to kill somebody," said Mapes. And the instant he said it, was like someone had flicked a light switch.

"You thinking what I'm thinking?" Asked Porter.

"Yea, and I hope it's just the suspicious part of me. Christ the kid's only eleven," said Mapes.

"Ok, I think we have enough," He shouted at the office manager across the room. "Thank you very much, but could I impose on you again and use your telephone?" he asked.

Mapes dialed the number of the county coroner and waited. On the forth ring he picked up.

"This is sergeant Mapes, have you been able to check those dental records yet? Ah ha! I see…. Thank you," he said and put down the phone. "It's a match, it's definitely the Stone boy and he's definitely been murdered. What time you got?"

"Three o'clock," said Porter.

"Well it looks like we go back to Fairfax and kill two birds with one stone, no pun intended. We'll inform the mother first, then we'll talk to Seizer," said Mapes.

Elaine Stone kept repeating the word "no" as she stood in the doorway of the narrow 1910 townhouse until finally collapsing on the threshold unable to repudiate the overwhelming evidence the officers presented. Both detectives reached to catch her when she fell but she dropped like a stone. When they tried to help her up she resisted and wanted only to sob into the worn wooden doorframe.

"Just leave me alone," she screamed.

"If you need anything Ma'am we'll be right across the street for awhile," said Porter. "We're sorry for your loss."

They left her still sobbing in the doorway and went to speak to Bert Seizer.

"Do you ever get used to this part of it?" Asked Porter

"Notifying next of kin?" Mapes asked.

Porter nodded. "Yea does it get any easier?"

"Not really. After a while it doesn't show on your face anymore but it's still the kind of thing you think about when you're alone… you never forget it"

"So are we just going to leave her there?" Porter asked looking back.

"I don't know what else you want to do, she want's to be left alone."

Mapes knocked on the door and Bert Seizer answered almost immediately.

"Come in my wife said you'd be by," he said. "I guess she told you some of what happened?"

"She did but we need to hear from you exactly what went down yesterday morning," said Mapes.

They followed him into the dining room and he motioned for them to sit down. They both noticed his swollen cheek and black eye but didn't say anything at first. The three men were sitting at the table when Peggy Seizer came into the room. She looked as though she was coming to sit down but her husband stopped her pointing toward the kitchen.

"Why don't you go make some coffee?" He said.

With his wife gone he began to tell them the same story they had already heard except for when he took his son to the basement to administer his punishment.

"Look I can imagine what you're thinking. You think I'm some kind of a monster don't you?" He asked.

"Like I told your wife it isn't our place to tell you how to discipline your child. Obviously you've been doing it a while and he hasn't run away before. What was so different this time?" Mapes asked.

The man lowered his head in a posture of guilt and regret.

"He was different yesterday, he has been acting strange for a few weeks but yesterday he just came apart on Elaine Stone, granted she pissed him off, but he would have never spoken like that to an adult before, no matter what. That's the way I raised him, to respect his elders."

"Anyway I brought him downstairs to the basement and I took off my belt and... Look I love my son but he wouldn't say he was sorry and he started screaming at me; calling me names. He's never acted like this ever."

"Miss Stone suggested that you question him about what he knew about her son's disappearance, did she not?" Asked Mapes.

"She did, and I did ask him, but he swore he didn't know anything except that Ron mentioned he wanted to go to the ocean."

"If you don't mind me asking Mister Seizer, what happened to your face?" asked Porter.

"Oh this," he said touching his cheek. "I uh... slipped on a piece of coal and fell against the stairs yesterday."

"Was this when your son was getting punished?" Mapes asked.

"No it was when he ran up the stairs I tried to catch him but I slipped."

"I see, and your son didn't tell you anything regarding Ron Stone?"

"No, just what I already told you."

"I'm afraid that homicide will also be looking for your son for a different reason Mister Seizer. You see Ronald Stone is dead, he was murdered," said Mapes.

Bert Seizer didn't flinch when he heard the news but instead became defensive.

"What does his death have to do with my son? Are you suggesting he had something to do with a murder?"

"We're not suggesting anything, but we definitely want to talk to him as a person of interest. He's been sullen and moody, by your own admission, he insulted his friend's mother, and he defied his own father, and if you ask me I think he did a lot more than that. To me, all of this acting out spells involvement of some kind. Whether it's directly or indirectly I believe he knows something." said Mapes.

Bert Seizer stood up, angry at the detective's last remark. His fingers twitched, giving Mapes the impression that the man had entertained the thought of taking a swing at him.

"I'm going to ask you to leave my house now," he said pointing to the front door.

"You might want to rethink your attitude Sir if you expect police help," said Mapes as he and Porter walked to the front door." We will find him and when we do I hope for your sake you've been honest with us."

"Get out," Bert shouted.

Mapes nodded and they left.

On the way back to the precinct, Mapes made his usual stop pit stop at the liquor store.

"Sorry Porter but it's been a tough day and I need a quick bracer."

Porter, as usual, had no comment. He kept his eyes on the windshield as though he were sight seeing.

Finished with the daily ritual Mapes got back in the car and pulled back into traffic.

"What's your take on the old man?" he asked, belching out the window.

"He reminds me of my old man. He loves his kid but he thinks that not being strict is bad parenting," said Porter.

"So you don't get the impression he's hurt the boy?"

"No, I'm not sure if he has or not. If he has he may not think he has. People really believe that a few bruises are a small price to pay for saving their kid from becoming a juvenile delinquent or worse."

"How about you, what do you think?" Asked Mapes.

"Well to be honest I hated my old man for the beatings I got but then, look how I turned out, I'm a law abiding citizen with a healthy respect for authority. So was he wrong? Would I have turned out different if he hadn't been the way he was? I don't know," said Porter. "How about you?"

"Me, my old man was a drunk. I don't remember much about him. He ran his car into power pole when I was five and killed himself. My mother raised me and she didn't believe in whippings. So what do you think that proves? Not a goddamn thing. The only thing I got from my father is my fondness for the spirits," he said smiling. "But as for the Seizer kid, I think his dad may have gone too far and pushed him over the edge. I hope we find him before he does something really stupid."

"Maybe that's the problem, maybe he already has," said Porter.

"Then he doesn't need anybody else to beat him up, he needs help. And if he doesn't get it he'll be like a wild animal caught in quicksand. The more he fights it the deeper he goes.

"You surprise me Mapes, I would have never figured you for a bleeding heart. The poor delinquents had a rough childhood that's why he's evil. Besides I always thought you didn't like kids anyway," said Porter.

"You playing devils advocate on me Porter? I know for a fact you coached little league," said Mapes.

Porter laughed and took out his notepad. He thumbed through it and said, "I have a quote here that says, 'These kids are mean as rattlesnakes.' Isn't that what you said about the young ones in the Gunther gang?"

"I might have, but this kid don't rank with Gunther gang. He's only eleven and he's in deep shit. And who says I don't like kids? And what the fuck are you doing quoting me in your notes anyway?" Mapes questioned.

"Just trying to learn from the master." Porter laughed. "And who else is going to bust your balls?"

Chapter Twenty-seven

Dicky Williams had been sitting on his front steps when Mapes and Porter told Elaine Stone that her son had been positively identified. He saw her collapse in the doorway saw the looks on the officer's faces. It wasn't hard to figure out what had just happened. He kept still as he watched them cross the street and speak to the Seizers.

The image of Everett Foss coming down the sidewalk carrying a paper bag caught his eye and he motioned for Everett to join him on the steps. He held his index finger to his lips to make sure Everett didn't attract the detective's attention. But the officers seemed to be having a serious conversation and gave Mrs. Seizer their full attention.

If they had noticed the boys they might have remembered the description from the fourteen-year-old gang member about seeing a light skinned boy with white hair poking around the body. However, by the time the detectives were through talking to Peggy Seizer, Dicky and Everett were half way to the fort.

About twenty feet from the fort Dicky gave a loud whistle. In one corner of what was once a window appeared the face of Carl Seizer.

"Yes," he said excitedly. "I'm starving. You guys brought food right?"

"Yea, here I made you a couple of baloney sandwiches," said Everett handing him the brown paper sack.

"Here's a Ale Eight," said Dicky pulling out a bottle of ginger ale he had stuffed in his back pocket.

Carl snatched up the bag and opened the soda with his teeth. Everett winced watching him do it. Rubbing his fingers over his own front teeth he said, "I still don't know how you guys do that."

"It's easy," said Dicky.

"Yea, especially when you're starving. I would have broke the bottle open and drunk it out of broken glass," said Carl between gulps.

"Did you sleep here last night?" Asked Everett.

"Yea I slept here, and hey, can one of you guys steal me a blanket? I froze here last night."

"I got an old one in the basement we used when the cat had kittens but it's clean now, I think," said Dicky.

"Was it really dark here? I bet it was really dark and scary here last night," said Everett.

"I got a flashlight. If I hear something that don't sound right I just turn it on," Carl explained.

"How many times you turn it on?" asked Dicky smiling.

"I don't know, a few times, I guess. I kept thinking it was my dad looking for me," said Carl, downplaying the fact that he'd been up most of the night jumping at every sound.

"You're going to need more batteries then," said Everett.

Dicky and Everett laughed.

"I don't figure I'm going to stay here long enough to need more batteries," Carl said finishing the second sandwich.

"What are you going to do?" Asked Everett.

"I plan on getting me some money and splitting to Florida where it's sunny all year round."

"How?" asked Dicky.

"I don't know, steal it if I have too. My Dad's going to be sorry he ever used that fucking belt on me. They're all going to be sorry," said Carl.

"Your Mom too?" Asked Everett.

"Yea her too, she could have stopped my dad a bunch of times but she just stayed in the kitchen and made cookies," Carl argued.

"Cookies ain't so bad," said Everett.

"I've seen his dad's whippings before man, he gets crazy," Dicky said, looking at Everett. "It looks like he went berserk on you this time man," said Dicky lifting the back of Carl's shirt.

Carl was striped with welts, from neck to ankles, some of them with scabs. His lower lip was also swollen with a scab from a backhand to the mouth.

"What did you do?" asked Dicky.

"He called Ron's Mom a whore," said Everett.

"No shit?" said Dicky laughing. "Man that's rich."

Carl smiled also, momentarily but his thoughts soon returned to the severity of his situation and he again grew sullen. Despite his bravado in front of his friends he was actually lost as to what he would do next

"Oh shit I almost forgot, the cops came to Ron's house this morning and told her they found him. She was a mess man. She fell down in the doorway and she wouldn't let the cops touch her.

"Then everybody knows he was shot now?" Asked Everett.

"Well yea they'd have to, and they went over and talked to your Mom next. I saw them, said Dicky pointing at Carl.

"About what, about Ron or me?" Asked Carl.

"Come on man, they had to be talking about you," replied Dicky. "But maybe it's because you split, there ain't no way they could know about anything else."

Carl threw the pop bottle against one of the stonewalls causing a starburst of green glass, and walked out into the hollow. He wondered if they had spoken to his father. His father had to be angry. He was convinced that soon everyone would know he had killed Ron.

"I got to get out of here, their going to come looking for me man, I know it. I got pissed yesterday and hit my dad with a shovel"

"Crimany Christmas!" Said Dicky.

"And that ain't all, I told him about Ron."

"Everything?" Asked Dicky.

"Yea, I said I did it. So if the cops talked to my old man they know it was me that did it," said Carl. "I got to get some money and then maybe I can get on one of those barges on the river and take it someplace. Maybe I can get to the ocean where it's warm and live on the beach."

"Don't you need money for food? Asked Everett.

"Well yea, but I can collect pop bottles on the beach and cash them in for food. And it's warm there all the time so I only need shorts and my tee shirt. And you know what? I can maybe build a shack out of palm trees to live in, like Robinson Crusoe. It will be really neat," he said.

Carl's face betrayed his optimism. He was hurting. The welts were bearable, he knew they would heal, but the pain in the pit of his stomach had been his constant companion since the shooting, and it was getting worse.

He wanted to go home and sleep in his room: to wake up fresh in the morning and find out it was all over; to find out it was just a bad dream. He wanted his father back but he wanted the father that took him to Reds games and hugged him when he got home from work. Not the father that peeled the skin off with a belt. Not the wild-eyed, frenzied disciplinarian. Not the father whose frown made his blood run cold. There was no changing his fate and he knew that. He was running out of options and soon he would have to make a move.

Dicky felt relieved that Carl had told someone. Now he was off the hook. It would have been easier to lay the blame for on the Gunther gang so that all of them could have gotten off clean, but this was second best.

The whole idea of the shooting had traumatized him and clouded his thinking. He would need months of therapy to rid him of the guilt and pain. He would become quiet and sullen, unable to cope with life. After all, he had lost his innocence. No one would find him culpable in an accidental shooting, not at thirteen years old. Dicky liked Carl and genuinely felt bad for him, but he was also pleased by the way things were working out for him. 'After all, he thought, he had been through enough just dealing with his own problems. None of this was his fault anyway. This was second best.

Everett wished he could say something to make it easier for Carl. He felt Carl's pain, he could hear the edginess in his voice. He saw the cloud that came across his eyes when he spoke about Ron or his father. Carl wasn't the bully he used to fear anymore. Alone and scared Carl accepted his fate and there was nothing Everett could do about it. After years of living on the same block, their relationship would have evolved into lifetime friends. But because of a split second tragedy, their friendship was reduced to a few sandwiches in a brown paper bag and a goodbye. Everett wanted to cry but neither of the older boys were crying and he was still afraid of being called a baby. Remembering the day after the shooting when they all hugged and cried together made him feel good. During his own times of stress, he took comfort in that. He would never forget it. It was the first time any of the boys had ever shown affection. He wasn't sure what he was feeling now or how to put it into words, that the bond of friendship was something sacred. He couldn't say it but he felt it.

Chapter Twenty-eight

"Ok what do we know about this kid?" Asked Mapes, standing by the squad room chalkboard ready to write.

"Well, we know he was eleven years old, white and from a broken home," said Porter.

"Why would you think that to be important in a homicide case?" Asked Mapes.

"Because Kids from broken homes are more likely to have too much time on their hands and statistically gravitate towards trouble, whether it be acting out at school or engaging in petty crimes; even joining a gang. His age would usually determine the level of trouble he could get involved in and his ethnicity would also tell us something about his penchant for trouble," Porter answered. "Colored kids are more apt to get involved in crime at a younger age than white kids."

"You realize their ain't a colored kid in the Gunther gang, Right?" Asked Mapes.

"Well I was speaking statistically," said Porter.

"I wasn't looking for a thesis on the kid anyway, I was looking for something more in the realm of facts that relate to the homicide, but you're right though, we have to know who the kid was to get a feel for who did this," said Mapes. "How about we start with, gunshot victim with a right temporal wound shot at point blank range. Number two, his killer had to be looking straight at him and there were no defensive wounds. He either knew his killer or he didn't see it coming, or maybe both."

"You know what's been bothering me is, how come there were two bodies dumped in the river and they both end up washed ashore on the same stretch of shoreline? What's the chance of that, unless maybe they were dumped at the same place?" Asked Porter.

"Now you're talking," said Mapes. "Ok we need to talk to somebody about river currents."

"Why don't we just ask Shark where he dumped his body and we'll probably be pretty close to our kid."

"Shit, I forgot about Shark," said Mapes angry with himself for not thinking of it first. "Good call."

The deputy working lockup opened the door to the interrogation room and pushed Jack Short into the room and down in a chair opposite Sergeants Mapes and Porter.

"Shark how's county treating you?" He asked in a friendly tone.

"I've been in better," Shark answered suspiciously. "Why what do you want?"

"We want to talk to you about where you dumped the body," said Porter.

"I shouldn't be talking to you without my attorney present," said Short.

"Why? Were here to help you. You already confessed to the murder, we don't need anything from you on that. What we do need is for you to tell us where exactly you dumped the body. We need to know for another case," said Mapes.

"Why would I want to help you? What, are you going to buy me a pack of smokes or something?"

"No, but I can talk to the DA about the possibility of a plea deal, you know like maybe second degree, five to fifteen instead of life," said Mapes.

"Can you guarantee that for sure?" asked Short.

"No, I said I would talk to him. But if he thinks you're being cooperative though, he's more likely to listen to me," Mapes answered.

"He's got a lot of juice with the D A," said Porter

"Is this about that other hit you guys tried to pin on me the first time?" Asked Short.

"Where exactly did you throw the body in the river?"

"In the wrong spot, didn't I? I should have noticed that bend in the river. I shoved it in right next to that old factory about a quarter mile up from where you guys found it."

"You mean near the church?" Porter asked, surprised.

"Yea If I had gone a little further up river, it would have got caught in the current and probably made it all the way to New Orleans."

"I take it this isn't where you always dump your bodies? Asked Mapes sarcastically.

"I'm done talking," said Shark. "So yous guys going to tell the D. A. how helpful I was?"

"Absolutely, just as soon as I get back to the precinct," replied Mapes.

Instead of going back to the precinct they decided to go see for themselves where the Shark had dumped his body in hopes of finding a crime scene.

They parked on Riverside Drive and walked down the cinder embankment to the rivers edge. The metal drums were still where the boys had left them when they played war.

They had no high hopes of finding a pristine crime scene but "to catch a break you have to work the case," Mapes said.

They split up and scoured the ground looking for clues. The summer rains had removed all traces of any footprints that might have remained. Porter noticed that there was a small break in the brush along the bank.

"This is the only spot where you can slide a body in the water without a machete," he said.

Mapes nodded but didn't look up from his search of the area around the one and only drum that was still upright.

Suddenly something glistened as he walked past. He reached down among the shards of green glass with his pencil and uncovered a partially buried shell casing.

"I got something," he shouted.

Porter looked up to see Mapes dangling the shell casing on the end of his pencil.

"What caliber?" Porter asked as he walked over to inspect for himself.

"It looks like a 9mm," said Mapes handing the pencil to Porter.

"I've never seen one like this. Probably fits in one of those foreign guns, German or Italian maybe," he said.

"You know... I have seen bullets like this during the war. The Germans used them in their Lugers. Yea, I believe this is from a Luger," said Mapes.

He then turned his gaze back to the ground and started toeing the dirt with his shoe in an effort to find more. After several minutes of looking he found three more shell casings.

"Mapes look at this," said Porter pointing to the two bottles still standing on the upright barrel.

Mapes surveyed the area and noticed more empty bottles piled next to the barrel.

"Target practice," said Mapes. "Somebody was here shooting bottles," he said looking up the embankment. "The hillside there would absorb most of the sound." Mapes scratched his chin and turned in a complete circle.

"What?" Asked Porter.

"This is our crime scene, the only thing around here is that old factory and the church down the road. Shit somebody could shoot all day down here and not disturb nobody," he replied.

"What about on the other side of the river?" Asked Porter. "You know how sound travels over water."

"What, over in Kentucky? Shit, you know how many of those hillbillies shoot off guns over there? Nobody would pay any attention to it. No! This place is perfect for a shooting gallery or a murder," said Mapes.

"You know John, there ain't no telling whose been shooting down here, maybe it was an accident and the shooter just panicked," said Porter.

"That's a possibility," said Mapes nodding. "But I'm not going to sign off on that just yet. About ten years ago we had string of killings targeting young boys.... The perp dropped the bodies in the river. We never caught the guy... hell we still don't even know if we found all the bodies. Some of them could have made it all the way to the Mississippi."

"Yea, I remember that, I was working traffic then. But wasn't his M.O. strangulation?"

"Yea but these guys evolve. What we need to do is check across the river to see if they've found anything. We'll start with Newport and go down as far as Louisville," said Mapes.

"I'll go call this in and get the lab rats down here," said Porter.

Chapter Twenty-nine

The night was warm and full of fireflies. Carl wanted one last look at his home, something to take with him besides all the bad memories.

He made his way to the back yard and climbed the oak tree just outside his bedroom window. The tree forked about halfway up and afforded a perfect vantage point to see several rooms including his room and the kitchen.

Carl's room was dark but the kitchen light shined brightly. Through the pane of glass at the top of the door the light from the kitchen also illuminated the back steps.

He could see his mother busily making something... probably cookies, he thought. He could almost smell them. His eyes filled with tears as he the thought of never smelling his mother's cookies again. This would be his last look at home before he left for good.

Carl's body tensed instinctively when his father entered the room. Just the sight made him tremble, even though he seemed normal again. He stopped and hugged his wife and then sat down at the kitchen table. His mother filled two cups of coffee and sat across from him. She reached across the table and took one of his hands and squeezed it. Carl thought his father looked almost sad. But he soon passed it off as his imagination seeing what it wanted to see. Still... Maybe he was.

Carl sat mesmerized watching his parents having an intimate moment. It was like he had never noticed that they loved each other. He couldn't remember when they had ever held hands or even uttered the words, 'I love you' in his presence. Had they been like this all along and he just hadn't noticed, he wondered? Receiving his share of hugs and kisses was all he concerned himself with before the accident; or if he was going to the movies or, would he get a new bike; how much would he get for Christmas? Was he so self centered that he noticed nothing about his parents? He had to answer yes. And now it was too late. It was too late to take back what he'd done. It was too late to take back all the hateful things he'd ever said; all the hateful things he'd ever done. It was too late to start over and be the perfect child his parents always wanted. His childhood had ended in that split second at the river.

Climbing down from the tree was harder that the climb up. His legs were cramped and his mind was still with his parents. He hesitated for a moment at the back door. The kitchen light went off and the back yard went dark. He took a deep breath and savored the summer smells of home and left quietly.

Passing Dicky's house he looked inside to see him feeding his father what looked to be oatmeal. With the wheelchair at the kitchen table and Dicky at his side, he dutifully and respectfully saw to his father's needs. Without speaking a word he went through his nightly duties without complaint. Carl had never seen that side of his friend either. It occurred to him that there was a lot he hadn't noticed. It was like being reborn with new eyes. But the new Carl was still trapped in a past life. He would live his life differently now, he told himself. He looked back at his home and then down the street to Everett's house. He felt sick, frightened and alone. Wiping the tears from his face, he walked away into the summer night.

By midnight Carl was at the river. As he made his way along its banks he watched the barges pass north and south on their way to places he only could imagine. When he reached the terminal on Highway 52 he could see the place where the barges load and unload. Long strings of light bulbs hung above the docks, dancing in the wind like tethered fireflies. He spotted a barge that looked as if it were being loaded. Quietly he made his way down to the chain link fence surrounding the terminal and climbed over it to gain access to the docks.

The strong smell of coal filled his nostrils. Many of the barges were hauling coal but some were stacked lumber, and others loaded with crates. A night crew of men was busy loading and unloading as well as several tugboats and barge pushers moving the massive steel containers from one point to another. Carl could not see which of these were departing. Deciding to wait until first light, he crouched behind a scrap heap of loose wood and empty boxes, and tried to sleep.

Chapter Thirty

The number of bodies found in and along the river was more than Mapes could have imagined. After checking with the Hamilton County Sheriff as well as the Kentucky police departments from Newport, Covington and Louisville, the list was 89. If he added the number of corpses pulled from the river by the Coast Guard it was well over one hundred.

"Shit, this river is a floating graveyard," said Mapes slamming the phone down in its cradle. So far I got twelve bodies of young teen boys but nothing linking them together. Hell, some of them were churned up in boat propellers and I'm not even sure there really murders."

Porter paused his search of the Kentucky side of the river to listen to Mapes vent. It was getting close to four o'clock and he knew that Mapes was probably thinking more about his beer and schnapps rather than the case. He had to admit to himself that he also needed a few hours away from the tedium of phone work. This was the unglamorous side of a detective's job; hours of pouring over files and the endless stream of phone calls. But at the end of the day it was this that usually produced the most leads; good old-fashioned police work.

"How's it going for you? Asked Mapes.

"The same, I got nothing to connect anything with anything. They do things different over there I guess, there's also a cross-counties jurisdictional rivalry going on, it sounds like. They think everybody who calls for case info is trying to steal their thunder," Porter replied.

"Or their chicken recipe," said Mapes. "They seriously guard their chicken recipes." Mapes laughed. "Why don't we call it for today and come back in tomorrow with fresh eyes. --- There! That's what I'm supposed to say. The truth is I'm beginning to think this was random. It was either an accident or he pissed somebody off and they killed him. If we can't tie any of these other cases to ours we go back and talk to Elaine Stone again and start over."

"And then what? Aren't we going to press Bert Seizer some more? I know there's something he's not telling."

"That's the last thing we do," Mapes said. "After we talk to her we interview the neighborhood kids.... The ones who said he was running away from home. I read the file, those kids all went down to the river on a regular basis to smoke cigarettes."

"And maybe they took a little target practice too?" Porter suggested.

"I don't know about that, the youngest is only nine. I doubt he has access to a gun, but who knows... the thirteen year old, maybe? Anyway at least tomorrow we'll also have the lab rat's reports. The thing about a homicide case is, it's like a fuzzy photograph; the more information you have, the clearer the picture gets until, Bam! One day you look at it and see the face of the killer. --- Of course that's the best-case scenario. The worst case is you might take it into retirement. This is the kind you never let go.... the ones with kids." said Mapes looking across the room at nothing. He looked exhausted.

"Yea let's get the fuck out of here," Porter agreed.

Porter was finding out that John Mapes was a basket of contradictions. On one hand he's full of the cynicism you'd expect from a thirty-year veteran and he was also an alcoholic like a lot of the other depressed career cops, yet he had just shown a side that Porter would have sworn didn't exist; he had a soft spot, and he was tenacious, in that he never gave up. Porter couldn't help wondering how many of these cases Mapes would be taking with him? He also wondered if he was looking into a mirror. Everyone had told him, "being in homicide is where the action is," but that it came with a price. Looking at his partner told him how much.

Detective Porter went home and changed into his shorts and went for a long run. This was how he shook off the day's pressures. He usually ran four miles every day and then followed it with a swim at the Y. On the way home he stopped at the same newsstand and bought a copy of the same evening paper. This time he also bought a magazine, True Detectives, which he did occasionally. That was the extent to which he would deviate from his daily routine.

"You know all that running won't do you no good if you get hit by a bus tomorrow," said the old man who ran the newsstand.

Porter laughed like he did every day when the old man said that.

"Yea but won't I look great in my new suit?" Asked Porter exactly the way he did every day.

"If anything you're predictable," his wife always said before she left him for a co-worker and moved to California. He was reminded of one of his father's gems of wisdom.

"Everybody sucks somebody's ass," his father used to say. "You might end up sucking some broad's ass while she's sucking somebody else's. Everybody wants what they want, and to get it you have to suck somebody's ass somewhere."

"And the older you get, you'd think it get's better, but it don't, it gets worse. You take that guy at the top; he's sucking some taxman's ass just trying to keep what he's already sucked ass to get."

"You have any idea how much ass I got to suck to keep a roof over my your head and food on the table. --- A lot! So I'm telling you, to be a success you better get used to it. Buy a lot of chap stick, I'm telling you."

Porter must have heard that rant a hundred times, and he loved him for it. It was his father's way of saying, "You do what you have to do for the people you love."

But he had spent four years sucking his wife's ass and she left him anyway. He figured the rule must not apply to cops.

The next morning was spent finishing the last of the Kentucky cases and making the determination that there wasn't any connection to the murder of Ron Stone. All of the bodies found on the Kentucky side of the river were male shooting victims, but all but three were black. And the ones who weren't black were too old to fit the profile of Mapes's child killer. He wished he had found the missing piece to the old case for his partner's sake, but as Mapes always said, "You get what you get, and you make the best of it." Porter felt that this particular Mape-ism was one that Mapes himself didn't really believe or else he wouldn't carry these cases with him so long?

After working alone all morning Mapes finally showed up carrying another file.

"So what did the lab rats come up with?" Porter asked.

"Out of four shells we got a partial print on one but so far no match. If the perp came in from out of state we might never find him. The print was sent off to the FBI but that could take six months even if they do find a match."

"The best news is they pretty much confirmed that the spot where the shells were found is our crime scene."

"How do they know that?" asked Porter.

"They brought a dog down there and he sniffed out a spot where it looks like they tried to cover up a lot of blood with dirt but all it did was keep the blood from washing away with the rain. They found a sample that had coagulated and matched it to Ron Stone's blood."

"So we talk to his mother now?" Asked Porter

"Yea but today is the funeral. We let her bury her son." he replied. "We'll go to the wake afterwards at her mothers house in Norwood. She's had a lot of time to think since we last saw her. Maybe she's remembered something."

The mother's house in Norwood was just off Madison. It could have been located on half the streets in Walnut Hills. It sat back on a raised lot with stairs that led up the embankment to a newly remodeled row house.

The block was full of cars and people were still arriving from the funeral. The detectives parked down the street and walk to the house. The front door was propped open and people stood on the porch holding plates of food.

Inside more people were milling about eating and talking. No one paid much attention to the detectives; they were just two more suits in the room. They stopped at the buffet table and surveyed the spread.

"I wasn't hungry till we came in here, Jesus what a spread. Do you think anybody would mind...?" asked Porter.

"We ought to find Mrs. Stone first, we might not be welcome after she talks to us," said Mapes.

"It's all right," said Elaine, standing just behind the two men.

Mapes did an about face and took off his hat. Porter took his eyes off the food and did the same.

"We're sorry for your loss. I hate bothering you today but we are still trying to find out who did this," said Mapes.

"Lets go outside," she said.

They followed her through the kitchen and out the back door. In the back yard was a picnic bench full of children eating and a row of white Adirondack chairs. Elaine sat in one of the chairs and motioned for the two men to sit in the two nearest her.

"I'm sorry about the way I behaved the last time you came to see me. I didn't want to believe Ronny was gone and I took it out on anyone who told me otherwise. I even called my own brother an asshole because he was trying to get me to look at the facts."

"Don't even worry about it. What you're going through right now I can't even imagine," said Mapes.

"What can I do for you then?" She asked.

Mapes was surprised at calm that had come over her. It was as though she had accepted what had happened and was at peace with it. He'd seen this before a few times but the people were Buddhists who meditated their way though adversity. Some Christians who actually believe their loved on was in a better place could also reach this level of peace but he had rarely seen it.

"Have you had the chance to think any more about anyone that your son might have known of an unsavory nature? --- Any body that might have a connection to the Gunther gang or to anyone doing drugs maybe?" Asked Mapes.

"I have given it a lot of thought and the truth is I don't know. You always hope your child never gets involved with people like that but you never really know for sure. I had no idea that he was going to the river, but I worked a lot, and when I wasn't working I thought more of my own problems than I did his." She said tearfully. "I loved my son sergeant Mapes but now I've doubted that I really knew him. I think he spent most of his time with his friends. If anyone knows what happened to Ronny it's them," she said.

"We have talked to Bert Seizer but we've yet to speak to the boys. You have heard that Carl has run away haven't you?" Asked Mapes.

"I did, but I wasn't surprised…. The way Bert whips that kid… We all have heard it. I believe that you have to switch a child occasionally, I mean that's the way we all were raised. But Bert, in my opinion goes too far sometimes. I mean, the kid's only eleven, for crying out loud," said Alice.

"I see, well some parents believe that you have to take a firmer hand with boys than you do with girls I know, but you say that it was more than that?"

"I do --- and I also believe that if you find Carl, I truly believe he knows what happened to Ronny," she said.

"And excuse me for asking but you aren't just saying that because of the ruckus he caused at the Foss's house, are you?" he asked.

Elaine smiled and shook her head. "I don't hold any ill feelings about that. He was under pressure too, and some of the things he said to me were hurtful but true. I've managed to come to terms with what I am and what I've been. I feel sorry for Carl, I really do. I hope you find him soon before anything happens to him."

"By the way, is the Foss family here?" Asked Mapes.

"None of them came, the Williams' the Seizers or the Foss's," said Elaine.

"Don't you think that's odd?" He asked.

"Not really" she said smiling. "We all have our own problems don't we?"

"Well thank you for your time, we'll let you get back to your guests now," said Mapes.

"Grab some food before you leave we've got tons," Elaine said.

"Actually I'd love too," said Porter. "I'm starved."

"We really have to be going Ma'am, but thank you anyway," said Mapes.

Porter looked like he'd been stabbed in the heart but he said nothing. They all went through the back door and passed the buffet table and then out the front door. Porter followed behind Mapes and quickly folded some bead together with meat and cheese as he passed. By the time they got to the car his face was stuffed with food. Mapes looked at him across the top of the sedan and shook his head.

By the time they got back to Walnut Hills Porter had finished his sandwich and was wiping his mouth with his coat sleeve. The Foss house always looked like no one lived there. The grass was overgrown, the concrete driveway was crumbling and all the windows were shut tight with dark drapes showing no light from within. Mapes parked the car out front and he and Porter walked to the door and knocked.

Several minutes past and repeated knocking before the latch could be heard turning from the inside. A bald man in his late thirties dressed in kaki pants and a sleeveless undershirt finally opened the door.

"Mr. Foss?" Asked Mapes.

"Yea!" Said the man.

"I'm sergeant Mapes, this is sergeant Porter, we are investigating the murder of Ronald Stone and we'd like to ask your son a few questions if you don't mind," Mapes said.

"What kind of questions?" He asked frowning.

The man appeared to have just been awakened from a nap. He also recked of stale beer and body odor.

"We are trying to get feel for who might have wanted to harm him. We need to know if your son noticed anyone hanging around lately who didn't belong. We're asking all the boys in the neighborhood for help. If there was something out of the ordinary we feel they would have noticed," said Mapes.

"Uh, ok just a minute I'll see if he's here," said Foss.

He closed the door, leaving the detectives to wait on the front steps. Several minutes later he reemerged at the door alone.

"He's out playing somewhere, I guess, Least ways he ain't here," Foss said looking at Mapes then at Porter. "Hey I'm out of work you know, and I kind of always wanted to be a cop, so I was wondering... you guys hiring?"

"I don't really know Mr. Foss, you'd have to go down to city hall and ask for an application," Mapes said.

"Yea ok, Mapes right? I'll tell them you sent me," said Foss.

"Mind if we look around the neighborhood for Everett and talk to him if we see him?"

"No, knock yourself out, he's should to be around somewhere close. He knows what he gets if he don't," Foss said with a chuckle.

The detctives did not laugh, but backed off the steps to leave, and then Porter turned to ask, "What does he look like?"

"He's about four foot with shorts and a striped shirt. --- Oh and he's a toe head like me... or like I was." He chuckled again.

The two men left and walked down the sidewalk towards the Williams house.

"Can you imagine that rube as a cop?" Asked Porter.

"The scary part is I know some cops just like that guy," Mapes answered.

"Yea well I guess that's a good thing then since he's listing you as a reference," said Porter.

"Yea that and ten cents will get him a cup of coffee."

Suddenly Mapes froze.

"What?" Asked Porter.

"The kid… his father said toe headed," said Mapes. "The gang kid, he said he saw some boys in the water with the body and one of them had white hair. --- A toe head remember?

"Shit, those boys do know something about the murder then," said Porter.

"Well, they knew Ron was dead long before any of the rest of us, and for some reason they kept quiet about it, that's interesting," said Mapes.

"I don't know how a kid goes through something like that without telling somebody?" Porter questioned.

"They could if they were scared," said Mapes.

They began to walk slowly down the street looking for any signs of children playing.

"You ever have any secrets this heavy when you were a kid?" Asked Porter.

"Naw, the biggest thing was me smoking my dad's tobacco just like these kids, but nothing like a killing."

"You said killing instead of murder, is that what you think it is now?"

"I don't know what it is. You saw that there was some kind of target shooting going on down there, anything could have gone down. You get a bunch of kids together with a loaded gun and there's no telling what's going to happen."

"Is it because they're so young you don't want to believe they're capable of murder?"

"Oh, I've seen a lot of things in thirty years. I know what people are capable of, including kids. But suppose I do want to believe the best about our innocent population? If I'm wrong I can take it," said Mapes.

"Is it just because they're white," Asked Porter.

"No it's just because they're kids," said Mapes.

"You remember the question they asked at the academy about if the department policy was to shoot to kill anybody pointing a gun at you, would you still pull the trigger even if it was a kid?" Porter asked.

"Yea, I remember," Mapes replied.

"Is there any difference in the way you would answer that question now compared to how you answered it then?" Asked Porter.

"What are you my conscience now?" Asked Mapes.

"No, just trying to find out who my partner is."

"No, the answer is still the same."

"And that is...?"

"Anybody pointing a gun at me is dead, period. Like I told them then, 'A kid with a gun can kill me just as quick as his daddy."

"What about you, how did you answer that one?" Asked Mapes.

"I was a young and stupid then. I told them I wasn't sure I could shoot a child. And yea, I found out that was the wrong answer. I only heard the part of the question that spoke about shooting a child. What I didn't hear was the given, that it was department policy to shoot anyone pointing a gun at me. The thing is, just between me and you, I still don't know if I could shoot a kid."

Mapes laughed. He remembered the large number of his classmates that got screwed up over that question.

"So if this Foss kid draws down on us we smoke them, right?" Asked Porter smiling.

"Right," replied Mapes.

Chapter Thirty-one

Everett and Dicky had seen the strip down Ford pull up and park in front of Everett's house and watched from behind a hedge as they talked to his father. When they saw the two men were comming down the sidewalk instead of getting in their car, both of them ran to the side of Dicky's house and on down into the hollow. As soon as they reached the fort they jumped behind the stonewall and crouched behind it.

They stayed in this position for at least ten minutes occasionally peering out over the wall to see if anyone followed, but no one did.

"Do you think they know?" Whispered Everett.

"I don't know, I hope not, but even if they did I don't have nothing to worry about. I didn't do nothing," said Dicky.

"How come you keep saying that? You told Carl that we were all going to get in trouble.... You because you're the oldest, and the oldest always gets the blame for something." Everett questioned.

"I never said that, I never said the oldest always gets into trouble. I said I might get into trouble. But look, I got to take are of my old man so they would probably let me go on account of hardship, just like they let my brother quit school so he could get a job."

"What about me then, I got a hardship, my dad don't have a job no more?" Asked Everett.

"Yea but you brought the gun, you're just the same as Carl," said Dicky.

"So you blaming it all on me now cause I brought the gun? Asked Everett. "You shot the gun too, you touched it, you get the blame too. Anybody who shot it gets the blame."

"Yea we'll see who gets what you little shit," said Dicky angrily.

"You're turning into a big asshole Dicky," said Everett.

"You better take that back you little turd before I pound your face in."

"Go ahead and see if I don't kick you in the mouth," said Everett backing against the wall and pulling his legs up against his body.

Dicky curled his fingers into fists and flinched as he thought through the impulse to hit Everett, but after a few moments he relaxed, as did Everett who had been ready to kick out with both legs in his defense.

"You better remember it was you who didn't want to tell anybody, and it was you who made us put Ron in the river. If you keep blaming me and Carl to the cops I'm going to tell them about what you did."

Neither of them spoke for a few moments and then Dicky stood up and looked toward the trees that bordered Owl's Nest Park. There were two silhouettes of men just beyond the tree line. Both men wore hats and dark clothes.

"Shit! They came all the way down into the park looking for us," said Dicky. "I mean you. They went to your house; they probably want to talk to you. Maybe it's just about Carl being gone," Dicky said.

"You think so?"

"Yea I bet that's all it is. You're going to have to talk to them sometime cause they know where you live and they'll just keep coming back till they find you."

"Yea, well it don't have to be today," said Everett as he watched them pass. "You don't think they already found Carl do you?"

"Fuck! I don't know. I never figured on that. Well if they did, and Carl told them everything, then they're looking for both of us," said Dicky. "Oh shit! Oh shit! Oh shit! Let me think. What do I got to do?" Said Dicky pacing around the inside perimeter of the fort.

"Do you think we have to run away too, like Carl?" Asked Everett.

"Hey man I can't run away I got to take care of my Pop. He can't do for himself no more," said Dicky, with a tear in his voice.

Everett sat back against the wall and stared into the opposing wall. The stones were not all the same he noticed. They had rounded edges but they were all different shapes of grey rock. He had never paid any attention to the wall before; only now when he thought he might go to jail did he begin to notice how beautiful they were.

"If Carl squealed, then my dad knows I took his gun," said Everett, his voice quivering.

"Yep," said Dicky. "I wouldn't want to be you right now. What are you going to do, run away?"

"No, I'm just going to go home and see my Mom.... and my Dad, I got to tell somebody anyway. I can't do this no more man I can't," said Everett almost crying.

Everett stood up, he felt a flood of relief that he was about to stop living a lie. It would feel good to confess just like it did the day he told the priest. Dicky remained in his crouched position and watched. He was puzzled by the look on Everett's face.

The two shadows at the tree line passed again walking in the opposite direction. Everett walked through the doorway and stood for a moment and then bolted toward the park without saying a word.

When Everett reached Owl's Nest Park, the detectives were just rounding the front gate on to Fairfax.

"Hey," Everett yelled as they disappeared through the gate.

He stood for a few moments waiting for the men to reappear in the park entrance, but they did not. Running now he made it to the entrance in less than a minute. The detectives were just getting into the car when he rounded the corner.

"Hey," he shouted again, now running as fast as he could.

The car then made a u-turn and drove down Fairfax, away from Everett, with no idea he was running his fastest to catch them. When at last he was at his driveway he gave up and watched the car disappear in the distance.

Tired and out of breath, his gaze shifted to his house and the front door. There was no use in prolonging the inevitable, he thought, and headed for the front door.

Once inside he saw his father sitting where he always sits, in his favorite chair watching television and drinking a beer.

"Hey Dad," he said walking closer.

"Everett, buddy how you doing, did the cops find you?" He asked, obviously in a good mood.

"No Dad they didn't talk to me. I saw them and I ran as fast as I could but they drove away before I could catch up," said Everett.

"Well no matter, if they want to talk to you bad enough they'll come back. Hey you know your old Dad might get a job as a cop, what do you think of that?"

"That would be cool dad, I guess, but.... did the cops say anything about Ron?"

"Not much, they just wanted to ask you some questions. I told them before you didn't know nothing. Do me a favor sport and get your Dad another beer."

Everett did as he was told and retrieved a beer from the fridge and handed it to his father. He stood at his father's side for a moment after he had given him the beer, contemplating his next move. He wasn't drunk yet, this was a good time, he thought. Just as he was about to speak his father scratched the top of his head and then swatted him on the rear saying, "Go on outside and play now and let Daddy watch TV, go on now."

Again he did as he was told. He had an urge to turn back and tell him, but he did not. He had enjoyed his father's attention and his good mood. It had been a while since he had called him sport or even asked him for a favor. It had been a while since his Dad was this nice to him and he didn't want to spoil it. The worst would happen soon enough, he thought. He couldn't help wondering though if he had just made a mistake.

Chapter Thirty-two

Daybreak came with a whisper of light dancing grey on the river. Carl hadn't slept very well, with the night crew banging tools and moving barges like bumper cars all night. The truth was he hadn't really slept well since the accident. The bloody face of Ron Stone was etched forever in his dreams. And though he seemed to be growing numb to it, nevertheless it made a sound sleep impossible. If saying he was sorry would have made everything all right, he would be sleeping in his own bed right now, he thought. The fact was, he couldn't bring that fatal bullet back, nor could he take back hitting his father, or calling Ron's mother a whore. All his misfortune had only proved to him what he always knew; that he was flawed. Why else would his father felt compelled to give him so many harsh whippings? It was just as well that he was out of their lives, he thought, but he had to learn not to cry whenever he thought about it.

The morning brought a hint of autumn with a wind blowing off the river that chilled him to the bone. Carl shivered as he patiently waited for an opportunity to jump aboard one of the barges.

Morning also brought a shift change and as the night shift left the docks and the oncoming dayshift was still milling around the office, Carl saw his chance to get aboard a barge and took it.

Quietly leaving his spot behind the trash heap he circled around wide to the left of the office crawling at times behind brush and tall grass until he reached the docks. He spotted a tugboat ready to start pushing the next barge out into the river. The pilot, high in the wheelhouse, was busy concentrating on his connection with the barge and did not see Carl slip aboard on the stern and disappear below. He found a warm spot in the engine room and crouched behind one of the massive diesels that spat smoke and was so loud it made his ribs vibrate. He yelled at the top of his lungs, "Hey"... but the sound was lost in the growl of the engine. Wrapping his arms around his knees, he settled down and waited for the boat to get underway. His adventure so far was frightening. He tried not to think about the fact that he was leaving everything he had ever known behind to run like a criminal. Huck Finn had his big adventure floating leisurely on a raft and spending warm nights asleep on river islands. It was Carl's favorite book and it gave him comfort thinking about it and comparing himself to Huck. He would try to think of this as his life's biggest adventure.

At last the engines grew even louder. The entire vessel vibrated and he could feel motion. He heard a moaning sound from the stress of the tugboat pushing against the barge. The engine room vibrated as though something was out of control and the air was a choking hot mixture of grease, oil and diesel fuel. This lasted for at least five minutes but it seemed longer. Once the boat got the barge moving and the momentum helped push it along, the engines settled down to a steady, but loud, hum.

Carl waited about a half an hour before he came out of hiding. He made his way back through the engine room door and stuck his head out to see the green of the riverbank passing slowly by. He was on his way. It was exciting yet terrifying. His stomach fluttered with the excitement and hunger. He realized it had been yesterday since he had last eaten. He moved forward and stuck his head out to see another crewman on the bow of the boat. Three steps out side and he ducked into the cabin to the crew's locker room.

Once inside he saw a table with two benches as well as two chairs. He opened one of the lockers and found the crewman's personal effects and spare sets of clothing. He also saw a wallet and opened it. Inside was forty dollars in cash. Carl took one of the twenty's and stuffed it in the pocket of his cut offs and left the other in the wallet.

Another locker contained a brown paper bag with two fried egg sandwiches inside. He was starved and the smell was enough to make him shake. Again he only took one and left one for the locker's owner. The sandwich tasted wonderful. His growling stomach finally settled down and Carl sat in one of the chairs and relaxed looking out the portals like a paying passenger on a pleasure cruise.

Outside he saw the head of the crewman bouncing in and out of view from the front portal. The man was heading towards the cabin. Quickly Carl crumbled the wax paper wrapping and shoved that into his pocket as well. He scrambled through the doorway and back inside the engine room.

While Carl was in hiding the tug helped reposition another barge to travel in tandem to their destination up river. Once together the tugs pulled out leaving the barge pusher to navigate the load to its destination.

When Carl decided to come out of hiding again the tug had detached from the barge and was headed downriver to pick up another load.

He raised his head to look out and noticed he was heading back in the direction he came. It was then he realized that he wasn't going to make it to the ocean on a river tug. He had to get off, but getting off the boat was going to present a greater problem than getting on, unless he waited until the end of the day and jumped ship when everyone left. So far no one had come in the engine room, but he worried about how long he would be so lucky.

An hour later the tug reached it's destination but it was not to dock, it was to assist two other tugs in pushing three coal barges into their docks to be unloaded.

Most of the day was spent going up and down river from one job to the next. Some tugs go with the barges to their destinations; he'd seen them pass while he and his friends choked on Pall Malls. It was apparent however that this tug had other responsibilities that did not require going further than a few miles either way.

A new sound now made the vessel vibrate. It sounded like a chain unraveling followed by a loud thump and then by silence; the engines had stopped. He could here men talking and laughing on the deck. Their banter grew louder until he heard the door to the cabin open and clank shut.

"What the fuck, did you eat one of my sandwiches Larry?" One of the men asked.

"No, I wouldn't touch that greasy shit you eat," said another voice sounding angry.

"Well somebody sure as hell did, I packed it myself," said the man, sounding very upset.

"Why don't you go up on the bridge and accuse the captain... see if he ate it," said the other voice followed by laughter.

"Well it's just I need two sandwiches to make it through the day that's all. Now I'm going to get hungry again before I get off."

"Jesus, you fat fuck you need another sandwich like you need to be divorced. --- Oh shit! That's right you are divorced. Hey maybe she just got tired of hearing you accuse her of stealing your lunchmeat," the man said chuckling.

"Fried eggs."

"What?"

"The sandwich, it was fried eggs."

"Jesus Christ Morty, why don't you go see if somebody's been sleeping in your bed too, you Goldilocks motherfucker?

The men finally grew tired of talking and finished the rest of their break in silence. Carl was relived to hear that no more was said about the sandwich. He also hoped that no one would check their wallets before leaving and notice money missing. He thought perhaps he should try to return it after the men finished lunch. This idea passed when he thought of not being able to buy food later. If he was discovered he could jump overboard and swim to shore if he had to. Carl couldn't swim exactly but he could tread water. He figured he could tread water long enough to make it to shore because the idea of drowning terrified him.

The tug raised it's anchor and got underway soon after the men finished lunch. The hum of the engines filled the room again as Carl settled in beside them and waited.

The warmth of the room accompanied by the steady drone of the engines made his eyelids heavy until finally he dosed off for some much needed sleep.

Carl was jolted awake by a large hand squeezing the back of his neck. He tried to squirm free but the hand held him like a steel vise as it lifted him from behind the engine. Dangling above the engine room floor he gazed into the face of a very large bearded man. The man wore a Greek fisherman's hat with dark skin and hair.

"Please I'm sorry, here, here's your money back," said Carl pulling a wadded piece of wax paper from his pocket.

"Fuck! It was you, you ate my sandwich," said the man angrily pulling the wax paper from his fingers.

The man went into a rage and shook Carl. The hand around his neck was now so tight that he had trouble breathing.

Carl choked and kicked in an attempt to free himself from the man's grasp but he could not. The man was furious with Carl because the sandwich incident had caused him to be the brunt of his co-workers jokes for the rest of the day. They were calling him Goldilocks by day's end and nicknames stick on the waterfront.

"So you a little stowaway, ain't you? Let's see if you don't come an board another boat and steal," he said and dropped Carl hard on the steel floor. He was gasping for air but still he tried to crawl away. He managed to crawl only a few feet when the hand came down on him again, this time on the back of his cutoffs. He was pulled backwards so hard that before he knew it his shorts were around his knees.

Carl quickly reached down to pull them up but a hand slammed his face hard against the deck.

"Please! Let me go, I won't ever do it no more I swear," he said, suddenly realizing that he was saying exactly the same thing he always said when faced with his father's own harsh punishment. He then stopped fighting just as he always did. Whatever was going to happen to him was going to happen no matter what he said or did. The dark man was grown up and grown-ups had all the power. With his face on the floor he could see a large monkey wrench under the engine mount, but it was at least five feet away; there was no chance to reach it. There was nothing he could use to defend himself like he had with the coal shovel. If his father's whippings had taught him anything they taught him that he must accept the pain and humiliation. He went limp and readied himself to receive another harsh beating, but what came was much worse. The bearded man had made up his mind; He had longings and he needed to teach this boy the lesson, the lesson of his young life. At least for now he wasn't going to be the brunt of everyone's jokes, he wasn't going to be his ex-wife's doormat, her toy to be kicked aside for a younger man, no! Tonight he was going to have it all, all his way. He had paid enough and deserved to feel like a man again, he thought. He would show this fat little sow just who really was Goldilocks.

The boats and surrounding docks were dark and deserted. Not even the night watchman in the guard shack on the edge of the parking lot was close enough to help. There was no one to hear his screams and pleas. And when it was all finally and mercifully over, when the dark sweaty man was spent, Carl wished he were dead.

The pain was so bad Carl blacked out. It was like a dark painful dream and he couldn't awaken. He thought he felt more heavy vibration like when the boat was moving but this sensation faded in and out. When he at last came around, he lay motionless until his memory returned and the blinding pain made him realized where he was. He waited for the man to deliver the blow that would take the pain away again. His felt paralyzed from the waist down. The pain went deep inside his torso. At first he couldn't speak. He could only make deep guttural noises like his throat had been cut. A trickle of blood tracking down his inner thigh told him he was not actually paralyzed. Slowly he lifted his head and tried to raise himself to his knees but the pain was excruciating. Turning his head to the side, he froze at the sight of the man's shoes. Now he could hear him breathing and as the man bent over him a few drops of sweat dripped cold onto the back of his neck.

"Please don't hurt me anymore I won't tell I promise, please, I won't tell," he cried when the man again picked him up.

Holding him by the back of his neck, the man dragged him through the hatch and out onto the deck. Carl continued to cry and beg for mercy.

It was when the man picked him up and slammed him into the deck that he lost consciousness. He knew nothing of being picked him up again and held high above the deck. He didn't hear the splash, or feel the pain as his body hit hard on the water. Consciousness did return with a few brief seconds of terrifying clarity just before he slipped away into the cold embrace of the river.

Chapter Thirty-three

Inadequate lighting, dingy green walls, and the smell of dirty ashtrays described every room behind the front desk at the Cincinnati Police Department, including the homicide squad room.

Mapes had just dialed detective Bliss in missing persons while Porter took his usual position in the visitor's chair beside the desk.

"Bliss, hey you got anything new on that missing Seizer kid? --- Well he has sort of fallen into my investigation of the Stone killing. No I don't have much either except for my gut feeling that everything happening in that neighborhood is related one way or another. --- Yea I think we should pool our resources on this. You and I both need to find this kid, granted for different reasons, but I promise to keep you up to date If you do the same…deal? --- Ok, catch you on the flip side."

Mapes put down the phone and stared at Porter.

"That Putz hasn't even been back to talk to the father yet, can you believe that?" Asked Mapes. "He says the mother calls every day to find out if any thing new turned up. But I'm feeling the dad is the key here."

"Why, hasn't he talked to him then, because of his caseload?" Asked Porter.

"Yea that's his whine every time I talk to him... I mean shit; you'd think every other person in Cincy was missing. We got a caseload too but we prioritize. You work the cases that need to be worked first and then you work in the other cases along the way."

"Except for those conundrums, right?" Quipped Porter.

"Yea except for the conundrums, of which I may add, this case is quickly becoming," replied Mapes.

"It's going to help when we find the Seizer kid but I think we should go down there early and talk to the Foss kid. --- That reminds me, did Earl from personnel get a hold of you?"

"No why?" Asked Mapes.

"Because he wanted to know if you were recommending the older Foss for a job. I guess he came down and applied. Earl said he threw your name around like you were married to his sister," said Porter grinning.

"Oh shit, what did you tell him?"

"I told him he was your brother-in-law and you recommended him highly." Porter laughed out loud.

"Thanks partner, I'll make sure your riding nursemaid the next vomiting drunk that gets hauled in," Mapes returned.

Mapes leaned back in his chair and closed his eyes while rubbing his temples.

"You got any aspirin, my head is splitting this morning?" asked Mapes.

"Sorry John there out in the glove compartment, said Porter. What's wrong, too much schnapps last night?"

"Too much beer, not enough schnapps, replied Mapes.

"Maybe it's time to slow down a little," said Porter.

"I have slowed down, when I was younger I was a drunk."

"So now you're not?" Porter asked sarcastically.

"An alcoholic maybe, but a drunk no."

Porter did not respond to the remark, he'd heard the answer before; drunks don't have to go to meetings, alcoholics do.

Just then the phone rang and Mapes answered.

"Homicide, Mapes here," he said.

"Mapes this is Bliss, I just heard the call about a domestic disturbance down there on Fairfax, I thought you ought to know."

"Who is it Seizer?"

"No it's Foss, I guess the old man just beat the shit out of his wife."

"Thanks Bliss I appreciated it, I'm heading down there right now, I'll let you know if I find out anything about the missing boy," said Mapes and hung up the phone. "Mount up Herb we're going down to talk to Foss."

Porter jumped from the chair and followed his partner to the car. Once inside Mapes asked for the aspirin and Porter opened the glove box and handed him he bottle. He took four pills and threw them in his mouth. Removing a metal flask from his lapel pocket he washed them down with a grimace.

"You took those with alcohol?" Porter asked shaking his head.

"You ain't my fucking wife Herb," Mapes barked. "Get your head on straight, we're going down to talk to the Foss kid and while were there we're going to lean on Bert Seizer. I'm tired of being lied to. Somebody's going to tell me something today or I'm going to loose my pension trying."

The drive to Fairfax was slow. It was nine thirty and the morning traffic was still heavy. When they finally pulled up in front of the Foss house there were already two patrol cars there. Alice Foss sat on the front steps with her arms around her three youngest children talking to a uniformed officer. In the driveway next to the porch, the dark silhouette of a man could be seen sitting in the back of the parked patrol car. As they walked up to the porch the officer turned around.

"You must be Mapes and Porter," he said. "I was told you were coming."

"What's going on here?" Mapes asked looking down at a bruised and bleeding Alice Foss.

"Let's go over here," said the officer, motioning them off the porch and out of earshot. "It seems the old man just found out this morning that he got turned down for another job and started drinking. To make a long story short things got ugly, he knocked his wife around a little and, according to his wife, tried to hit the oldest kid.

"Did he hit him?" Asked Porter.

"No the kid was too fast for the fat fuck. We've been called out here before on two other occasions for the same thing. The last time I saw them at the hospital and I gave the kid, Everett, one of my cards. I told him if his father ever got this bad again for him to call me. And that's what he did. I keep telling that poor woman she's got to get away from him but she don't listen. The court only holds him for a couple of days you know how it works. I tell you man one day he's going to kill one of them."

"Yea I hear you, but what are you going to do if she won't leave?" Remarked Mapes shaking his head. "Where's Everett now, I need to talk to him?"

"He's inside, he doesn't want to look at his father inside the police car."

"Why?" Asked Mapes.

"Beats me," said the officer.

Mapes and Porter came back to the steps. Mapes took off his hat.

"Excuse me Mrs. Foss, I'm sorry about your ordeal this morning. Is there anybody you'd like us to call for you…a friend or relative maybe?" Mapes asked.

"No I got nobody to call. Both my parents are dead, my sister moved to California and I ain't heard from her in ten years. Like I told the other officer, this is it for me. If I can't work this out I got nothing."

"It doesn't have to be this way Alice," said Elaine Stone just approaching the porch.

Everyone turned as she walked up and stood in front of Alice.

"Mrs. Stone," Mapes said nodding his head in her direction. Porter removed his hat and also nodded.

"Like I said Honey, it doesn't have to be like that. I had a man who liked to use me as a punching bag and I got rid of his sorry ass. I'm not saying it's easy cause it ain't, but me and Ronny we got by all right till…"

She looked at the ground instead of finishing the sentence but everyone heard the words anyway.

"Look he's going to jail and that's that, so why don't you come on over to my house and I'll make us some coffee? I got some cookies for the kids and me and you can have a talk."

Alice began to cry and Elaine took her hand.

"I should have been coming over to help you when you were going through the loss of your child. --- My god Elaine I never even came to the funeral. You ain't even had time to grieve proper and here you are over here with a hand out to me," she said through her tears.

"Shhh, come on now, come on over and we'll have us a good old-fashioned cry together," said Elaine.

Alice got up from the step and Elaine led her through the grass towards her house.

"Come on Kids we're going next-door, Sissy go get you're brother," said Alice.

"Excuse me, but we need to ask Everett a few questions first, if you don't mind," said Mapes.

"Um yea Ok just send him over when you're through."

The two women and three children walked behind the police car on the way next door. None of them looked over at her husband as they past.

Mapes and Porter found Everett sitting at the kitchen table alone, the picture of a little boy lost. Mapes pulled up a chair, turned it backwards, and faced him.

"You know who we are don't you?" Asked Mapes.

Everett nodded. "Yes sir."

"And you also know that we are investigating the death of Ron Stone?"

"Yes sir."

"Is there anything you want to tell us about what happened to your friend?" Asked Porter.

Everett turned his head away and his chin was beginning to quiver. Neither detective spoke but instead decided to let the boy tell it at his own speed.

"It was…. I didn't mean…. I can't," Everett stumbled and then broke into tears.

Mapes put his hand on Everett's shoulder. "Take your time son. Start at the beginning and just tell us how it all happened."

Everett took a deep breath and began again.

"We went to the river to play war. We all brought stuff. Ron brought his fathers hat and bayonet, Dicky dressed up in his dad's army uniform, and I forgot what Carl had, a canteen I think," he said looking Mapes in the eye.

"That's ok it's not important right now, just keep going," said Mapes.

"I brought a gun," he said, his whimpering now turning louder and harder. "I thought the gun didn't work. My dad said it didn't work. All the times he had it out he always said it didn't work"

"Then it was your Dad's gun that shot Ron?"

"Yes," he whispered turning his face away.

"How did it happen?"

"I dropped the gun and it went off. I almost shot Carl," he said, his face showing pain. "Anyway we decided to shoot pop bottles. Everybody got a turn and then the gun just went off. It went off and shot Ron. Ron's blood was all over us. He was talking and then he was dead," he cried.

He lowered his head, buried his face in his arms and wept. Mapes, trying to comfort the boy, put his arm around him when

Everett took him by surprise when he turned his head burying his red swollen face into the detective's shoulder. Mapes froze at first. He had no children of his own and no experience with a heartbroken child looking for comfort. This was as foreign to him as singing in public. Still he felt something that he had never felt before. After a few moments he lowered his other arm and patted his back.

"It was an accident, don't cry, it was a horrible accident but it's not your fault," he found himself saying in a reassuring tone.

Mapes turned slightly away from Porter's line of sight because he was seriously afraid that he might tear up. He didn't want that to end up as the joke of the day down in the squad room. Porter was not so intimidated. His eyes grew moist regularly especially when it involved children.

After a few minutes Everett began to gain control of his emotions and pulled away from Mapes.

"Tell us how he got in the river then?" Mapes Asked with his composure in tact.

"We were afraid that we'd all go to jail, so we gave him a river funeral and then pushed him in the river. Ron always said that the Ohio goes all the way to the ocean, and he wanted to go there someday. We wanted the river to take him to take him there."

"What were you doing when those boys from the gang showed up?"

"We pushed him in the water that day but then he came back and got tangled up in some bushes. Me and Dicky tried to get him loose but then these Gunther gang guys started throwing rocks at us and we had to run."

"Where is the gun now?" Mapes asked.

"It's in my Dad's drawer under his shorts," said Everett, his answer almost bringing a chuckle to Mapes who desperately wanted to change his mood to something lighter.

Mapes felt uncomfortably good. He had always wondered about what it must be like having children and why so many people swear by it; now he understood a little.

"Show me," said Porter.

They followed him into his parent's bedroom to the top drawer of his parent's dresser. Mapes reached inside and felt around from one end to the other; there was no gun.

"It's always there," said Everett.

"Maybe he put it in another drawer," suggested Porter.

One by one Mapes pulled everything from each drawer but still there was no gun.

"Do you know what kind of gun it was?" Asked Porter.

"It was a gun my dad said he took off of a dead German in the war. Dicky said it was a Luger."

"That matches what we already know," said Mapes.

"Do you know when your Dad last had the gun out?" Asked Porter.

Everett lowered his head again and answered, "Last night."

Is he still in the driveway?" asked Mapes walking out of the bedroom.

Both detectives ran to the front door and looked to the right for the patrol car but it was already taking Everett's father to jail.

"That's ok, that's ok we'll get the location from him at the station," Mapes said.

"What about your Mom, do you think she knows where he put it?" asked Porter.

Everett shook his head. "My Mom don't like it, she never knew where he hid it. Just like my Dad don't know where she keeps her cigarettes."

"How come you know everything?" Mapes smiled.

Everett didn't answer but returned the smile. Since the accident there hadn't been much reason for anyone he knew to smile.

Mapes looked towards Porter and then down at Everett and said, "I think we need to go next door and tell Elaine Stone what happened to her son.

"You want me to stay with Everett while you go talk to her?" Asked Porter.

"No, I want to be there, I should have told before. Ron was my friend," Everett insisted.

"What do you think?" Asked Mapes.

"Let's take him, I don't see what difference it's going to make," Porter replied.

"Fine," said Mapes taking Everett's hand and starting across the lawn.

Porter reached the door first and knocked. Momentarily Elaine opened the door and smiled at Everett and then the detectives.

"Thanks for bringing him back, Are you all through talking to him now? Come on inside Everett." She tried to take him by the shoulder to guide him inside but Mapes didn't let go of his hand.

"What is it?" She asked.

"We need to speak to you Mrs. Stone, it's about your son," said Mapes.

The uncomfortable pause at the door puzzled Elaine at first but then it hit her. Her gaze lowered to Everett. He looked at her for a moment and then ran to her throwing his arms around her waist.

"What is it Elaine?" Asked Alice just arriving in the doorway. "What's wrong with Everett?"

"We need to speak to Mrs. Stone privately," said Porter.

"No it's ok she probably needs to hear this too, doesn't she?" She asked.

With his hat in his hand Mapes began to speak, but as he did another face appeared in the doorway causing him to pause.

"This is May Williams, she's Dicky's mother," Elaine said. "Whatever you are about to say you can say to all of us."

"Well, Everett has just told us what happened to Ronny. It seems the boys were target shooting at the river when the gun accidentally discharged killing your son. I'm sorry," he finished.

Elaine immediately put her hand to her mouth and started to weep. The two other women gasped. Finally Elaine put her hand on Everett and said, "Oh my God, you children knew this the whole time and you told no one?"

"Dicky knew this the whole time and...?" Asked Mrs. Williams.

"Whose gun was it?" Elaine asked.

"It was my dad's," said Everett.

"Everett, why didn't you tell someone?" Asked his mother.

"There still only children," said Porter. "They were all afraid of going to jail."

"Why would you think that honey?" Asked Alice.

"Dicky said his Dad's friend hit somebody so hard it killed him and he went to jail. He didn't mean to kill the guy but he still went to jail," said Everett.

Elaine turned to Alice and buried her face in the woman's shoulder and continued to cry. Everett looked up at Mapes for support.

"That was different," he said. "And obviously he's an adult. It's a little different with adults."

"Excuse me... I'm so sorry Elaine but I need to go home and talk to my son.... Again I'm sorry," said May Williams pushing her way past the detectives and on out the door.

The revelation in the doorway had the effect of setting the neighborhood on its ear. Families questioned their relationships and started talking to each other in some cases for the first time.

Everett had purposely left out the part about Carl holding the gun when it discharged. He had planned to tell them but it didn't come out and no one asked. After a while it didn't seem to matter. Adults didn't seem to care who did what, only why no one told.

It all boiled down to a matter of honesty and trust. Some parents wondered if they had failed to teach those lessons and then some blamed society. Not one asked their children.

"Dicky's going to be mad," said Everett. "I squealed."

Chapter Thirty-four

The fourth floor of Covington's Saint Elizabeth hospital was usually quiet. It was where they kept the intensive care patients as well as the comatose.

Kenton County Sheriff's detective Emmet Love got the call to investigate an assault victim being treated on the fourth floor. The emergency room doctor who treated him was waiting at the nurse's station when he arrived. As he walked up, the doctor came out from behind the station with his hand extended.

"You must be the detective I'm supposed to meet, my name is Doctor Harland."

"How did you know I was a cop I haven't flashed my badge yet?" Asked Love.

"I've worked EMR for a long time I can usually spot a cop pretty easy," said the doctor. "Comes from years of treating gunshot wounds over in Newport."

"I don't know if I should be pleased or pissed," he said smiling.

Emmett Love was a tall solidly built man about forty with short-cropped grey hair; too good looking to be a cop with a last name to match.

Dr. Harland was from an old Kentucky family also tall, very thin and a trustworthy face with a demeanor that could have successfully been applied to selling worthless swampland while drinking mint juleps at Churchill downs.

"What have you got for me?" Asked Love.

"This way," the doctor said gesturing towards the left of the station.

Love followed him into a single room and saw a young boy laying eyes closed surrounded by tubes and monitors.

"Who is he?" Asked Love.

"We don't know. He was brought in last night. A fisherman on the river pulled him out stone cold. Lucky for the kid he was an ex army medic."

"The guy worked on him and got him breathing again and then brought him here in his own car. We were able to patch up his wounds but he's in a coma. We don't know for sure how long his brain was deprived of oxygen."

"What kind of wounds?" Asked Love.

"A concussion for one thing, a few assorted cuts and bruises. He also looks like he's been whipped pretty badly but those wounds are older. The main reason he needs your help is, he was sexually assaulted."

"Jesus Christ, you mean he was beaten, sodomized and then thrown in the river like a piece of garbage? What kind of an animal does that?" Love asked shaking his head. He had experience with bar fights shootouts and moonshiners but pedophiles were new to him.

"You've never worked homicide, I take it? Asked the doctor.

"No I haven't, but I've been a cop for fifteen years and I know these predators are out there, it's just when you find one in your own back yard... I've worked a few child abuse cases but nothing like this," Love said with disgust. "Well, I need to check the missing children's lists on this side of the river and the other. Somebody has got to be missing this kid."

"He seems to be well fed and well groomed so I would think he would be from a middle to upper class family," said the doctor.

"Anything unusual about what he was wearing?" Love asked.

"No, see for yourself his clothes are right over here."

Detective Love walked to the small closet and took down the coat hanger containing the boy's cut off jeans, tee shirt and underwear. He meticulously went through the pants pockets and found only a crumpled twenty-dollar bill.

"The creep wasn't after money, I guess I can rule out a bum, Love mumbled to himself.

After carefully examining the shirt. He switched his attention to the shoes and socks in a small container on the closet floor.

"Buster brown shoes, not the cheap ones," he said.

Love walked back to the bed and stood looking at the boy. He then took his hand and held it.

"Somebody is definitely looking for you, buddy and I'm going to find them, I promise."

The problem with looking for missing person was, there was no master list. Every county and every city with a police department had there own records. Realistically, the only way possible to get a complete list was to call each individual jurisdiction within a fifty-mile radius of the river and ask questions. When Emmet got back to his office he immediately started calling. What the Sheriff's department did have was a master list of all police and county law offices in the states of Kentucky and Ohio.

Starting with his own state of Kentucky he spent three hours on the phone before turning his attention to the other side of the river. He decided to start with Cincinnati and radiate out like he'd done from Covington. The first call he made to Cincinnati P.D. wasn't fruitful, Detective Bliss was out and he had to leave a message.

Several more hours of calling went by before he got a call back from Bliss.

"This is Love's desk, what can I do for you?"

"Uh, the Love Desk?" Bliss queried.

"I'm Detective Love with the Kenton County Sherriff."

"I'm Sergeant Bliss with Cincinnati Police, you called about a missing person case?"

"Yes, we've got a boy down here in a coma we can't identify. I called to see if you have any missing boys who might fit the description. He looks to be about ten or eleven, maybe twelve. He's a little on the husky side, brown hair, brown eyes and he was wearing cut offs and a tee shirt, Oh and Buster Brown shoes with striped socks."

Bliss thought for a few moments and shuffled papers around on his desk looking for the right report.

"Yes, yes I've got a missing boy who's been missing for several days now. He's actually a run away if it's the same kid. He had some kind of scuffle with his old man and took a powder. His name is Carl Seizer. He's also a material witness to a homicide here so, you know, I think I'm going to turn you over to Detective Mapes and let him handle it. He can notify the family. I think he wants to talk to the kid first though."

"Like I said, the kid's in a coma he won't be talking to anybody for awhile. What he needs right now are his Mom and Dad."

"Yea, well I'm going to give this to Mapes anyway, he'll probably be coming down to see the kid. What hospital did you say he was in?"

"He's in Saint Elizabeth's."

"And what exactly are his injuries?"

"He has a bad concussion and…" Love hesitated, "He's been sexually assaulted."

"What!" exclaimed Bliss.

"Yea this poor kid's been through the ringer. You said he had a had a scuffle with his father, you don't think he could be involved in something like this do you?"

"Shit! I don't think so. From what we know, his father is stable, has a good job, not even a parking ticket on his record. He's been pretty strict with the kid I know, but I can't see him doing anything like that."

"And you're good with him being a runaway and not abducted?" Love asked. "The reason I'm asking is, it would fit if the kid had been abducted and then assaulted. That's the way it usually happens. And of course if that was the case I'd have to notify the FBI."

"All I can tell you is what I know for sure. His folks say he ran away, and hey, all he has to do is walk over the fucking bridge and he's in Kentucky. You guys don't have creeps like that over there?"

"Oh yea we got'em, it's just that if I can assume he was abducted, the Feds could mount a better hunt. You know I'm just a country Sheriff," remarked Emmet, tongue-in-cheek.

"Yea sounds like heaven to me, I'd trade case loads with you in a heartbeat," said Bliss. "But seriously, wait and talk to Mapes."

Chapter Thirty-five

Mapes went to county lockup to see Melvin Foss after the ordeal on Fairfax was all over. He was shackled and handcuffed when the deputy brought him into the interrogation cell. The look on his face said pain. Mapes remembered a self-portrait he once saw of Vincent Van Gogh just before the artist tried to commit suicide. The look was the same he thought, the look of a tortured soul. But wife beaters were all tortured souls, especially when they're paying for it, which was not often enough as far as Mapes was concerned. But he wasn't there to listen to his problems; he was there to find the weapon that killed Ronald Stone.

He had left Porter back at the office to return a phone call from detective Bliss of Missing Persons. Porter was anxious to hear what Foss had to say but the chance of finding Carl Seizer took precedence in his book.

Mapes waited until the jailer took off the handcuffs plus a few moments more while Foss rubbed his wrists like everyone does when they're uncuffed.

"I trust you slept well last night Mr. Foss?" Mapes said sarcastically.

"Look I know what you're thinking…that I'm this monster who likes to hurt his family but it just ain't true. I love my family, it's just that I'm going through a real briar patch right now trying to find work and support my family."

It occurred to Mapes that he'd heard a similar excuse from Herb Seizer referring to the beating of his son.

"I'm really not here to listen to your confession Foss, that's between you and your higher power or whoever you think is going to want your sorry ass after you die. Just a heads up though the one I talk to at the end of the day isn't partial to wife beaters. I'm here to find out what you did with that luger war souvenir of yours."

"What Luger?" Ask Foss.

His demeanor had changed quickly from sad and repentant to surly and defensive.

"The one you hide at the bottom of your skivy drawer, you know, the one you wave around to scare the shit out of the wife and kids when you're feeling the power," said Mapes.

"Like I said, I don't know what you're talking about."

"Ok champ, this is how you want to play it? I got statements from you're whole family. We can do this dance forever as far as I'm concerned. I can feel your paperwork getting lost. --- Oh and if you get a bad report in here you get time tacked on. I can seriously see you doing six months in here unless you cooperate."

"I don't know nothing about no luger," said Foss.

"Would it help your memory if I told you that your son and three of his friends took that gun to the river and one boy was fatally shot with that gun."

Foss flinched at the revelation that his son had taken the gun. He turned away from Mapes and looked for the jailer.

"Hey, take me back to my cell," he yelled.

Both Mapes and Foss stood up and locked eyes across the table.

"You're just making a bad situation worse," said Mapes.

"If you got no weapon then my kid didn't take nothing that killed nobody, and if I did have such a gun I probably got rid of it a long time ago," said Foss just as the jailer was slipping the cuffs on to take him away.

"I'm not trying to make a case against anybody you idiot, we just need to secure the weapon to close the case," Mapes shouted as Foss was led through the doorway.

Chapter Thirty-six

A quiet had settled over the neighborhood on Fairfax Avenue. Painful secrets were exposed and people were trying to adjust to their new realities.

Mapes had talked to both Dicky and Everett as to the whereabouts' of Carl Seizer and was told about Carl's Idea of catching a barge to the sea. He was also made aware of the marks on Carl's body, remnants of the last whipping before the boy left. Both detectives concluded that Herb Seizer had gone over the line with his punishments, the last of which, being the one that pushed Carl over the edge.

This was a time for pulling together. Even though Dicky couldn't really tell how much his father understood, he would hold his hand and talk to him every night including his involvement with the Ron Stone Killing. He had to believe his father was still in there. His eyes still seemed alive even though his body was not. Once he had even thought he felt his father squeeze his hand. His mother had taken up going to church again to do penance for failing in her parenting skills. She blamed herself for Dicky's fateful decision to keep the death a secret. At any rate the family seemed to be trying to work though it except that no one smiled anymore. Danny had even stopped his usual brotherly bantering and humiliation rituals. This bothered Dicky the most. He longed to be the brunt of one of Danny's practical jokes or a punch in the arm as he passed. This was a show of love between brothers that was likened to a hug. What existed now within the walls of the Williams home was a family broken. Just like when his father's stroke had turned his world upside, he wondered if his life would ever be normal again.

His relationship with Everett had soured at first because of the boy's confession to the police in front of his mother. Dicky was quick to blame him for his trouble at home. In the light of day he could convince himself that he was blameless, but it was in the dark of night that the demons of guilt came around like cold fingers in his back. Alone in the dark he was to blame for all of it including his father's stroke. Because he collapsed during a tirade for failing to help his mother, Dicky quietly carried the guilt.

Everett's house was still minus his father. Alice and the children were breathing easier without Daddy, even though Alice was visiting him in jail and again succumbing to his promises of a new leaf.

Mapes secured a search warrant for the gun, which turned up nothing during the search of the Foss property.

The only war souvenirs found were an extra large German combat helmet and several swastika armbands. No firearms or ammunition of any kind were found anywhere on the premises. Since nothing could be proven against Foss for ditching the gun, no charges were filed.

In keeping with the courts policy on staying an arms distance from domestic disputes, Foss was finally released with a court order to get counseling and a sentence of six months probation because of it being his third arrest for spousal battery. Mapes always believed that the law would take a more heavy handed approach to spousal abuse if it were the husbands getting the crap kicked out of them.

Chapter Thirty-seven

Soon after the Everett's confession, Mapes and Porter found themselves at the Seizer home. Bert answered the door and at first he stood frozen, expressionless and then like someone had thrown a master switch, broke down in the doorway.

"May we come in?" asked Porter.

"Yes, I'm sorry come in," he said softly, wiping his eyes.

"Peggy the detectives are here," he shouted upstairs.

The fast paced clicking of shoes on wooden steps preceded his wife's entrance into the living room.

"Have you found Carl?" She asked, before taking a seat beside her husband on her mother's floral loveseat. The entire living room had obviously been decorated by a woman, Porter thought, with floral patterns on everything from the furniture to the wallpaper.

"No we haven't found him yet we just came here basically, to inform you about what has recently transpired in the Ron Stone case," said Mapes.

"I am truly sorry about what happened to Ronny but I'm interested in finding my son. I want you to concentrate on finding my son. I don't mean to sound calloused but Ronny is dead and my son isn't."

Bert seemed uneasy at the mention of Ron's death and Peggy was the first to notice.

"What's the matter? Oh my God! Is he dead?" She asked bringing her hand to her mouth.

She looked frantically at Mapes through wet eyes, while trying to ready herself for the bad news by clutching the arm of the loveseat.

"No, no we don't have any evidence of that," said Mapes attempting to calm the woman. "I came because I wasn't sure if you still have conversations with your neighbors across the street," said Mapes.

Peggy shook her head without speaking like she didn't understand the question. Her husband however, looked away.

"I can assume you have not, Mapes said. "Well the two boys, Everett Foss and Richard Williams have given statements that the shooting of Ron Stone was an accident that happened when they were all target shooting down by the river. It was a bunch of kids playing with a gun, Ron was shot when the gun accidentally discharged."

"And Carl was involved?" Asked Peggy.

"Yes as I said they were all target shooting when the accident occurred."

In the middle of Mapes description Bert again started to weep.

"What's the matter Honey?" Asked his wife putting her arm around him.

"Is there something you want to tell us sir?" Asked Porter.

"It's just that I already know what you're not saying,"

"About the beating you gave him?" asked Mapes.

"No, about Carl shooting Ronny," he said.

Mapes and Porter looked at each other in surprise as the new piece of the puzzle fell into place.

"What do you mean Carl shot Ronny, Carl wouldn't shoot anybody?" His wife demanded.

"He told me he did that day in the basement. He said it twice. He said, 'I killed Ron.' I knew he meant it because he wanted to hurt me with it, because I whipped him so hard."

"You want to tell us exactly what happened that day Mr. Seizer?" Asked Mapes.

"Carl had been acting strange for at least a week," said Bert.

"He had been, at least a week," confirmed Peggy.

"Anyway I didn't know it was because of the shooting, I thought he was starting to act out the way so many teenagers do these days. He was shouting at Elaine Stone and calling her a whore in front of the neighbors like some out of control juvenile delinquent. I wasn't going to have a juvenile delinquent in my house. I grabbed his arm and took him in the basement and took my belt to him."

"This time was different though. This time he ran from me and he fought me. He, he started to yell back at me. The harder I whipped him the more he yelled. It was like he was crazy.... And then I saw it.... He grabbed a coal shovel and hit me with it.... And I saw it. It was then... I saw it," He said dropping his head.

"You saw what Mr. Seizer?" asked Porter.

"I saw me," he said. "Carl was me."

Mapes let him calm down a bit before continuing.

"Mr. Seizer, the boys told us that Carl was going to try to hop a boat or a barge somewhere and try to sail downriver to see the ocean. Any idea's where he my go to do this, there are a lot of places to look along the river. Is there anywhere that he might be familiar with to go, like somewhere you might have gone together perhaps, It would help narrow the search?" Asked Mapes.

"Well uh, let me see. There used to be a place we went fishing a couple of times and I remember passing cargo terminal with barges and tugboats. Carl used to talk about being a tugboat captain someday." He said with a thin smile. "It's about five miles upriver from here, on the Ohio side," he said.

Porter wrote down the directions and the two men stood to leave.

"Please find my son Sergeant… please, before something bad happens. I know I'm to blame for all of this. It's clear to me that Carl felt he couldn't come to me after the accident. I just want my son back. Please!" He begged, reaching over to touch the sleeve of Mapes coat.

Chapter Thirty-eight

The day he spoke to Foss about the luger, Mapes returned from county lockup to find Porter on the phone with Peggy Seizer. This wasn't unusual, she called everyday for an update on the investigation. The only thing different was, this time Porter had held something back. He had just gotten off the phone with Emmett Love in Covington about the possibility that their young John Doe was actually Carl Seizer.

Upon discussing the news with Mapes they decided to visit the hospital first to make sure it was Carl before telling the Seizers.

Equipped with a recent picture from his file, they drove across the John A. Roebling Bridge to Covington Kentucky.

Emmet Love was waiting for them when they stepped off the elevator onto the forth floor. Mapes extended his hand first.

"John Mapes, This is my partner Herb Porter."

"Emmet Love," he said, gesturing for them to walk down the hallway. "I want to tell you I'm committed to finding who did this. I got kids almost the same age and I'll tell you what... I'd kill the man who ever did this to mine."

As they turned the corner into the room the nurse had just finished changing the boy's bandages.

"Damn you weren't kidding when you said somebody beat the shit out of him," said Porter. "My god."

The trio stood speechless staring at the swollen, almost unrecognizable human form before them. Mapes took out the photo and held it out for the other two to look at.

"What do you think, is it him?" asked Mapes.

Their eyes darted from the boy back to the picture several times before anyone spoke. No one wanted to commit himself at first. Shaved and bandaged, and only part of his face showing, it was difficult for the detectives to be definitive. That part of his face that showed was his eye and left cheek, both of which were badly swollen.

"I think it's him but I'm not positive," said Porter. "According to his file he doesn't have any distinguishing birthmarks, but his blood type is A positive and he has had his tonsils out."

Mapes lifted the chart from the table and looked it over.

"Well his blood type matches but it doesn't say anything about his tonsils," he said.

"Let me call a doctor," said Love.

When Love left the room Porter asked, "What's your gut feeling John?"

Mapes went to the bedside and lifted the blanket uncovering his legs. The lash marks from his father's last whipping were clearly visible like the faded stripes on a white tiger.

Love had been gone for several minutes and then returned with a doctor in tow.

"I'm back," said Emmet.

The doctor went to the bedside with a tongue depressor and opened the boy's mouth.

"He's definitely had a tonsillectomy," he said in a thick accent.

"It's him," said Mapes. "He has the right blood type, no tonsils and this boy has definitely been whipped, he has the scars to prove it.

"They whip kids like that over here too. Spare the rod and spoil the child, isn't that what they say?" Emmet questioned.

"You know if a stranger did that to a child he'd be put away for a year but the boy's own kin..." said Porter.

"Yea, I don't like it either but it's not my job to change the law, just enforce it," said Mapes.

Back at the nurse's station Porter used the phone to call Carl's parents. Mapes and Love watched Porter's face as he delivered the news. It was clear that the news broke their hearts. He laid the phone down for a moment and bowed his head. He could feel Peggy Seizer's pain bleeding through the receiver at his side. All of his years in traffic and vice had never prepared him for this case.

Mapes took the receiver from his hand and held it to his ear. Porter grabbed the bridge of his nose with two fingers like a person suffering from a severe headache.

"Yes we'll wait till you get here," said Mapes and then hung up.

One hour later Bert and Peggy Seizer arrived to take charge of their son. Carl remained in a coma despite his mother's persistent preening and whaling as she hovered over him. His father sat by the bed looking like a man on death row. Mapes hoped that the picture of his son lying helpless and beaten burned a permanent picture on the man's brain. Each had their own reasons for blaming themselves, he for his beating and she for not recognizing what it was doing to their son. With all of the strategies available on parenting, none of them guarantees success, but to fail without trying is a greater sadness.

Chapter Thirty-nine

The three detectives left the hospital in total agreement that they needed to find a bar. Even Porter the only professed non-drinker agreed. He was still recovering from the trauma of delivering bad news. Mapes was down from the first mention and pleasantly surprised that it was Love who made the suggestion.

The bar Love recommended was frequented by local Kentucky cops. It was near the waterfront and looked like it had seen better days. Most of the other buildings on the block were boarded up, just the place for cops to unwind away from the public. Love ordered the drinks while Mapes grabbed a table in the back, making sure to sit back to the wall, facing the door.

Porter's choice was a straight shot of tequila, Love was a bourbon rocks man, and Mapes had his usual beer and schnapps.

"You ever wonder why it is you do this," Love asked, because sometimes I do?"

Mapes was surprised at the admission. Most cops develop a hard exterior and rarely talk about those few cases that actually get through; the ones that sit on your chest at night like a two hundred pound porcupine.

"I know what you mean," said Porter. "Lately I've wondered if I made the right choice coming to homicide."

Mapes wasn't surprised to hear Porter's admission. He had been wondering the same thing.

"Look, we do it because, who the hell will if we don't?" Asked Mapes. "Somebody has to do it... take this case for instance, are you willing to let it go? Could you let it go? Fuck no, and neither can I."

"Yea I know, I said sometimes," replied Love defensively. "It's the ones that involve kids that get to me."

"Those are the ones you got to work the hardest because if you don't, those are the cases that follow you. Somebody has to stand up for them, somebody has to stand up for the kids" said Mapes.

"Is that why you're still on this case, I mean you've established this was an accidental shooting. I would think you'd be anxious to put this one to bed."

"Yea but there's still the missing weapon and I don't have Carl Seizer's account of the shooting. Granted it's a technicality but it's all about dotting my eyes and crossing my tees."

"Crossing your tees eh," Love chuckled, holding up his glass.

Mapes and Porter responded and held up theirs.

"I'll drink to that," said Mapes.

"Here, here," said Porter.

"To crossing your tees then," said Love.

They all touched glasses, drank and then sank back down into the booth to reap the spirit warming rewards of a good stiff drink. Mapes had been watching as one by one the bar was filling up. Day shift was over and those officers were headed in for a welcomed drink. Love held up his hand for the waitress to bring another round.

"You have any leads on the Seizer case?" asked Mapes.

"Not yet, I haven't talked to the man who brought him in yet. I'm waiting till he gets off work and then I'll have him take me to the spot where he pulled the kid out. But I'm also hoping the kid's going to come around soon and tell us something."

"On our end, the other boys involved said that he was planning to try and catch a barge to the ocean," said Porter.

"All the way down the Ohio to the Big Muddy?" questioned Love. "It'd be faster to catch a freight cross country to Atlantic City."

"Yea well, he's only eleven," said Porter.

Porter's statement brought a halt to their conversation. The reminder that Carl was just eleven years old brought them back to the seriousness of the crimes committed against him.

Mapes stood up and finished his drink. He stepped into the isle and waited for Porter. Love remained seated.

"We'll be in touch," said Mapes.

Love nodded, "same here."

Emmet sat alone in the booth for a moment thinking about his philosophical conversation with Mapes before he noticed the wall clock and realized it was time to go and meet Carl's savoir.

When Love arrived at the Weidemans beer warehouse also near the waterfront he realized that he could have walked from the bar. Sitting on the bumper of a fifty Buick special was a small dark haired man dressed in an army fatigue jacket and jeans.

Love pulled up and leaned over to open the passenger door.

"Frank Mingo," he shouted.

The man jumped up from his seat on the chrome bumper and came to the door.

"Yea, Sergeant Love, right?" Asked Mingo.

"Yea, hop in," said Love.

The man got in and closed the door. A closer look at the man revealed he was also dark skinned.

"Which way do I drive?" asked Love.

"Turn left and drive down river about two miles. When you get to big smokestack turn in and drive about a quarter of a mile to the right, that's where I go fishing. That's where I found him," said Mingo.

Love followed the man's directions until he came to the spot Mingo had talked about. The large smokestack belonged to some kind of paper mill using river water for both cooling and waste. The coal fired furnaces belched black smoke into the fading light of the Cincinnati skyline.

"This factory sucks up river water to cool its motors and then spits it back out. Catfish like the warm water I think," said Mingo. "Least ways I catch a lot of them here."

"Why don't you tell me how you came to find him and then show me where exactly it was, Ok?"

"Yea sure," Mingo replied. "I was right over there," he said pointing to a small clearing by the water. "And how is he doing, the kid, how is he?"

"He's doing as well as he could be, I guess, thanks to you. So you were fishing over there and then what happened?" Love asked.

"I had just reeled in a big catfish, a five pounder. He was splashing and thrashing when I got him close to shore. So I grabbed him by the gills and I flipped him up on the bank and them I put him in my cooler. I had already caught three catfish and the last was way big enough, so I picked one out of the cooler and through it back in the river for the Great Spirit."

"Hold on, the Great Spirit, are you Indian or something?" Love asked.

"Or something, I'm Shawnee, my people have lived here along the river since there was a river," said Mingo. "Anyway you always pay tribute to the Great Spirit by throwing one back, and besides you may catch him again when he's bigger."

"Ok then when did you see the boy?" Love asked.

"I didn't see him I heard him, said Mingo. "I had just thrown the fish back and I heard it hit the water, you know, with a splash. I started to pack up when I heard another splash. I looked up and then I heard another one. I knew it couldn't be the fish so I put down my cooler and listened. I heard one more splash then I saw where it came from and I squatted down so the lights of Cincinnati was behind the splash... and then I saw it. It was an arm. It came up out of the water and then slapped against it making a splash. Then I pulled off my jacket and dove in. The current is slow right here because there is a sand bar just beneath the water line about five feet out. That's why I was able to catch him before he floated away."

"Wait, he was splashing, you mean he was trying to swim? He must have been conscious then?" Asked Love.

"I don't know that. It could have also been nerves jerking his arm. Or maybe it was a water spirit that brought him to me to save, who knows? Anyway I pulled him out and he wasn't breathing so I started pushing on his diaphragm to try and get it going again. I worked on him for ten, maybe fifteen minutes and nothing.

I put my head on his chest and I didn't hear a heartbeat so I pounded his chest one time hard. Then he spit out the water like the fountain in downtown Cincy and started breathing. I rolled him on his stomach and pounded out the rest of the water."

"Was he conscious, did he say anything? Love asked.

"No, I could see that he was hurt. His shirt was all tore up and his pants were around his ankles. He had bruises and cuts all over his body. A bad spirit, a Matchemaneto, possessed whoever hurt that boy," said Mingo

"I can live with that explanation except this bad spirit had two legs," replied Love. "So then you threw him in your car and drove him to the hospital, right?" Love asked.

"Yes," answered Mingo.

"Did you see or hear anything else before you pulled him out, you know like a boat maybe?" Love asked.

"No, I only heard the splash," said Mingo.

"Think hard, it's a big river, maybe the boat was out in the middle? Love asked.

"There are always sounds in the distance, sometimes closer; barges and tugs, pleasure boats, you know like that."

"Maybe a barge went by, or one of those paddle wheeler's full of tourists?" Love suggested.

"No.... I saw a tug; I remember it was alone headed upriver. I never paid any attention to it. There are always tugs and barges after a while they become invisible, you know?"

"Yea, I know. If you think of anything else, you can call me at this number," said Love handing him a card from his wallet.

The man took the card and put it in his coat pocket. Love drove him back to the warehouse and dropped him off.

"Is it all right if I go to the hospital and see the boy?" Asked Mingo.

Love thought for a moment before answering, "I think that would be a good thing, maybe he remembers you. From what I know, you're the only man in his life, who hasn't made him suffer.

Chapter Forty

It had been two weeks since Everett had seen Dicky, the only one of his friends still on the block. There was Tucky who lived further down Fairfax but he was twelve and always tried to lure Everett into his backyard playhouse to strip down and play doctor. Everett tried avoiding him whenever he could. The only person he ever told about it was Ron who told him to stay away from him. Everett had told Ron, that Tucky made him feel like he had just stumbled in the girl's bathroom.

But Ron was gone and Carl was in the hospital. He went out every day hoping to see Dicky sitting on his porch waiting to go do something but so far he seemed to always be indoors.

Maybe he was still mad, thought Everett or perhaps his mother wouldn't let him come out. Whatever the reason, it made living on Fairfax a lot lonelier than it used to be.

Mel Foss was back living at home and still drinking. He also hadn't spoken to his son since he came back. Everett tried on several occasions to start a conversation but his father only Ignored him, staring at the TV like a man in a trance. The cop he called when his father went off the rails must have told him that's why he was still mad, Everett thought.

The morning Everett decided to go knock on Dicky's door was when he realized that summer was almost over. Labor day was next week and then school. He needed a friend back in his life, especially somebody who had just shared in the same tragedy. There was only one person. The way he figured it, he had nothing to loose. He stood on the porch in front of the big wooden door and gathered his courage. At last he gave it three hard, loud knocks and stepped back.

May Williams answered the door and stood looking down at him without speaking. It was as if she was trying to decide whether or not to slam the door in his face.

"Hello Mrs. Williams can Dicky come out for awhile.

She smiled slightly and reached through the door to tousle his hair.

"Hello Everett, you know I think that Dicky needs to come out and play today. He's been sitting in his room for too long. Wait here a minute, I'll go and get him," she said.

Everett sat down on the steps and waited. From inside the house he heard yelling; both from Dicky and his mother. The shouting got louder and he also thought he heard scuffling like two people wrestling.

"I don't want to," he heard Dicky say as his mother dragged him to the front door.

When she finally opened it she shoved him out, still complaining. A loud click followed as she locked it behind him. Dicky struggled in an attempt to get it open but finally gave up.

Breathing heavy and still seething over being made to do something he didn't want to, he turned and glared at Everett.

"What are you doing here squealer?" He snapped.

Everett said nothing. Dicky took a step back from the door and kicked it. Everett watched him for a moment and then spoke.

"Want to go to the park and watch the football guys practice?"

"No."

"They got that sled thing down there and the guys are pushing it around with the coach standing on it yelling stuff at them."

"No"

"You want to go down in the hollow and catch turtles."

"I said no, I don't want to do nothing."

Everett left the steps and walked around to where Dicky stood.

Stepping in front of him he said, "Don't be mad at me anymore. I had to squeal, it was the day the cops took my dad to jail. He thinks it was all my fault, and now he won't talk to me either. My Mom said I had to talk so they could find Carl and so Ron's mom could get closure. Nobody got sent to jail, the cops said nobody would," said Everett with a tear in his voice.

He had never felt so lonely and so desperately in need of a friend. Dicky was feeling the same although he wouldn't admit it, especially to Everett. But Everett's admission was true and he knew it.

"My Mom said the same thing. She made me squeal too," said Dicky at last. I ain't mad at you no more I'm just pissed about everything. Ever since my dad got sick I keep asking God for things to get better. But they don't get better, things just keep getting worse and my dad keeps getting worse. I think God must be taking a long smoke break or something. My mom says we might have to put him in a home. It's like nothing goes right lately. Hell man ain't nothing gone right in a long time."

Everett moved next to him and put his arm on Dicky's shoulder. He felt much better. He wanted to hug Dicky but he didn't dare, he didn't want to be told to go play with Tucky. Feeling good was enough.

"Did your Mom tell you they found Carl?" asked Dicky.

"No, my Mom ain't been talking too much since my dad got home."

"Yea he's in the hospital and everything," said Dicky.

"What's wrong with him?" asked Everett.

"His Mom told my Mom that he fell and hurt his head and they might have to keep him in the hospital for a long time."

"Maybe he slipped when he jumped on the barge" Everett suggested.

"I don't know he fell somehow, anyway they got him staying at a hospital over in Covington."

"Maybe we should go over and see him," suggested Everett.

Dicky thought about the football team that practiced in Owls Nest park.

"Maybe... so is the coach yelling really loud about how stupid they are and they hit like girls?" asked Dicky smiling.

"Oh yea man you ought to hear him," said Everett.

"Ok lets go and watch for a while," said Dicky slapping Everett's hand.

Chapter Forty-one

A thunderstorm was approaching Cincinnati from the southwest bringing the possibility of Tornados, the weatherman said. The rain and wind had moved in overnight, toppling trees and power lines. Emergency crews were out in force making it hard to get around the city without experiencing substantial delays.

Mapes was at work on time but Porter had to drive all the way from Norwood. At eight thirty he flounced in shaking his overcoat and umbrella like a wet dog, showering the first three desks in the squad room as well as their occupants.

"Sorry, it's crazy out there," he said passing three frowning detectives on the way to his desk and a smiling John Mapes.

"Having you for a partner is like having Milton Berle for a partner. There's never a dull moment," said Mapes.

"Laugh it up, it won't be so funny when the tornado hits. I know, I was in Kansas once and I saw one. It will scare the shit out of you John," said Porter.

"Think you could gather yourself enough to look over this map of the river, I've found three places where they still move Barges near where Bert Seizer said he used to take Carl fishing?" Asked Mapes.

Porter took a few minutes to carefully hang up his rain gear, and remove his goulashes before taking the map.

"Yea I know this section of the river. I haven't been there in years but yea; I remember there was some kind of Barge terminal there somewhere. I used to date a girl who lived close but you know how it is when you're young and in heat, you don't notice much else."

"I looked in the phone book but I can't find a listing for anything to do with shipping or barges on that stretch of the river," said Mapes. " I've put in a call to the port authority too but they haven't called back yet"

"Maybe it's not there anymore. Maybe they moved or something. You know I remember reading in the paper that they were planning some big terminal complex down there so everything could come and go out of one spot, but I don't know if they ever went through with it or not," Porter replied." You know there are also all those private marinas where he might have gone to look for a boat ride, if that's the case it's like looking for a needle in a haystack".

"We got to start somewhere. Maybe we should take a drive down there and have a look," said Mapes.

"You're still planning to continue investigating this case then?" Porter asked.

"Why wouldn't I, checking into what happened to Carl Seizer is just tying up loose ends and I don't like loose ends," said Mapes.

"You don't feel this case belongs to sex crimes then?"

"This is still my case till I say it ain't," Mapes growled.

"So what if he walked across the bridge into Kentucky, are we going to check out that side of the river too?"

"I'm sure Detective Love is capable of doing that but if he needs help we will be more than happy to oblige," said Mapes frowning at Porter. "Look Herb, if you want to transfer back to Vice I can arrange that."

"It's not that, it's just that we already have a heavy caseload that gets bigger every day and I've been wondering lately if our victims wouldn't be best served by turning this case over to another department, that's all."

"You're entitled to your opinion, but as long as I'm senior detective here I still call the shots, and I say we finish this case. Now what I want you to do is prioritize that stack of reports and push the John Doe's to the back. Concentrate on the ones that are a slam-dunk first. We'll work on these till lunch and then were going to go look at boat docks. Do you think you can live with that?"

"I can live with that… would you rather I kept my mouth shut or tell you what I think?" Porter questioned, angry at being discounted.

"I don't suppose you could wait until I ask you what you think?" questioned Mapes.

"It's been my experience that when a boss asks for my opinion he really doesn't want it unless I agree with him," replied Porter.

"True, at least we agree on something," said Mapes handing him a stack of files.

At a quarter past twelve Mapes and Porter left for the river. By one they were cruising the stretch of shoreline where Bert remembered the barge terminal. What they found was fenced off area overgrown with weeds and a faded sign that read, "Buckeye Transfer."

"Well that explains why I couldn't find their phone number," said Mapes.

"I wonder if there are anymore places like this still in operation on this stretch of river?" Asked Porter.

"There is one more that was in the book. It's down river a little further and they are still in business," said Mapes pulling back out on the roadway.

A few minutes later they were pulling up to the office of the Tri-Modal Delivery and Transfer terminal. The office was twenty yards from the docks and barges. On one side of the property stood coal silos and on the other a warehouse. The perimeter of the property was overgrown with weeds, some as tall as five feet.

Mapes carefully surveyed the property, leaning back on his heels to get a three hundred and sixty degree view. He noticed there was only one light bulb over the office door and a string of six over the dock area. He concluded that it would be easy for a child of eleven to skirt the office through the perimeter's weeds and jump aboard a barge or tug.

Entering the office Mapes unfolded his wallet to show his badge.

"I'm detective Mapes this is my partner detective Porter. We'd like to ask you a few questions," he said to a surprised foreman sitting behind his desk.

"Ok what's this in regards to?" the man asked.

"We're trying to trace the route of a boy who was assaulted last week and we have reason to believe he might have come through here in an attempt to jump a tug."

"I only work dayshift but we ain't seen no kid like that. I've been here for five years. If ever we see a kid on the premises we rum them off," said the foreman.

"We suspect he would have tried to gain access at night," said Mapes.

"Well I guess I can't speak for the night crew but if he did get to the dock it wouldn't do him no good to jump a barge. Lately all we been shipping is coal, a little pig iron but mostly coal. If he's sitting on a coal barge somebody's going to see him, but a tug maybe. He might have been able to slip aboard a tug and hide."

"You got a list of tugboats you've used this last say... two weeks?"

"Sure do, there's only been three to take away the night shift's barges. It's the same three all the time, he said. "The Laurence E. Taft, The Ashley Lee, and The Lorelei, she's a new one come up from Paducah. Those are the only ones we've been using on morning runs lately. You know how it is we use who the union tells us to, besides Business is slow in August. Come winter we're going to be up to our asses in work hauling coal; Tugs and barges running in and out of here twenty-four hours a day."

Mapes nodded and decided there was nothing else to be gleaned by talking to the foreman. Perhaps he would have to come back and talk to the night foreman if nothing else panned out, he thought.

"Well thanks for your help, you've given us something to go on," said Porter.

"This kid, you said he was assaulted, what happened to him?" Asked the foreman.

Mapes thought for a minute and then decided to level with the man. He figured most of the teamsters working on the docks were family men and would probably help ferret out a pedophile if they could. He wasn't sure if they would turn him over to the police or dispose of him on their own, but he decided to give it a shot anyway.

"He was beaten and raped, an eleven year old boy beaten within an inch of his life and raped," said Mapes feeling his blood pressure rise.

"Jesus sweet Mary!" Exclaimed the foreman.

"You can spread that around if you want. If any one out there knows of someone they think might have done this, have them contact me," he said handing him his card.

The foreman took the card, stepped to one side and tacked it on the office bulletin board on the wall near his desk.

"If we find this asshole we'll be in touch, you can take that to the bank," he said.

The rain and wind began to increase on the drive back along the river, whipping the trees and bushes like prairie wheat.

Then an earsplitting clap of thunder shook the vehicle, followed immediately by a blinding flash of light that stunned both detectives. The tree that fell across the road was the next in the succession of adrenaline surges to shock their nervous systems. Mapes had hit the brakes when the lightning struck which was the only reason the tree didn't land across the hood of the car.

"Shit!" yelled both men almost in sync.

The wind and driving rain increased to a point where it shook the car.

"God damn Herb, are we really going to get that tornado?" Asked Mapes.

"Are we all right?" questioned Porter patting himself down as though checking for wounds.

The tree completely blocked the road. Mapes got out to see if it could be moved but it could not.

"Well shit! I wonder if we can get out the other way?" he asked.

Mapes turned the car around while Porter put in a radio call to have the city workers remove the tree. He had never been up this section of road that skirted the river heading northeast.

"Look at the map in the glove box and see if Mehring Way runs into Sixth Street somewhere," said Mapes squinting at the windshield in an effort to see through the heavy sheets of rain pounding the vehicle.

"No it doesn't directly but if you take a right up here in about two miles it does run into Sixth, Porter replied.

"Good then we take Sixth all the way back downtown."

The rain and wind was so intense it made travel on the two-lane road very slow. Passing Tri-modal they could see their crews working feverishly to finish loading the outgoing barges.

About a mile before their turnoff the river took a sharp bend to the left exposing a marina where private boats as well as a few commercial boats were docked. Mapes stopped before the road turned the other direction and stared through the blurry windshield at the boats.

"What is it?" asked Porter.

Mapes didn't answer immediately but reached under his seat and pulled out a pair of binoculars. Peering through them for a moment he then handed them to Porter.

"What does it say on the side on that tug up there?" He asked pointing to the tug surrounded by smaller private boats.

Porter squinted through the lens for a moment and then answered.

"The Lorelei," said Porter finally.

"That's one of the three boats we need to look at," said Mapes. "If the other two are docked here it'll save us some leg work"

Mapes found the drive leading to the marina and made the left turn to the gate. The rain and wind in tandem made it difficult to stand without holding on to something, but they got out and walked past the gate, holding fast to the railings, on down the wooden dock to the boats.

"I can't believe you talked me into ruining a perfectly good suit," said Porter pulling his hat down over his face.

"Me either," said Mapes doing the same. "Can you read the name on that other tug?" asked Mapes.

Porter stopped and peered through the heavy rain.

"The General Owen, not ours," he said.

The boat was tied to the dock by its stern and bowlines. The vessel looked deserted. There was a sconce light on just to the right of the side entrance. There were three decks including the smaller bridge at the top; all were dark.

"What do you think, they're taking a rain day?" asked Mapes.

"A tornado day maybe," said Porter as they now stood in front of the tug.

"I suppose I wouldn't want to be out there right now either," said Mapes, "Hell, I don't want to be here, right now. But since I am I guess we should go aboard."

"Without a warrant?" asked Porter.

"Yea, I thought I heard someone yell for help, said Mapes stepping over the rail with some difficulty and onto the deck.

"Hello, anybody on board? He shouted.

Mapes pushed open the side hatch and walked in followed closely by Porter.

Once inside they were in a passage; to the right, went up to the bridge and to the left went to the crew's quarters and engine room. In the crews quarters they found a schedule that included the names of those crewmembers and the days they work. There were at least six crewmen on duty at all times.

"Copy down theses names," said Mapes.

Porter took out his notepad and copied down all eight names on the schedule. A small galley and six wall lockers took up the rest of the crew's quarters. Mapes pushed open the next hatch and peered down the steps into the dark engine room. He lingered at the engine room for a few moments like he was listening to a voice that Porter couldn't hear. Finally he returned to the crew's quarters and back down the hallway.

"There's no use looking in the bridge I'm satisfied to have the crew list. We'll see if this matches what we get from the union. Let me see it," said Mapes reaching for the list.

He studied it for a moment and then began reading the names aloud.

"Brian P., Ray S., Larry V., Gene F., Terrell S., Ben S., Louis T., and Mort G. Jr.

Back at the office Porter put in a call to the tugboat workers union and ask for the boat owners and skippers of the three tugs in question. After explaining why he wanted this information the union was glad to cooperate. Before three o'clock he had all of the information he ask for, including the list of crewman aboard each vessel.

Porter went to the Lorelei first and checked the union list against the boat's schedule from the crew's quarters. Here he found a discrepancy. The union had no record of a Mort G. Jr. in their record of crewmembers but after checking the list of tugboat captains he found the name of Mort Green listed as the skipper of the Lorelei and Mort Green was listed also as the owner. This made sense Porter thought, that it would not be necessary for the owner's son to be union.

Mapes had enlisted the help of the longshoreman to obtain a list of men working the docks for Tri-modal as well as two other nearby docks. He and Porter spent the rest of the day on the phone compiling a list of names and addresses.

It was almost four when Mapes called Emmet Love's office in Covington. Love answered on the first ring.

"What are you, sitting on top of the phone?" Asked Mapes jokingly.

"No, I was just about ready to leave the office," Love replied.

"The reason I'm calling is to let you know that we have a lists of the tugs and barges working the week Carl disappeared. I've also got a list of the crewmembers as well as longshoreman. I figured that anybody having to do with moving, pushing or loading is a suspect. We're going to start running down all the names tomorrow; at least on this side of the river, " said Mapes.

"That's great! I talked to the man who brought Carl in and he says he's sure he saw a tug go by right about the time he pulled the kid out," Love said. "I'm going to follow up on this side of the river tomorrow, maybe we should plan to check back say, about three."

"Sounds good, talk to you tomorrow," Mapes finished.

"I got a feeling we're close to wrapping this one up," he said, interrupting Porter by throwing a pencil in his direction.

"Yea why's that?" Porter asked putting the pencil above his ear.

"Because my nose itches. Whenever I'm getting close my nose starts itching," said Mapes smiling.

"That's got to drive you crazy," said Porter sarcastically.

"Don't get me started," replied Mapes.

Chapter Forty-two

People in a coma don't always lay motionless with their eyes closed like they're asleep. Sometimes they open their eyes, make facial contortions and even appear to be smiling. It's the reason most loved ones hang on so long before giving up to the inevitable, even if the patient is brain dead.

Carl had only been in a coma for three days when he startled his sleeping mother by snapping awake like he was coming out of a bad dream. He sat up in bed, made several guttural sounds, and collapsed back into a coma.

Peggy Seizer was frantic in her efforts to get someone to come in to check on him but when a doctor was summoned, he found Carl in the same condition he had been in for the last three days.

She had spent everyday with him since she was notified of his condition. His father would arrive after work about five o'clock and stay until nine or ten and then take his wife home to get some sleep and begin the whole ordeal over again the next day.

It was on the fourth day that fatigue began to set in on both Peggy and Herb. By eight o'clock both couldn't keep their eyes open and decided make it an early night. It was painful tearing herself away from her son but she realized that she wasn't going to be able to keep up this kind of a schedule forever. Guilt however is a powerful motivator.

At 8:45PM Frank Mingo came to see Carl. The fourth floor was quiet and only occupied by an occasional nurse making her rounds. He approached the bed and laid his hand on the boy's forehead as if checking for fever.

Carl did not move, even when Frank began to chant. Frank Mingo was praying. With eyes closed he prayed in his own way and in his own language. The hospital wing was quiet. Visiting hours were almost over, so Mingo kept his chanting low so as not to cause a disturbance.

In his mind he was talking to Carl and Carl was talking to him. Mingo was convinced Carl had a run in with the bad spirit.

At the end of his chanting he laid a small leather pouch on Carl's chest. The pouch contained a few beads, a feather and sand taken from the spot where he had pulled him to safety. This was a medicine bag filled with spiritual items to protect Carl from further harm.

Mingo had turned to leave when a voice took him by surprise.

"I saw Ron," said Carl to a startled Frank Mingo.

Mingo turned and walked back to his bedside.

"Hello, My name is Frank, I...." Mingo was interrupted.

"I saw Ron"

"Is Ron a friend?"

"I saw Ron in the water, I saw Ron in the water," repeated Carl.

Mingo had no idea who Carl was referring too but he did understand how the water could hold a person's spirit. He concluded then that the person he spoke of must be a dead friend, possibly a friend who died in or near the water and who's spirit still remained there.

"Hold on partner I need to tell somebody you're back," said Mingo.

As much as he still believed in the teachings of his elders, Mingo was also a trained Medic and knew that healing was a combination of science and the spirit. It was time for the doctors to take over.

He ran to the nurse's station but found it still empty. On the counter was a bell; he rang it several times vigorously.

A large woman with red hair came out of a nearby room and hurried to the station.

"I'm sorry but visiting hours are over," she said in an even well rehearsed voice.

"I know, I got here late, but you need to call a doctor. The comatose kid in 412 is awake," said Mingo.

"Oh My!" she said, and hurried to the desk and picked up the phone.

Mingo returned to Carl's bedside. He was awake but didn't respond immediately when Mingo came in. His eyes appeared not to be focusing.

He looked around the room and then at Mingo through hollow eyes. Finally he locked onto Mingo's face.

"Where am I?" He asked.

"In the hospital, you've had a concussion," replied Mingo.

"Is my Mom here?" He asked.

"Not now, she was but it's late. I'm sure the doctor will call her," Mingo answered.

"Who are you?" Asked Carl.

"My name is Frank Mingo, I pulled you out of the river, he replied. "Do you remember?"

"No."

"You said you talked to Ron, is he a friend?"

Carl nodded and seemed to remember something. His cheeks drew up like he was going to cry. Mingo stopped questioning and held his hand.

A few minutes later a doctor and two nurses rushed into the room. Mingo stepped aside and let them work. The doctor administered several eye and reflex tests while the nurses checked his vital signs.

"Are you a relative?" The doctor asked.

"No, ah," he said pausing for a moment, "I'm a friend."

"I'm sorry then I'm going to have to ask you to leave. You can visit him again tomorrow," said the doctor.

"What the hell," said a nurse holding up the medicine bag.

"That's a gift," said Mingo. "I brought it as a gift, it's like a good luck charm."

It was then Carl snatched the bag out of the nurse's hand and clutched it tight against his body.

"Apparently he likes it," said the doctor. " But I'm going to have to take it for now we have to change your bandages and I'm afraid it's not sterile. We'll give it back when we're finished, I promise," the doctor said prying it from Carl's hand.

"I'll go now then," said Mingo.

"Just a minute I'd like to talk to you before you go," the doctor said. "Please just wait outside in the hallway I'll be right out."

Mingo nodded and went out to the hallway and waited for the doctor like he was asked. A few minutes later the doctor came out.

"I remember you, you were the one who brought him in the other night. You saved his life," he said. "You were a medic or something during the war, right?"

"That's right I served in Europe," said Mingo.

"So what do you do now, are you in medicine still?"

"No I work in a beer warehouse," he said smiling.

"Seriously you should get back into medicine, you're good and you seem to care, you could work for an ambulance service or fire department or even become a nurse. I'd be willing to give you a recommendation if you need it. With your background it wouldn't take much to get you certified," the doctor said. "That is if you're not too attached to your beer warehouse."

"Thanks, I might take you up on that," Mingo replied.

"And this thing," said the doctor holding up the medicine bag, "Do you believe in this?"

Mingo saw the skepticism in the doctor's eyes. He' seen it before in other people who questioned his beliefs.

"What I believe is this; people need two things to get well; first they need a good doctor with the right diagnoses and second they need to believe they will heal. Sometimes they can get that kind of trust from a good doctor but sometimes when the spirit is badly injured, they need something more, and believing in a little magic doesn't hurt." I'm sure somebody must be praying for him to get past this. Don't we all ask for a little magic once in a while?"

The doctor looked him in the eye for a long moment and decided he was sincere. He nodded, and tossed the bag in the air, catching it with his other hand.

"I'll see that he gets his magic back," he said smiling. "And think about what I said, not using your kind of training would be a waste."

Chapter Forty-three

Life at the Everett's house remained quiet since his father came home. Everything was out in the open now about Ron's death and Everett's involvement. He was sure he would get in trouble for taking the gun or surely for telling the police about it, but his father never mentioned it.

The bouts of drinking had increased, he was drunk almost always now, but his loud and angry tirades had stopped. He spent his days locked in front of the TV and rarely spoke to anyone except Alice.

It was as though the life had been sucked out of him. Everett almost wished for his old father back even if it meant a slap across the lips once in a while. At least then he'd received some attention.

One morning early Everett overheard his mother crying, a soft lonely cry that crept up the stairs from the kitchen like steam from the teacup.

After wiping the sleep from his eyes he slipped downstairs in his pajamas and sat on the last step to listen.

"We're down to the last of our savings and the strike fund is gone. Everybody on the picket lines is doing it for free. I tried every place I can think of to find work but nobody's hiring," said his father.

"Maybe I can ask Elaine if they need somebody where she works at the diner. I've waited tables before," she said.

"No," his father growled. "No wife of mine is going to support me. I'm the man of the house. I'm supposed to provide for my family, how do you think that would look if you were the one working and I was the one keeping house. No! I'll figure something out."

His mother began to cry again. "What are we going to do, I only got enough food in he house for about three more days and then that's it."

"Shut up!" His father's voice grew louder now but still not as loud as before, not like the old days. "Are you trying to make me feel like I'm a piece of shit? I said I'd figure something out, now shut up about it."

Everett heard a kitchen chair topple over as his father stood up and then the kitchen door burst open as he stomped past him on his way to the front door. His entrance into the dining room was so sudden that Everett had no chance to run back upstairs. He sat on the step cowering against the stairwell wall looking up to see him as he passed. His face was a snapshot of desperation, like a man on a ledge.

Everett made his way into the kitchen to find his mother picking up the chair.

"Good Morning sweetheart, you ready for some breakfast?" She said forcing a smile.

"Mom, I can help get us some money," Everett said burying his face in his mother's robe.

"Oh god! You heard us didn't you? she said scooping him up into her arms.

She hugged him tightly and cried into his small shoulder.

"I know you can honey, I know you're Mommy's little man, but you heard your daddy he's going to figure something out. So don't you fret about it, she said attempting to sound cheerful.

Five days went by and Everett watched the food supply get smaller. Their last meal was a pot of navy beans that his mother managed to stretch over three days. On the sixth day his mother came home crying again because the corner grocer wouldn't extend her anymore credit.

Everett's father had been leaving every morning the way he used to when he had a job but he always came home drunk and barely able to walk. At weeks end his father came home loud and angry the way use to when he became violent. He shouted and threw a chair. He broke Alice's antique lamp and put his foot through the glass-covered portrait of her mother that hung in the living room.

Everett over heard him say that the bar he frequented refused to serve him anymore until he paid his tab.

Even for a child It was plane to see that his parents were at the end of their rope.

The following morning Everett got up early and went downstairs to the kitchen. He grabbed a piece of bread from the breadbox and slipped out the back door. The red American Flyer wagon that he hadn't ridden in several years was wedged between the house and the side fence. Though rusty and covered with weeds and cobwebs it still rolled. After a few minutes with the garden hose and an oily rag it was back on the road.

Starting from the next block over he went from house to house and up and down each block, knocking on doors asking for soda bottles. Three times he filled the wagon to its brim and then emptied it at the corner market for the deposits.

Long neck soda and beer bottles were worth two cents each and by days end he had made two dollars and twenty-seven cents. A loaf of bread cost twelve cents at the corner market. Three pounds of hamburger was eighty-nine cents and a dozen eggs were thirty-nine cents. Everett loaded his wagon and headed home. He was tired but he also felt good. It was the feeling of accomplishment that made it all worth it. He couldn't wait till he got home to surprise his mother with the food and the rest of the money.

He put his wagon away and entered through the back door. His mother was sitting at the kitchen table smoking a cigarette. This was the first time he had actually seen her smoke. She had always kept her habit a secret except to the thief who stole them to smoke at the river.

"Everett honey where have you been all day?" she asked.

Everett couldn't contain his surprise. He backed in through the doorway and then turned around and sat the grocery bag on the table and reached into his front pocket and pulled out wadded dollar bill and the remainder in loose change. He dumped it all on the table in front of her.

"Look Mom I been working. Now we can eat and look there's more money for tomorrow," he said excitedly.

"What did you do? How did you do this Everett?" She asked astonished.

She began moving the coins around with her fingers into like piles as she counted.

"I went out with my wagon and collected pop bottles. Sometimes me and the guys do that when we want to go to the movies or if we want candy and cokes. I can go again tomorrow if you want," he said.

With a tear in her eye she pulled him to her and held him.

"Bless you sweetie, your Mommy's little man aren't you?"

She pressed his face into the shoulder of her housedress. He loved her smell---A comforting blend of tobacco, wine, with a hint of perfume. There was also another aroma, an unidentifiable X-factor that, combined with the rest, was her smell, and it always made him feel safe.

This day was the best he had felt in a long time. While his mother made dinner from the food he'd brought home. Everett walked around the house smiling and allowing himself to be playful with his sister and brothers. It was the first time in a while that they had all been in the kitchen together. And best of all it was the first time in a long while that he'd seen his mother happy.

Once dinner was ready everyone sat at the table waiting for their father to get home. Alice had made hamburger sandwiches on white bread with a can of pork n beans she found in the pantry. It was after five and he still hadn't come home. Alice assumed he was out looking for work but she wasn't really sure since he had left that morning like Everett, without a word.

Alice finally made the decision to go ahead and let the children eat before the food was completely cold. Half way through the meal they heard the front door slam. Everyone froze. They had all been conditioned to fear the sound of a slamming door.

The sound of his footsteps getting closer to the kitchen made the younger children stop eating and slide out of their chairs to stand in the comfort of their mother's arms.

Everett however was anxious to gain his father's approval for his initiative and remained seated. When the kitchen door swung open and everyone saw the flushed red face of their drunken father, no one, including Everett, had any illusions of that he was going to be pleased.

"What's this?" He shouted in a sarcastic voice.

"Everett went out today with his wagon and collected pop bottles around the neighborhood. He brought home enough for us to eat for a few days, wasn't that wonderful?" she asked. "Look", she said, reaching in her apron pocket and dumping the money on the table next to his plate. "Sit down and eat honey."

Mel looked down at the food and the money. Everett could see his father's mood grow darker then looked at Everett, still seated at the table and nodded. At first Everett took this to mean that is father was nodding his approval and smiled. The other of the children stayed put, clinging to their mother's apron.

Mel continued to glare at him and continued nodding. Everett quickly realized that this was not the fatherly approval he sought.

"So nobody trusted me when I said I'd figure something out," he barked, pounding his fist on the table shifting and his gaze to Alice.

He reached into his pocket and pulled out a wad of cash and shook it under his wife's nose.

"Where did you get that?" She asked.

"None of your fucking business where I got it. I got it because I'm supposed to get it. I'm the man of this house, not you," he shouted looking back at Everett. "You! You drag that wagon around the neighborhood begging for pop bottles and making me look like a fool.... Making me look like a... a...I don't know what all who can't take care of his family," he yelled sweeping his plate of food and Everett's money onto the floor with one swipe of his arm.

Sissy began to cry and while the younger boys cowered into their mothers apron.

"You think you can be me big shot?"

"No Daddy, I'm sorry," Everett cried.

I ought to put a bullet in you, you little shit, I ought to put a bullet in all of you," he shouted pulling the luger from his jacket pocket. "Then you won't be ashamed of me no more"

The children were all crying now. Alice moved away from her husband and closer to Everett taking the younger children with her.

"Please don't, nobody is ashamed of you. Please, you're scaring the kids to death. Don't do this," she begged backing up against the stove.

"I got no dignity left Alice, I got no fucking dignity left," he screamed. Mel held up the luger and shook it at her. "The only thing I got left that makes people listen is this. I can get respect; I can get my dignity back. All I have to do is be willing to pull this trigger. And you know what Alice? I'm there… I'm there!"

Out of the corner of her eye Alice noticed that the cellar door was ajar. Reaching behind her she grabbed the iron skillet, still full of hot hamburger grease and flung it at her husband. As soon as the skillet left her hand she scooped up the children and pushed them through the door, pulling it shut behind her.

Mel yelled in pain when the skillet hit his head but Alice saw none of it. She paid mind to her husband until her children were safely inside the cellar.

"God Damn you fucking bitch," he screamed.

Mel pounded on the door but it didn't budge. He had fortified it after the last tornado warning with extra supports and hinges as well as three more latches. The cellar was impenetrable.

He soon gave up pounding the door with his fists and threw a chrome kitchen chair against it. Alice heard the chair bounce off and her husband pick it up. He then began banging the chair against the door, but still the door held. At last he gave up and collapsed against the cellar door exhausted. Alice put her ear to the door. She could hear his heavy breathing on the other side.

"You gave up on me Alice," he said in almost a whisper, his lips touching the door as he spoke. "Everybody gave up on me." She could hear the muffled sound of her husband crying. She said nothing. Alice was conditioned to keep quiet when he got emotional. Her heart wanted to open the door and hold him the way she used to in the old days; those wonderful days when lying in each other's arms meant something. But her recent experience at being the focus of his anger, held her back. She suddenly realized that if he decided to shoot through the door he might injure her or the children so she moved further down the stairs into the basement, held her children tight, and waited.

After a while house grew quiet. They all heard the front door slam but no one moved to get out. Alice kept the door locked for the better part of an hour until she was sure he was gone. When she did finally open the door she opened it very slowly and peeked through the crack into the empty kitchen.

Still shaking she called the police. Soon officers arrived and Alice at last felt safe. The police searched the house to make sure he wasn't hiding somewhere waiting for them to leave. The officer offered to have a car stay to watch the house the rest of the night and Alice accepted. Before the police left she asked them to be sure to pass on the information about the gun to Mapes. When Mel came back, Alice wasn't sure if she could go though this all again. She didn't want to believe that he was capable of killing her or the children. What she wanted to believe was that if she could get him to face his addiction to alcohol that their life would get better. But being without a job had taken the biggest toll on him. Melvin was a proud man but his self-esteem eroded with every day that he was out of work. Alice was an expert at trying to understand him. But that night she finally understood that she couldn't keep on taking the abuse, no matter what the reason. Alice decided to call her only friend for help.

Elaine Stone had become a pillar of the First Fundamental Baptist Church since her son died. Alice felt close to Elaine even though she thought it strange that the only person who had offered a hand of friendship was the mother of the boy killed by her husband's gun.

Elaine did respond to Alice's call and agreed to take in the children for the night. Alice, however, spent the night on her own couch, securely wrapped in her own blanket, holding a butcher knife.

Chapter Forty-four

It was late in the day when news reached the desk of Detective Mapes that Carl Seizer had regained consciousness. By then he and Porter had investigated every name on the list of tug and dock workers who were at or anywhere near Tri-Modal on the dates in question. The only list of names that seemed to make any sense was The Lorelei. Every crewmember from the other tugs had alibis. Running down the names of the longshoremen working at Tri-Modal also proved to be a dead end.

The bottom line was, they were down to eight names and the chance that any of them were involved was a shot in the dark.

"Grab your coat were going to Kentucky," said Mapes.

"The Kid?" Asked Porter.

"Yea, he's awake," Mapes answered.

Carl had been moved from intensive care to a second floor room that he shared with another boy. His head wound was almost healed and the anal tears and internal injuries had also healed but were still very painful. The worst of his injuries however could not be seen or treated by a physician.

Carl spent most of the days looking out the window at the changing trees. Autumn was coming early. School started soon and the weather would be getting colder and wetter. None of this seemed to matter anymore. Since his awakening he had gradually stopped talking. He would respond to the medical staff by nodding and shaking his head: "Does this feel better? Are you in pain? Would you like a pillow," all answers requiring only a yes or no?

Peggy Seizer was more than happy that he was responding at all. His father's attention prompted something different. His daily question, "How you doing sport?" was answered with a glare from Carl.

Herb Seizer was trying. He desperately wanted his son back. He had sought counseling during Carl's recuperation and learned much about himself and where he went wrong with his brand of heavy handed parenting. Most parents, he learned were passing on what they themselves received. He decided that if his son could forgive him, the chain of severe punishment passed on from generation to generation would stop with him.

But the look on Carl's face told him that he wasn't ready for any forgiveness yet. Carl still hadn't forgiven himself.

Mapes and Porter walked into the hospital room to see Carl in a wheelchair looking out the window and his mother sitting near him quietly knitting. Both detectives respectfully took off their hats and approach the window.

"Hello Mrs. Seizer... Carl," said Mapes. Porter nodded.

Carl didn't respond to their greeting but continued to stare out the window.

"We need to talk to your son. We need to find out who did this. If he could tell us anything it would help," said Mapes.

"We need to speak outside," his mother said in a low voice.

Mapes and Porter followed her out of the room and stopped just outside the door.

"He isn't saying much yet, the doctors think he's still in shock," she said in almost a whisper. "He barely talks to me and he won't say anything to Bert yet. My husband is so heartbroken about what happened to Carl. He blames himself for everything."

"I'm sorry about what you're all going through, but the time to get this guy is now. If he could remember anything..." said Mapes.

"The only one he's talked to since he's been back is that Indian man who saved him," she said.

"Frank Mingo?" asked Mapes.

"Yes, that's him. He gave Carl some kind of Indian charm. --- Carl won't let go of it. I've tried to take it off while he's asleep but he wakes up and starts crying. It's like he's afraid to be without it. It bothers me that he's so attached to that pagan thing but I don't know what to do about it," she said.

"Well if it helps him…" said Porter.

"I'd still like to try, if you don't mind," Mapes said.

"Go ahead, if you catch who did this, I hope you kill the son of a bitch," Peggy spat. "Sorry."

The detectives returned to the room and Mapes pulled up a chair next to Carl.

"Carl I'm detective Mapes, Is it all right if I talk to you?"

Carl continued to look out the window but said nothing.

"Looks like fall is coming early, doesn't it?"

Carl said nothing. Mapes looked at Porter who gave him a shrug.

"Carl I need your help to try to find out who hurt you. We need to catch this guy before he hurts anyone else."

Mapes noticed that the boy flinched when he said, "the man who hurt you," but he still remained silent. Mapes was getting impatient and felt like shaking him back to the real world but then he thought about it and decided that anything physical may make him worse. He decided to give it one more try.

"Carl, was the man who hurt you... was he... was it on a tugboat?"

Carl did not speak but screwed up his face like he was going to cry and began rocking back and forth in the wheelchair.

Mapes knew he had struck a nerve. Peggy reached over and pulled on Mapes's arm. When he made eye contact with her she shook her head. She felt Carl had had enough questions, he was visibly upset now. Having just gotten a raise out of him for the first time Mapes wanted to keep pressing.

"Carl please," he said to no avail.

Mapes slumped in his chair and took a deep breath. He turned again to look at Porter when he noticed Emmet Love standing in the doorway. Emmet motioned for Mapes to join him in the hallway.

Just outside the room detective Love stood next to a small dark skinned man wearing jeans and a polo shirt held tight at the neck with a beaded slide of Native American design.

"John this is Frank Mingo, he's the man who saved Carl and brought him in.

"Good to finally meet you," said Mapes extending his hand to Mingo. "I understand you were a medic during the war, where did you serve?"

"Yes, I was in Europe around Bastogne," said Mingo shaking hands with Mapes and Porter.

"Battle of the Bulge," said Porter nodding.

"Yes, It wasn't called that when I was there though they named it later. We were just The Battered Bastards of Bastogne," he said smiling.

"Say Frank I just had a thought, Mrs. Seizer says you have a connection with the boy... he talks to you," said Mapes.

"Sometimes when it's just me and him," he said.

"We're trying to nail the bastard who did this to him, maybe you could go in there and talk to him and see if you can get something we can use."

Mingo looked in the room and saw Peggy Seizer glaring at him. "I don't think his mother likes me," he said.

"No it isn't that, she thinks that talisman you gave him is some kind of pagan good luck charm," said Mapes.

"I wasn't trying to piss any body off, I just wanted to give the boy something to hold on to when he was lost. Besides we all look the same to same divine spirit no matter what we call him," said Mingo. "But if she doesn't mind I'd be glad to help."

"Let me talk to her," said Mapes.

Mapes returned to the room and left the three men to wait.

"So, I take it you didn't have much luck either?" said Porter.

"No, I have basically the same list you worked from but I got nothing. I do have someone working on background checks to see if any of theses guys have prior sex crimes, but that may take weeks," said Love.

Love and Porter peered inside the room and saw that Mapes was still pleading his case to Mrs. Seizer.

"You know, I can't get passed the fact that this whole thing started with the accidental shooting of Ron Stone and then snowballed out of control into this," said Porter shaking his head.

"Yea it happens some times, it's like people loose the connection with their kids," said Love.

"I think a lot of parents talk at them rather than to them," said Porter. "But then what do I know, I don't have any?"

"It sounds like this kid's folks treated him like a piece of furniture before," Love said.

"Worse, it seems to me. Nobody would purposely tear up a piece of furniture, it cost's too much, said Porter. "You got any kids?"

"A two year old daughter," replied Love pulling a picture from his wallet.

"Ah yea! She's beautiful," said Porter.

"And you know I would never in a million years lay a hand on her. At least that's the way I feel now, I guess I don't know how I'd react if she came to me one day and said Daddy I'm pregnant," said Love smiling.

"You still wouldn't touch her, I sense that about you," said Porter handing back the picture.

Just then Mapes and Peggy appeared in the doorway. Mapes had his head cocked to one side like he had been through an ordeal.

Mrs. Seizer was frowning as she left the room. She walked slowly past Frank Mingo and said. "I'm trusting you to go easy on Carl. If he doesn't want to talk don't push him."

After she left Porter asked, "What did you say to her?"

"I finally told her, 'look we may have a chance to catch this guy if we move quick before he gets spooked and leaves town. We want to make sure he doesn't do this to any body else. If you say no to this and he has a chance to hurt some other poor kid, it's on your conscience'."

The other men nodded their approval.

"You ready?" said Mapes to Mingo.

"Yea, I guess so," he replied.

"Then let's get started," said Mapes.

Mingo walked inside and approached Carl. Sitting in the same chair that Mapes used, he scooted closer. He noticed the medicine bag hanging from the boy's neck and he smiled.

"Glad to see this has brought you some comfort, said Mingo reaching over and touching the bag.

Carl didn't respond. His gaze remained fixed somewhere outside the window.

"Do you feel like talking... maybe a little?" he asked.

Mingo was having the same luck as Mapes, trying to get him to talk. Finally he remembered the night he came to see the boy. The night the boy spoke about seeing his friend Ron in the water. Mingo then began to chant, the same prayer that his father had taught him; the same prayer his people had been chanting, to the Great Spirit for thousands of years.

Carl heard the chant but not as words. It was more like a bee buzzing in his brain, getting louder and louder until it was right between his eyes so loud that it blocked out all other sound, all other thought, and all other feeling.

Then the buzzing began to lessen and he started to hear the words. The words were strange to him but he understood somehow that they were meant to comfort him. Finally he turned his head toward Mingo and looked him in the eye. Mingo stopped chanting.

"Remember me," Mingo said.

Carl nodded. "You saved me," he said in a weak voice.

"I'm glad you're back," said Mingo. "Do you remember what happened to you?"

Carl turned his face away and his eyes began to tear up. He again nodded.

"Do you remember who hurt you?" Mingo asked almost in a whisper.

The boy began to cry now, and again he nodded.

"Who was it Carl, who hurt you?"

He started to cry harder now. "His name was...he was"

"Who, who was it"

"His name was Morty," Carl said between sobs.

Frank reached over and put his arms around the boy and Carl fell into him sobbing. He held him until the crying started to subside. He looked toward the door and saw Porter and Mapes looking in and holding back Carl's mother who was also crying. Frank turned back to Carl and as he did he noticed the other boy who shared the room. He appeared to be the same age as Carl. He had been watching intently during the entire conversation.

Finally the boy said, "He talks in his sleep, he said he wanted off the boat and he promised he wouldn't tell."

Turning again to the door he nodded to Mapes and the detective released Peggy Seizer. She ran into the room and Mingo handed him over to his mother's outstretched arms.

Mingo got up and took one last look at Carl before leaving the room. Once outside he asked, "Did you hear?"

"I heard most of it but I didn't hear the name he gave you," said Mapes.

"Morty, he said the name Morty."

"Mort Green, he and his son work the Lorelei," said Porter.

The three left together with a stop at the lobby to make a phone call. Porter called Tri-Modal and ask if the Lorelei was still working. To his chagrin he learned that the Lorelei had not worked their docks for almost a week. His second call was to the union to ask if they could tell them where the tug was now working. He was informed by the tugboat union, that the Lorelei was in dry-dock for the next week, but that they couldn't give a location.

"Ok how many Marinas are big enough to accommodate a tug in this area?" Asked Mapes.

Love and Porter looked at each other, and then at Mapes.

"Anybody?" Asked Mapes. "All right, the deafening silence answers that question."

"Maybe we could call the port of Cincinnati and ask," said Love.

"Wait a minute, what time is it?" asked Porter.

"Four-thirty," Mapes answered.

"They're closed," said Porter.

"Well shit, we finally get a lead and were standing around with our thumbs up our ass," said Mapes.

Suddenly Porter snapped his fingers. "The marina where we first found her," he said.

"Yea but I don't think it's set up for commercial dry dock, there were too many small boats docked there," said Mapes.

"Ok so we go over and it ain't there, you got anything else going on?"

"Yea I'm a half an hour past due for a shot of schnapps," snapped Mapes. "But let's go anyway... you coming Love?"

"Yea sure, if there's a chance at all of getting this guy I'm in," he said.

"Maybe they're all finished with their repairs or maybe they never were in dry dock," said Porter.

"I said... we were going, didn't I?" Mapes growled.

Chapter Forty-five

The sun sat lazy on the western end of the Ohio, painting orange faces on any commuter near the river. Traffic was heavy but that was to be expected after Five O'clock.

No one knew quite what expect even if Mort Green was on the boat. Was he a large violent man or a small pasty-faced sewer rat that pushed his urges on only the small and weak?

There was also the matter of two Mort Green's; was it the father or the son. It had also been a long time since any of them had to fight. It wasn't that they'd forgotten how or were afraid; it was could they stop once they started. Each man carried a mental picture of the tortured eleven year-old and adrenaline levels were high. The police had a name for it; it was called "dancing on a suspects face," or just "dancing."

When they arrived at the marina, the Lorelei sat docked in the exact spot where they had seen it before. The marina wasn't deserted like the last time they were there, the day of the tornado warning. This time people were on board their boats; some getting ready for a weekend of fun and some working on their boats, painting or sanding and some sat on the edge of the engine hatch with tools in their hands.

The Lorelei took up an entire section of dock. There were no other boats near. The light near the aft door was on as well as one in the wheelhouse. As they grew nearer to the wheelhouse two silhouettes could be seen sitting, apparently engaged in conversation.

Love was the first to reach the boat and he easily slid over the rail onto the deck. Porter followed him over the rail and then Mapes, whose encounter with the rail was made more difficult because of his increased bulk.

Love opened the first deck hatch and yelled inside. "Hello aboard the Lorelei."

The trio entered the vessel and stood for a moment waiting for an answer. There was a door on either side of the covered deck and a stairwell in the middle.

"Hello," Love shouted again.

They moved closer to the inside stairway that led to the upper deck when they got an answer.

"Who's there?"

"It's the police we need to talk to you," said Love.

"About what?" Asked the man from the wheelhouse.

"Why don't you get your ass down here and find out," spat Mapes.

Suddenly a light came on in the lower deck and footsteps were heard coming down the stairs. Two men emerged from the stairwell; one older man of medium height in his mid to late fifties with gray curly hair and round in the middle like Mapes. The other man was taller, younger and thicker but not fat, with black curly hair and beard.

"What is this about?" Asked the older man.

"Are you Mort Green?" Asked Mapes.

"Yes why?" He answered.

"We have a young man, excuse me, a child of eleven, over in Saint Elizabeth's hospital who says somebody aboard this boat assaulted him," said Mapes.

"What! That's crazy we don't let kids aboard, this is a tugboat not a pleasure boat," said the older man angrily.

It was then something dark passed over the older man that made him glance at the other one.

"Are you Mort Junior?" Asked Porter.

"No, he's my first mate, ah... Bob Jones," the older man interrupted.

"That's funny, we've seen your crew list and there wasn't anyone named Bob Jones anywhere on it," said Mapes.

"That's because he's new," said the older Green.

"Ok then, let's see some I D," said Love.

Without warning the younger man took a step behind the older one and bolted out through the other doorway onto the deck and over the bow to the dock. Also without warning, Emmet Love pushed the older man aside bounded through the doorway in pursuit.

Porter was tempted for a moment to join Love running the man down but realized he was too late to be of much help. Love and the other man were already out of sight.

"He's new, huh? Said Mapes.

The older man sat down in one of the three chairs and put his head in his hands. "What was I supposed to do, he's my son," he said.

"That poor kid laying up there in the hospital who just had to have his colon sewn back together, is somebody's son too," spat Mapes.

"Shit! I can't just wait here I'm going to head down the dock and see if Love needs any help dragging his ass back," said Porter.

Love was twenty-five yards behind the man and gaining as they ran down the docks past startled boat owners. Love was in full sprint and had no chance to reach his weapon without loosing stride.

"Stop or I'll shoot," Love shouted anyway figuring the man couldn't see behind him, but he still didn't stop.

The man ran to the end of the dock to the base of a chain link fence topped with barbed wire. His look up at it for a split second and then darted off in the other direction toward the harbormaster's office. Once he was there he jumped the side gate and ran to the stairway that led to the tower, the place where the harbormaster could survey the docks and vessels in his trust.

Love was only ten paces behind him now as he bounded up the steps three at a time. Once at the top, the man kicked open the office door and ran inside. When Love reached the top he also entered the tower to find another door open to the catwalk that surrounded the tower. Once outside he came upon the bearded man standing on top of the railing looking down, like he was contemplating a jump. There was nowhere else for him to run.

Love had his weapon out now and pointing at him.

"Get down off the rail there's nowhere else to go," he said walking slowly toward him.

Love peered over the rail to see that there was nothing below him but more wooden dock, ten feet wide in both directions.

"I can't go back," he cried, his face contorted looking like a tortured soul from a Goya painting.

"You can't make it to the water from there," Love said.

"I know," he said.

"You want to commit suicide, well shit, why didn't you say so in the first place," said Love holstering his gun.

"I'll just wait here and have a smoke till you get done," he said. "What do you want me to tell your dad, cremation or burial?"

Love leaned against the rail as though he were waiting for a bus. The bearded man kept his eyes on the pier below. He was at least thirty feet off the ground with nothing soft to land on.

Several times he flinched and Love thought he was on his way but then at the last second he leaned back.

"Come on Morty I haven't got all night, either do it or get your perverted ass back here," said Love.

"I can't," the man screamed.

Love threw the cigarette down and began walking closer.

"Come on Morty jump, do the right thing. You fucking coward do it and save yourself the humiliation. Think of your poor father. What is a trial going to do to him and his business? Everybody's going to know what a perverted coward his son is," Love taunted steadily walking closer to the man perched on the rail.

"Shut up," the man screamed at the top of his lungs.

Love was only inches from him now.

"Want me to give you a little shove Morty?" said Love putting his hand on the man's leg. For a split second Love contemplated pushing him off and saving the tax payers the expense of dealing with him. Especially since he felt that Mort Green Junior was less than human.

Suddenly, Mort collapsed backwards onto the catwalk in a heap like a sobbing wretch caught in a trap. Love stood over him shaking his head and then looked over the edge to see an astonished Herb Porter looking back at him.

Love rolled him over and cuffed him. "Get up, sewer rat," he barked.

The man complied with a helpful jerk from Love. By the time he was ready to head downstairs, Porter was already in the tower latched on to Mort's other arm.

Once on the dock they pushed him in the direction of the Lorelei and started walking.

"What was all that about, some new way to psych down a jumper that I've never heard of?" Asked Porter.

"He's down isn't he?" Said Love

"He might have jumped though," said Porter.

"No a chance in hell, you know why?"

"Why?" Asked Porter.

"Because he is a coward. Anybody who can do what he did is a coward."

"Yea but I thought suicide was the cowards way out," said Porter.

"I don't know if that's true for the ones that hurt kids. They are the scum of the earth. For them I'd rather see something a little more painful." replied Love.

The two men said nothing for a few minutes until they rounded the dock and saw the Lorelei about ten feet ahead.

"Do you really think suicide is the cowards way out," asked Love.

After a few moments of silence Porter said, "No, for some it's their only way out and it isn't cowardice, it's just despair."

The elder Green's goodbye to his only son was more of a tear laden glare as he watched him being loaded into the unmarked police car to be taken to jail, possibly for the rest of his life.

Mapes threw the keys to Porter and got in the backseat with the prisoner. "You drive," he said, "I feel like dancing."

It took twenty minutes after the arrest before they were at the Hamilton County jail, booking the swollen faced Mort Green Junior.

Mapes went in with Green while Love and Porter waited in the lobby.

"Just give us a few minutes to start the paperwork and I'll give you a ride back to Covington," said Porter.

"I'll just call my wife, she can be here in fifteen minutes, Love replied.

A few moments later Mapes stormed out from the inner office and headed straight for them.

"Let's go Herb we got a situation," he said.

"What?' asked Porter.

"Trouble at the Foss house."

"You want to come Emmet?" Asked Mapes

"In for a penny In for a pound I guess," he replied.

Chapter Forty-six

Alice Foss and her children had moved in with Elaine Stone at her invitation. It was a big house with lots of room and Elaine was comforted to have more children in the house. Mel Foss hadn't been seen or heard from in days. With a warrant out for his arrest Alice thought he might have gone to eastern Kentucky, where he had family. At any rate, she liked sleeping in the same house as her children. Alone in her house was nerve racking without police presence and the truth was, she wasn't sure what her husband would do.

On their third night in the house Everett was sitting at the kitchen table eating a cookie and looking out the window into the blackness of the hollow behind the house, when he thought he saw a flash of light. Moving closer to the window, he pulled the curtains apart and, pressing his nose against the glass, watched a bit longer, holding his breath so as not to fog up the glass.

Again he saw several flashes of light, he was sure of it.

"Hey mom come here I think I see somebody with a flashlight down in the hollow."

A minute later Alice joined him at the window and both of them gazed into the dark together.

"What are you looking at?" Asked Elaine.

"Everett thought he saw someone with a flashlight down in the hollow," replied Alice.

Now there were the three of them looking into the hollow but no more flashes of light materialized. Soon afterwards they all lost interest and returned to doing what they were doing. Everett continued looking but saw no more light.

Mel Foss was on his hands and knees with a flashlight looking for the luger he had thrown into the hollow the day he was arrested. When he first stepped out his back door that day he saw the grill of the police car pull up in the driveway and quickly sent the gun spinning over the treetops like a sailcat.

He had made sure to stay clear of Fairfax Avenue during the day since then to avoid arrest. But now he was desperate and angry and needed the gun. After almost a half an hour on his knees he at last found what he was looking for.

The kids found a TV show that consumed their interest while Elaine and Alice sat at the kitchen table talking.

"Are you having second thoughts yet about having young children around?" Asked Alice.

"Certainly not! I love having the kids here. I love having you here. I spoke to Charlie at work and he says if you want to go back to work he's willing to give you a shot," said Elaine.

"Golly Elaine I haven't worked for so long, Mel wouldn't have it. I'd love to try though if you think I could do it," she replied.

"Honey if I didn't think you could do it I wouldn't have offered."

"Mel always told me my place was in the home, he was really old fashioned that way."

"My ex was the same way, he thought my place was in the home while his place was out screwing everything in a skirt," Elaine said smiling. "But I feel liberated since I've been on my own."

"Is there anything you would change now if you could?" Asked Alice.

"I would have stayed home a little more I suppose," said Elaine looking away. I know everyone thinks that I neglected Ronny but he was such a good boy and we had a good relationship. I knew how independent he was and I took advantage of that when I should have stayed home more, I realize that now, but I don't think it would have made any difference. He loved being with his friends and he would have found a way to be with them. So what happened probably would have happened anyway. My pastor says that sometimes God uses a tragedy to make something good happen somewhere else."

"And you believe that?"

"I have to believe that. I have to believe there was a reason that Ronny died, a reason I may never see."

Alice reached across the table and took Elaine's hand and squeezed it.

"Shall we join the kids and see what's so interesting on television?" Said Alice.

"Sounds good."

Elaine picked up the coffee cups and set then in the sink and reached over to flick the light switch near the door when the back door exploded inward shattering glass and falling off one hinge. The porch light silhouetted Mel Foss standing angry in the doorway.

Both Elaine and Alice screamed when it happened. Elaine fell on the floor trying to get away from the flying glass and Alice jumped back into the doorway to the living room. Within seconds Alice was surrounded by her frightened children.

"Daddy?" Asked Sissy.

Mel flicked on the light with his free hand, in his other he held the luger. He walked past Elaine and took his wife's arm.

"We're all going home now Alice, " he said squeezing her arm so tight she thought it would break.

"Leave them be Melvin, please," said Elaine just getting up off the floor.

"You stay out of this whore, I don't want to shoot you but I will if you don't shut up," barked Mel.

Alice felt the chill of hopelessness flooding back into her body. Her instincts told her to fight but she couldn't see a way out without putting Elaine and the children at risk. She knew it was useless when he was drunk unless she happened to stumble across a way out, but it wasn't here at her friend's expense. She also knew if she could get them back home that Elaine would surely call the police.

"Don't Elaine, it's ok I'll go with him, I want to, really," she said. Come on kids we're going home with daddy."

Mel followed behind with the gun pointed at his wife's back as they left Elaine's house and headed home. On the way out Mel yanked the phone off the wall and threw it.

Just outside the front door Everett tried to break free and run for help but his father grabbed the back of his shirt just as he made his move. Now with his hand containing Everett and the other pushing the gun barrel against his wife's back, they walked as if they were glued together across the lawn and into the house.

Mel shoved his wife toward the couch in the living room and pushed on her shoulder forcing her to sit. Everett collapsed on the couch next to her while the rest of the children scooted up in her lap. Mel stood at the end of the couch hovering over them with the gun.

"Now, we're all a family again. This is how it should be. A family is supposed to always be together, always," said Mel loudly. "Sissy run and get Daddy a beer."

The child looked at her mother for guidance.

"I'll get it," said Everett, standing.

"No you don't, you're going nowhere," said his father pushing him back down.

"It's all right, go to the kitchen and bring back a beer for your father," said Alice.

The girl slid off her mother's lap and ran into the kitchen. Minutes later she returned carrying a long necked bottle of Weidman's. Mel took it from his daughter and opened the bottle with his teeth spitting the cap on the floor. He then moved to the overstuffed chair in front of the television and sat down. Taking a long lingering swill he sat the bottle on the floor and exhaled deeply.

"Now what?" Asked Alice. "What do you want us to do?"

"I want you to shut up and everybody just go back to being a family again... like I said before."

"Can the kids go upstairs then?" Asked Alice.

"No!" He shouted. We're all going to stay down here and be a family God Damn it! How many times do I have to say it?"

Mel had grown agitated with Alice's questions and jumped up from his chair and stuck the gun in her face.

"You're always pushing me aren't you? You think you know everything. It's like you're always talking down to me like I'm a kid or something. Just go to work Melvin and bring me home your paycheck so I can spend it. You just sit there while I run everything," he shouted sarcastically. "You never even ask me what I think; you just go and spend it. Just drink your beer stupid and let me handle everything cause you're too stupid to figure it out."

"I never called you stupid ever, I wouldn't do that, you're my husband Mel. Why do you always say things like that, you know it ain't true?"

"Shut up you're back talking, I'm in charge, I'm the head of this house, I'm the man, I say what's what," yelled Mel as he hit her across the mouth with the gun, chipping her tooth and cutting her lip.

Alice grabbed her mouth and started crying. The children slid off her lap and also began to cry.

"Don't hit her no more dad look, you knocked her tooth out," said Everett reaching in her lap to recover the broken piece of tooth.

"Shut up you sniveling little mama's boy before I knock out your teeth," said Mel recoiling his arm as if he were going to strike the boy.

"Please stop this Mel please, this ain't you talking, I know it ain't. You need to get help, we all need help, please," she said crying through her blood stained fingers.

"I need help," he screamed, "Is that what your good buddy Elaine says about me? And what did you say? I bet you two had a good ole time saying things behind my back, didn't you? You probably told her what a no account hick I am…can't find a job like a real man, didn't you?"

Just then they all heard a knock. Mel looked wild eyed at the door. "Who is it," he shouted.

"Hamilton County Sheriff you need to open the door sir," came the reply.

"You get away from here and leave me and my family alone, you hear me?" He yelled leaning against the door.

"We can't do that sir we have a warrant for the arrest a Melvin Foss. If that is you, unlock the door and come on out or we'll have to break it down," the officer said.

"Anybody comes in here and I'll kill my wife...then I'll kill myself, you hear? You just stay out of here."

The voice at the door went silent as he retreated to his car to radio for instructions. Mel made sure all the drapes were pulled and windows shut as he ran around the room in a frantic circle.

"Let the kids go Mel they got nothing to do with this, said Alice.

"They got everything to do with this. Those kids are part of me so if there's something wrong with me there's something wrong with them too."

"But Mel there just kids... please, I'm begging you, let them go. Kill me if you want but let my babies go, please," begged Alice sobbing.

"Get all together here," he ordered scooting everyone close together on the couch. "We're all going to sit here close together so if they all come through that door to kill me, Were all going to die together like a family."

"Why does it have to be this way Melvin, I love you, the kids love you. You're a good man. You don't have to do this.

"Yea, how come I don't feel like all this love going on. I ain't had nothing go my way in almost a year it seems like. First I get demoted, then they cut my hours and then I get laid off. It seems to me that somebody somewhere is trying to say, 'your a piece of shit Melvin'." Suddenly the phone on the kitchen wall began to ring. Mel became more agitated with every ring until finally he jumped up from the couch and ran to the phone quickly turning to make sure everyone on the couch stayed seated.

"Who is it?" he shouted.

"This is Detective sergeant Mapes of the Cincinnati Police, Is this Mel Foss?"

"You know damn well who this is and I told you before to leave me and mine alone," said Foss.

"You must have spoken to the Sheriff who was here earlier, I just got here and I'm here to make you a deal," said Mapes.

"What kind of a deal?" asked Mel sounding skeptical?

"I'm here to make sure this all ends well for everybody including you of course," he said. "Here it is. You let the kids come out first and then Alice. And then you come out and we all go downtown and talk. And you have my word that nobody shoot's you."

"Ok I got a better deal, ain't nobody coming out, and you all leave and I promise I won't shoot nobody, how's that?" Mel said.

"Come on Mel we both know you don't want to hurt your family, you aren't that kind of person."

A few moment of silence went by before Mel spoke again. When he did speak he was crying. "I don't know who I am anymore. Last year I could have told anybody who I was but today… I got to go now," he said in a low voice and hung up.

Mapes and Porter stood behind their car parked directly in front of the house. There was another car in the driveway and a car on each end of the street blocking entry to Fairfax. Another officer stood behind the car with the two detectives with a rifle and scope. Sergeant Love took a position at the corner of the house with weapon drawn.

"Do we have anybody trained to talk to this yokel?" Asked Porter.

"Yea, me," said Mapes. "By the time they get a shrink down here this thing will all be over one way or the other."

"That's what I'm afraid of, there are kids in there," said Porter. "So what are we going to do?"

"Well I guess I'm going in, get him back on the phone," said Mapes.

The telephone inside the house rang again. This time Mel was standing by the phone.

"I told you to leave us alone," he shouted into the phone.

"Mel look I'm coming in. I'm not armed… If we don't talk this out my boss is going to take charge here and neither of us want that."

Before Mel had a chance to answer Mapes was gone.

Next came a rap on the front door.

"Shit," Mel said running to the door.

"Open the door Melvin," said Mapes. Mel took a quick step to the couch and grabbed Everett and dragged him back to the door. When he opened the door Mapes saw Mel Foss standing behind his son with a gun to the boy's head.

"I want you to back off my porch right now and let me and my family have a few minutes of peace together and then you'll have your answer, I promise you'll have your answer," said Mel very softly and without emotion.

It was as though a switch had been thrown, and a calmer serious twin had replaced the crazy out of control Mel Foss. Mapes didn't like it. Something wasn't right. Mapes didn't understand, and then he did. He looked Everett in the eye and saw the fear. Mapes knew then Foss had made up his mind to kill his family.

Everett turned suddenly into the gun and grabbed the barrel pulling it down. At the same time he screamed to his mother. "Run Mom run now!"

Alice couldn't see what was happening at the door but she immediately reacted and ran to the kitchen with the children and pushed them out the back door, telling them to run.

Mapes also reacted and reached for the gun, as the three of them struggled for the gun, but before Mapes could get a good grip on it, Mel jerked it free and turned it inside away from Mapes and into the midsection of his wife, running back to help Everett. He then pulled the trigger twice at point blank range.

Everett was safe. His two brothers and sister were safe. His father was handcuffed and on his way to jail. Elaine came over and sat sobbing on the floor with her arms around Alice. Alice was shaken but alive.

The last bullet fired, the one that had emptied the gun forever, was the one that killed Ron Stone at the river's edge.

Chapter Forty-seven

September weather was unseasonably warm. Labor Day was over and school was about to start. Elaine and Alice had officially become roommates and Mel Foss was serving a sentence for attempted murder and aggravated assault. Alice had also forgiven him again and takes the children to see him once a month. Mapes and Porter received accommodations for bringing the Fairfax incident to a conclusion without loss of life. Although Porter felt Everett should have received the award because it was he that remembered that the gun was empty when he fought his father in the doorway.

The only thing left unresolved was Carl's dilemma. Carl had paid the heaviest price all for his part in the accident. His already bad situation at home just got worse as his conscience twisted his feelings of guilt and his tenuous relationship with his father by turning him into a fugitive. On the run and vulnerable he ran into the worst of predators.

Now Carl was home and healing. The leaves of autumn were turning the streets of Cincinnati into a splash of reds, browns and yellows. Mornings were becoming brisk and darkness came nearer to dinnertime.

Carl's days were spent mostly sitting on the front porch in a wheelchair wrapped in blankets. He had missed the first two weeks of school and would probably miss another two. His body was almost healed but the scars on his soul from the summer's ordeal would take longer.

It was a day like this that Dicky and Everett decided to finally come and pay him visit. They walked up to the porch but Carl didn't acknowledge their presence at first.

"Hey Carl, how you been man?" Asked Dicky.

Carl still looked away. He wasn't sure how much they knew about his injuries and was reluctant to let down his guard. He didn't want to discuss his ordeal aboard the Lorelei with anyone right now, especially his friends, who, he thought, might look at him differently if they knew. And even if he wanted to, how could he tell them?

The one thing the boys had in common was their loss of innocence.

"Are you mad at me?" Asked Everett.

Carl turned his head to look at Everett and asked, "Why would I be mad?"

"Cause I squealed," said Everett.

"We all did," said Dicky.

Carl nodded.

"We should have told when it happened. We weren't thinking about Ron or his Mom.... only ourselves," said Dicky. " And that was my fault... sorry you guys."

Carl nodded again and said, "Shit man we all did things we shouldn't, didn't we Everett," he said, giving him an easy punch to the arm and making him smile.

"We did," Everett said.

Carl also smiled. It was the first time he had smiled for at least a month. It felt good. Although none of the boys said it they all felt the same. It felt good to smile again.

Chapter Forty-eight

Within a week Carl was up taking walks. His father would get up before work and accompany him on his early walks. Bert Seizer was desperately trying to get his son back. He had changed. He was a new Dad trying to forge a new relationship and forget the past. As Carl healed so would his relationship with his father. For the first time they were communicating, he was amazed how much he didn't know about his son. However close they would get though, he knew that his scars, the guilt he felt at not being there to protect his son, would never go away.

A month had past and the boys were all back in school and life on Fairfax had settled down to something resembling normal. It was a cold and windy Saturday morning in October when Carl came knocking on Dicky Williams door accompanied by Everett and carrying a brown grocery bag.

"What's going on?" He asked, sticking his head out the door and still dressed in his pajamas. "Shit it's firkin cold out here!"

"Come on and get dressed you have to come and help me do something," said Carl.

"What?"

"Just come on I'll tell you when we get there."

Dicky was warm and hungry for breakfast and the thought of going out on such a cold dreary morning didn't really appeal to him, but he saw the serious look on Carl's face and decided he'd better go.

"I'll be down in ten," he said and ducked back inside.

The boys sat on the porch to wait with Everett sizing up the bag to try and guess it's contents. Finally he asked. "When are you going to tell me what's in the bag?"

"When we get where we're going," said Carl. "Did you bring everything I told you?"

"Yea I brought 'em. Here I go again," said Everett shaking his head.

Dicky finally emerged from the house eating a piece of toast, and trying to put on his jacket.

"Ok so what's this all about?" he asked with a mouthful of toast.

"We're going to say goodbye to Ron," Carl said.

"We're going to a graveyard?" asked Dicky excitedly. "That's cool!"

"No, cause that's not where Ron is," answered Carl.

"Where is he then?" Asked Everett.

"He's still in the river, I saw him," said Carl.

Dicky looked at Carl as if he was crazy but Everett nodded and stood next to Carl.

"What do you mean he's still in the river he's not in the river he's supposed to be in heaven flying around with wings on and everything, that's what his Mom says?" Dicky questioned.

"Well he's not, he's in the river. Like I said I saw him. When I got hurt I was floating in the river and Ron was with me. He smiled at me and it made me feel better until Mingo pulled me out and saved me. Mingo says that he's still in the river until we go and release him."

The boys kept walking toward the river while they talked.

"Who the hell is Mingo?" Asked Dicky.

"He's a really cool Indian guy who was fishing the night I was drowning and he jumped in and pulled me out. He knows everything about the river spirits," Carl answered.

"It all makes sense to me," said Everett. "Tonto is always explaining stuff like this to the Lone Ranger on TV."

"Dicky shook his head and mumbled, "The Lone Ranger."

"Well we put him in the water and gave him a water funeral so that's why he's still there," said Everett. "We must have done it wrong."

"My mom said it told in the paper how some guy assaulted you. Did he catch you on the boat and kick your ass then throw you in the river?" Asked Dicky.

Carl then nodded. "Yea that's what happened."

Soon the boys slid down the red cinder embankment past the old abandoned factory and walked to the water's edge. Most of the green was gone from the river brush leaving the banks looking naked and lonely.

The boys stopped at the spot where they had pushed his body in the river and stared out across the water.

"So what are we supposed to do?" Asked Dicky.

"First we're supposed to do a chant but Mingo says we can sing anything we think will make him happy. Then we give him a present. Something he liked when he was alive.

"What?" I'm not doing that that sounds stupid, who is this guy Mingo, he sounds like a real queer," said Dicky.

"He is not Dicky, and you are going to do this with us if you're any kind of a friend to Ron.

Dicky began to feel guilty again. He thought he'd gotten past it but being here was making him feel sick again.

"It's going to release Ron to go to heaven to see the Great Spirit...It'll make you feel better. It'll make us all feel better," said Carl.

Dicky leaned over and put his hands on his knees and took two deep breaths to fight off the nausea. Soon he stood up and said, "Ok let's do it. What kind of happy song?"

"Mingo says his people chant something but that a happy song will do it. Don't we know a happy song?" Carl Asked.

"Well what about a commercial like on TV they're all happy songs," said Everett.

"Like what?" Asked Dicky.

"How about the Happy Tooth commercial where he sings, brusha brusha brusha, use the new Ipana, nah nah nah nah," said Everett.

"Do you know the rest of it?" Asked Carl.

"No"

"What about the Bob Hope song he always sings, you know, Thanks for the memories, nah, nah, nah in the park nah, nah, nah," sang Dicky. "But I don't know the rest of that one either."

"Geez we got to know something," said Carl. "Hey what about that Easter Song here comes Peter Cottontail, I mean even Gene Autry sings that one."

"No I ain't singing no Peter Cottontail, I wouldn't have sung that one to Ron when he was alive," said Dicky.

"How about one from Sunday school, the one that says 'deep and wide there's a river flowing deep and wide.' You just keep singing those same verses," said Dicky. "It's better than that damn Easter song.

"Ok let's sing," said Everett.

"Wait not yet," said Carl. "Gimme the smokes."

Everett reached in his pocket and pulled out three cigarettes.

"Oh shit are we back to doing this again, Back when we were bad?" Dicky laughed.

"Well we're better than we used to be aren't we?" Asked Everett.

"We are," he said, "we most definitely are."

"This is something we all used to do together here," said Carl as he lit up.

"Ok everybody take a hit and sing," said Carl.

The boys puffed on the cigarettes and began coughing and trying to sing Deep And Wide. They managed to get through two verses and half a cigarette before Everett threw up.

"Ok that's good," said Carl.

"Now what? Asked Dicky.

"Now we give him something that he took great joy in, said Carl"

He then reached inside the bag and produced the most beautiful dried and mummified cat they'd ever seen.

"Wow that's bitchin," said Dicky.

"Let me see," said Everett. "Oh yea! I remember that day...the day I gave him my Sailcat."

"I remember how cool it was when he sailed it over that lady's fence into those sheets. It was like it was alive and it went wherever his mind told it to go," said Carl.

Carl stepped closer to the river's edge and closed his eyes.

"Thanks Ron. You can go home now."

And with a flick of his cocked arm let the cat fly.

It started out low like a hovercraft just above the water then it hit a thermal and spun faster and higher till it was at least twenty-five feet off the ground. It sailed to the left and caught another updraft and flew even higher, till it was so small it could barely be seen. And then it took a nosedive toward the water almost out in the commercial lane where the barges go. It should have made a splash when it hit the water but it didn't. No one could see where it went in. As far as they knew it kept on going across the river and onto the deck of a barge that was headed to the ocean.

The boys stood smiling as they tried to make it out in the morning mist. It felt good to smile again.

The End